3-31-2015

F

Dorothy
Must Die #2

THE WICKED WILL

RISE

THE WICKED WILL

DANIELLE PAIGE

HARPER
An Imprint of HarperCollins*Publishers*

ISBN 978-0-06-228070-1 (trade bdg.)
ISBN 978-0-06-240613-2 (special ed.)
ISBN 978-0-06-238221-4 (int. ed.)

Typography by Ray Shappell
Hand lettering by Erin Fitzsimmons

15 16 17 18 19 PC/RRDH 10 9 8 7 6 5 4 3 2 1

❖

First Edition

THE WICKED WILL

ONE

The Emerald City was burning.

As I zoomed away from the smoking chaos and into the moonlit night, carried in the furry, twig-like arms of a monkey, the skyline crackled over my shoulder in a fury of glitter and flames. It looked like a little kid's birthday party gone horribly wrong, the formerly majestic towers and skyscrapers collapsing in on themselves in confetti-bursts of jewel and glass. It could have been beautiful, except for the dense, black mushroom cloud of smoke that hovered ominously over the skyline.

I was a long-ass way from Kansas.

My feelings about that might surprise you. Unlike some people, I had never been particularly eager to go back there. When it comes to clichés, there's one that I'm starting to believe might actually be worth repeating. *You can't go home again.*

Exhibit A: Dorothy. She tried to go home twice, and see how that turned out?

Exhibit B: the Wizard. He couldn't even manage to make it home once. (Okay, maybe that had something to do with the fact that he was traveling in a janky old hot air balloon, but still.)

Then there's me, Amy Gumm, trailer trash nobody from Flat Hill, Kansas. While I liked to think of myself as about as different as you could get from people like them, it was hard to ignore that we had certain things in common.

For one thing, we had all been carried here from the real world by some unknown force, and while I don't think anyone had yet figured out what that force was, I had my own theories about why we were the ones who had been chosen.

It's just a theory, remember. Nothing proven, or even close. But I sometimes wondered if the thing that linked me, Dorothy, and the Wizard was the fact that, back where we'd come from, none of us had ever fit in. Whether we knew it or not. Maybe all three of us had been born in a place we didn't belong to, and had been waiting to be found by a home that we could really call our own.

Look, I can't speak for anyone except myself. I don't even know the first thing about the Wizard, and only a little more about Dorothy. So maybe I'm wrong. It's just something I've thought about. But here's the thing: once you've traveled to the dark side of the rainbow, you've reached the end of the line. If you can't make Oz home, you're pretty much out of luck.

As far as homes went, Oz wasn't exactly the most hospitable, but at least I could call it mine. And now it was burning.

My rescuer was Ollie, the monkey I'd once saved from Dorothy's clutches. Flying at our side, his sister Maude was carrying my unlikely companion: Ozma, Oz's mystery princess with mush for brains, whose many secrets were only now starting to become clear to me.

Even as we sped into the clouds, the ground blurring below us, I was puzzling out the details of how we were flying at all. You've heard of winged monkeys, right? Well, Maude and Ollie were not exactly those—or at least they weren't supposed to be. Not anymore. Although they'd been born with wings, they had both had them removed.

Ollie had cut his own wings off, to free himself from Dorothy's enslavement. As for Maude—I still shuddered when I thought about how she had lost hers. I hadn't just seen it happen. I had been the one to do it, sawing them from her back myself using only a small dagger.

Now this was a new Oz, not the pleasant, magical kingdom you've heard about. That was a long time ago; long before I'd shown up.

In Dorothy's Oz, you did what you had to do. You made hard choices. You traded flight for freedom, if you had to, even if it meant losing a part of yourself. Sometimes, in Dorothy's Oz, you had to get your hands a little bloodied. Okay, maybe a lot bloodied.

But even in Dorothy's Oz, there was still magic, which meant that what was removed could sometimes be replaced when you had the right spell, which was how the monkeys were now flying with paper wings that were buzzing like dragonflies', vibrating so fast they were just a blur.

The wings didn't look like much. They were just two pairs

of glued-together newsprint and scraps that barely looked like they should be able to support the weight of Ollie and Maude themselves, much less a sixteen-year-old girl like me. But here we were, a thousand feet above the ground and going higher by the second. That was magic for you.

Yes I know it all sounds completely insane. To me, these days, it was just life. It's funny how quickly you adjust to insanity.

And if you think all that's insane, try this on for size: in the past several hours, I had tried (and failed) to assassinate Dorothy Gale, the Crown Royal Bitch of the Magical Land of Oz. I'd cut the Tin Woodman open and ripped out his heart with my bare hands. It was still beating with a mechanical ticktock in the bag I had strapped across the bodice of my torn, bloody servant's costume, where I'd stuffed it for safekeeping.

I had done all that. I was still getting used to it. But there was one thing I knew for sure that I hadn't done. I hadn't set the city on fire.

But someone sure had, and now, as I watched the flaming city disappear behind me, I thought I knew who. I suddenly understood that everything I'd been doing back in the palace had made me only a small piece in a much more complicated machine. While I hid in the palace, the Emerald City had been under attack by the Revolutionary Order of the Wicked, the secret cell of terrorist witches for whom I had become a trained operative. While I had been infiltrating the palace ball, disguised as a servant as I tried to kill Dorothy, they had been laying the city to waste.

I could only trust that they had their reasons. In a world

turned upside down like this, where sweet little Dorothy Gale was evil, Glinda the Good was eviler, and most everyone else was either scheming or scrambling to stay out of the way, there were crazier things you could do than putting your trust in people who called themselves *wicked*.

Not that I really did trust the Order entirely. But trust was almost beside the point. I was one of them, whether I liked it or not. And while I trusted some of them more than others, I had left *all* of them back there.

Mombi. Glamora.

The people who had saved me, who had taught me to fight; to be strong.

Nox. The person who had forced me to become who I was now.

They were still back there in the flames, and I was flying away. It was impossible not to feel like I had failed them. I'd had one job to do, and I'd messed it up completely.

"We can't leave," I said to Ollie for the fifth time since we'd left the ground, my voice hoarse and tired, my legs sore from where he was clutching me tight. I was gripping his fur even tighter. (I'm not afraid of a lot, but I've never liked heights. At least it was better going up than down.) "We have to go back to the city."

I had to say it, even knowing it was no use—that there was no turning around.

"I told you," Ollie said in the same weary tone of resigned finality he'd had the first four times.

"I can't just let them *die*," I pleaded. "They're my friends."

Once upon a time—how long ago had it even been?—Ollie had owed me his life. But there were lots of once upon a times in this place, and he and I were even now. I think.

"*You* can't die," Ollie said firmly. "And that's what will happen if we go back there. You'll die. They'll die. Oz will die. This is the only way."

"Your friends know how to protect themselves," Maude said. "They'll find us in the North where it's safer."

"North, south, east, and west," Ozma burbled uselessly in a tuneless warble. "No such thing as backward."

I sighed, ignoring her. I knew that Ollie and Maude were right. But my last glimpse of Nox back in the city kept flashing through my mind: his dark, always-messy hair, his broad shoulders and skinny, sinewy arms. The determined tilt of his jaw, and that look of almost arrogant pride. The anger that was always coiled deep in his chest finally ready to burst out and strike down everything that stood in his way, all of it to save Oz, the home that he loved.

No, not just that. To save *me*, too.

I had learned so much from him. He'd taught me who I was. Now I might not ever see him again, and there was nothing I could do about it.

"Where are we going?" I asked flatly. Now the burning city was just a tiny orange dot in the vast blackness below us, and then it was gone as if it had never existed.

"To the North," Ollie grunted. "To the Queendom of the

Wingless Ones. Now don't you think you should try to get some rest?"

I didn't really blame him for not wanting to talk. It had been a long and confusing night. But I had so many questions that I barely knew where to start.

Among the biggest of all of those questions was Ozma. She looked perfectly comfortable, cradled in Maude's arms where she was singing a little song to herself, the only one who didn't seem bothered by anything that had happened tonight. As a gust of cool air hit us and carried us sailing higher into the sky, her hair whipped around her face and she gave a squeal of delight, like this was just a ride on the Tilt-A-Whirl at the county fair. Her green eyes were so bright that it almost seemed like they were lighting our way.

Ozma whooped, wriggling happily as Maude struggled to keep hold of her.

"Hold still, Your Highness," Maude grumbled. "I can't go dropping the daughter of Lurline, can I? Queen Lulu would never let me hear the end of it."

Ozma frowned at the name. "*I'm* the queen," she said with an edge of annoyance.

My eyes widened a little in surprise when she said it. Technically it was true—she *was* the queen. Technically. But Ozma had never quite been all there, and this was one of the first times I'd heard her say anything that actually sounded half-lucid. I studied her face, looking for signs of intelligent life, searching for any trace that remained of the kind, majestic ruler that I'd heard she'd been before Dorothy Gale of Kansas had worked her magic and wiped her brain.

As she blinked back at me, I only saw more puzzles. Who *was* she?

Was she the dim-witted queen who I'd seen back in the palace, wandering the halls like someone's senile great-aunt? Was she the powerful descendant of fairies who had supposedly once been the best ruler Oz had ever had?

Or was she really Pete, the emerald-eyed stranger who had been the first person to greet me when I'd crash-landed in Oz; the kind-faced gardener who had risked himself to keep me company when I'd been a captive in Dorothy's dungeon; the mystery boy who, at the wave of the Wizard's hand, had transformed before my eyes into the dizzy, birdbrained princess babbling at my side?

Pete had been all of those people, somehow, and I'd just discovered that he and Ozma were one and the same. What did it all mean?

"Pete?" I asked. I had to believe that he was still in there somewhere. But Ozma simply looked at me sadly.

"Come on," I said. "If you can hear me, Pete, talk to me."

Ozma furrowed her brow at the name, and for a second I thought I saw a glimmer of recognition flickering behind her eyes. Was that him in there trying to get out? "Pete," I said again. "It's me. Amy Gumm. Remember?"

"I once knew a girl named Amy," Ozma said, her eyes glazing over again. With that, her jaw slackened back into an expression of placid boredom. She blinked twice and covered her perfect red mouth with a delicate hand, laughing at a private joke.

"There's magic all around!" she said. "Oh my. The fairies know! I'm a fairy, too!"

I rolled my eyes and gave up, holding on for dear life as we flew higher and higher into the sky. When we passed through a thick cover of damp cotton-ball clouds, the black sky opened up like it was a stage and the curtain had just been raised.

The stars revealed themselves.

I already knew that the stars were different in Oz from the stars I'd known on earth, but from this vantage they were *really* different. They took my breath away.

For one thing, they weren't a million miles away in space. They were right here and they were everywhere around us, close enough to reach out and touch. They were flat and five-pointed, none of them bigger than a dime; they reminded me of the glow-in-the-dark stickers I'd taped to the ceiling of my bedroom when I was just a little kid, before my dad had left and before my mom and I had moved to the trailer park. Almost, but not quite: these stars were brighter and sparklier and cold to the touch. Rather than being fixed in the sky, they were moving in a pattern that I couldn't get a handle on—they were configuring and reconfiguring themselves into brand-new constellations right before my eyes.

"They never get old," Maude said, sensing my awe. "As many times as you see them like this, they're always a surprise. This is probably the last time I'll see them," she said sadly.

When I glanced into Ollie's eyes, I saw that they were wide and filling with tears.

I looked at his paper wings, and wondered again how he had come to wear them. I know it sounds strange, but he had always been proud of being Wingless, proud that he'd been able to sacrifice the thing he loved most about himself in order to keep his freedom.

I decided to broach the subject as gently as I could. "Are you ever going to explain where exactly you got those?" I asked him.

"I told you," he said tersely. "The Wizard gave them to us. They're only temporary. But they were necessary."

"But *why*?" I asked. "And—"

Ollie cut me off. "I promised I would protect you. I needed the wings to get the job done. And they'll be gone soon enough."

"But the Wizard . . ."

Ollie squeezed my arm. "*Later*," he muttered. "For now, no talking. It's good to fly again. It feels like being a kid. Just let me enjoy the stars."

I don't know if it was the mention of her name or what, but suddenly I felt a wriggling in my pocket and remembered what—*who*—I was still carrying: Star, my pet rat. Star had come here with me all the way from Kansas, and somehow, she'd stuck by me through everything. There were times—like when I'd been trapped in Dorothy's horrible dungeon far below the Emerald Palace—when I was pretty sure I would have gone crazy without her to keep me company.

I pulled her out and placed her on my shoulder, feeling her

sharp little claws sinking through the fabric of my dress and digging into my skin.

Back in Kansas, I'd hated Star, who technically, had started out as my mom's rat, not mine. I've always heard that rats are supposed to secretly be really smart, but if that's true, Star must have been playing hooky in rat school. Back home, she'd always been mean and stupid, interested in nothing except running on her squeaky wheel and biting my hand when I tried to feed her.

Being in Oz had changed her, though. In Oz, it was like she had grown a soul. She had become something like a friend—my oldest friend in the world, these days, and we were in this together. I sometimes wondered what she thought of everything that had happened to us.

I wish I could have talked to her about all of it. I mean, animals talk in Oz, right? But not her. Maybe she was just the strong, silent type.

Star snuggled up in the crook of my neck, and we coasted along silently into the night, the stars brushing against my cheeks like little snowflakes. The clouds stretched out in every direction like an infinite ocean. I dipped my fingers in and let them skim the surface, scooping up little cottony pieces just to watch them melt into nothing in my hand.

Up here, things were peaceful. We couldn't see the burning city anymore. It was just us and the stars. I could almost imagine that Oz was still the place I'd read about in storybooks, the magical, happy land of Munchkins and talking animals, where witches were wicked but could be killed with nothing more than a little old-fashioned Kansas elbow grease and a bucket of mop water.

I was still imagining the Oz that could have been—the Oz I should have found—when I felt Star's little body slacken against my neck. She was asleep.

That did it. You might think it would be hard to relax in a situation like this—and believe me, it was—but between the twinkling stars and the wind on my face, the swooping up and down as Ollie sailed into one current after another, and the comforting, steady feeling of my rat nestled in my shoulder, soon I was asleep, too. I didn't dream.

When my eyes fluttered back open, the sun was a red wedge on the horizon. Morning was dawning, and all of Oz was spread out below us like an old crazy quilt. I'd never been in an airplane before, but somehow I had a feeling that this was better. We were flying low enough now to make out the details of the landscape—the purple swatches of farmland bordered by toy-sized villages; the winding, glittering rivers and the hazy, jagged mountains to the north.

In the distance was a dark, forbidding forest that stretched as far as I could see. I had a feeling that was where we were headed.

But as I watched the scenery below us, I noticed that something was happening down there. Something was changing. All across the grassy plain, I could see little pinpricks of color appearing and then spreading. When I looked more closely, I realized they were flowers, blossoming by the second. A few minutes later, the grassy plain wasn't grassy at all—it was an enormous, ever-changing expanse of blossoms popping up in every color I could imagine. Some were big enough that I could count the petals from all the way up here.

The forest ahead of us was changing, too. At first, I thought that it was just because it was getting closer, but no. As we approached, it became easier to make out the fact that the trees were actually getting taller, twisting up into the sky, gnarling into each other, the branches wrapped in thorny, snakelike vines.

The trees had faces.

The wind howled, and I shivered before I realized that it wasn't the wind at all. It was the trees. They were screaming.

"The Fighting Trees," Maude said in surprise, noticing them at the same time that I did. "It can't be . . ."

"What's going on?" I asked, looking up at Ollie.

"Dorothy hated the Fighting Trees. Exterminating them was one of the first things she did when she rose to power," Ollie said. "If they've returned . . ."

"But *how?*" Maude asked him sharply.

Ollie just shrugged and raised his eyebrows at me. "Did your friends do this?" he asked. I didn't know. All I knew was that the world was rewriting itself before my eyes. Like a story being torn through with a red pen.

Whose story was it, I wondered?

Suddenly someone else spoke: "The magic is returning," Ozma said, like she was explaining the simplest thing in the world. I did a double take. Had she really just spoken in a full, totally intelligible sentence? Ollie and Maude were both staring at her like she'd grown a third eye.

But before she could say anything else—before we could ask her any questions about what she'd said—Ollie screamed.

"Rocs!"

I looked up and saw what he was talking about: two dark, giant birds were speeding straight for us, beating huge black wings and shrieking in an earsplitting chorus.

So much for the cheery little birds that Oz was *supposed* to be home to.

"Amy!" Maude barked. "Can you . . ."

I was already on it, mumbling a spell under my breath, trying to gather up a fireball in my hands as Maude and Ollie wove and zigzagged to avoid our attackers.

It was no use. The birds were on top of us before I could summon more than the tiniest flame. They screeched madly and circled over our heads, their big black wings blocking out the sun, and then they dove for us.

All I saw was their fearsome, strangely human faces as they slashed their long, razor-like beaks into Maude's and Ollie's wings, ripping them from their backs with the ease of someone tearing open a bag of potato chips. Then, as quickly as they'd appeared, the birds were speeding off into the distance, their work done. The air was filled with shredded bits of paper that had held us aloft, scattering on the breeze.

For a moment we all hung in the air like Wile E. Coyote in a Road Runner cartoon. Then we were falling.

The ground was getting closer by the second. Ozma whooped with joy. This was the second time in less than twenty-four hours that I'd found myself plummeting toward certain death, and I was getting kind of sick of it.

But I didn't scream. Instead, I felt strangely calm in a way that I can't really describe. It was like everything outside of me was happening in slow motion while my brain kept on moving at normal speed.

Once upon a time a girl named Amy Gumm had come to Oz on a tornado. She had fought hard; she had been loyal and fierce. She had done things she'd never in a million years imagined that she would.

She had learned magic; she had been a spy. She had lied, and stolen, and been thrown in the dungeon. She had killed, and she had not regretted it.

She had been both good and wicked and everything in between. She had been both at once, too, until it was hard for her to even tell the difference anymore.

That was my story. *Well,* I figured as I tumbled from the sky toward certain death, *at least the ending will be killer.*

TWO

Full disclosure: I'm sort of a witch.

Fuller disclosure: I'm a pretty crappy witch.

Not like crappy as in *wicked*, although, hey, maybe I'm that, too. Who knows?

But really what I mean by *crappy* is, like—you know—not very good at it. Like, if there were a Witch Mall, Glamora would work at Witch Neiman Marcus, Mombi would work at Witch Talbot's and I would work at the Witch Dollar Store, where people would only come to buy witch paper towels, six rolls for ninety-nine cents.

I just never really got the hang of the whole spell-casting thing. For a while I thought it was because I'm from Kansas—not a place known for its enchantedness—but lately I've started thinking I just don't have a talent for magic, just like I don't have a talent for wiggling my ears or tying cherry stems in knots with my tongue.

Sure, I can do a few spells here and there. For instance, I can summon a tracking orb with not too much trouble. I've managed to teleport without accidentally materializing inside a wall or leaving any body parts behind. I have a magic knife that I can call on at any time. I can finally throw a decent fireball. (It took forever to learn, but fire spells are now my specialty.) And I've actually gotten pretty good at casting a misdirection charm that makes people ignore me as long as I tiptoe and don't draw too much attention to myself.

It's not as good as being invisible, but, hey, it's saved my ass on more than a couple of occasions. That's sort of how it goes: my magic is strictly the in-case-of-emergency kind. In nonemergencies, I prefer to do things the normal way. Call me old-fashioned. It's just easier.

But falling out of the sky from five thousand feet probably qualifies as an emergency, right? If Maude, Ollie, Ozma, and I were going to land without becoming pancakes served Oz style, it was going to take some serious witchcraft.

So as we plunged through the air, I just closed my eyes, tuned everything out, and concentrated, trying my best to ignore the fact that I probably had about fifteen seconds to get the job done. I couldn't think about that.

Instead, I focused on the energy that was all around me. I tuned into its frequency and gathered it all up, channeling it through my body as the wind whipped fiercely past me.

Once, I'd seen Mombi do a spell where she reversed gravity, turning the whole world upside down and sending herself, along with her passengers, all shooting up into the sky. Like falling, but in the wrong direction. Or the right direction, depending on how you looked at it.

I wasn't so sure I'd be able to pull off that trick, but I hoped that even my bargain basement version of Mombi's designer magic would be good enough that my friends and I just might be able to walk away from this. Or at least crawl away. Or whatever.

And maybe because it was do-or-die or maybe it was something else, but for one of the first times ever, it came easily to me. I reached out with my mind and twisted the magic into something new; something that could help.

The first rule of magic is that it gets bored easily—it always wants to be something different from what it is. So I imagined it as an energy re-forming itself into a parachute flying at our backs. I imagined it catching its sail in the wind, imagined it opening up and carrying us. It was like drawing a picture with my mind, or like molding a sculpture out of soft, slippery clay.

When I opened my eyes again, we were still falling, but our descent was slowing by the second. Soon we were floating like feathers, gliding easily toward the earth.

It had worked.

I can't say I wasn't surprised.

"Someone's been practicing her tricks," Ollie said. There was a hint of suspicion in his voice, but mostly it was just relief.

"I guess I just got lucky," I said. It was kind of a lie. It hadn't felt like luck at all. It hadn't felt like I had known what I was doing either. Somehow I had just *done* it. But how?

I tried to put my doubt aside. This wasn't the time for me to be questioning myself. It had been a gentler landing than I'd been planning on, but I felt as exhilarated and exhausted from the feat I'd just accomplished as if I'd run a marathon.

I picked myself up, dusted off, and tried to collect myself. My body was aching, sore from the trip, and my mind raced as I sifted through everything that had just happened, knowing that I had to stay alert. I had a feeling that the rocs hadn't attacked us by coincidence, which meant that, for now, we were still in danger.

And yet it was hard to be too worried when I saw where we had touched down: I was looking out over a sea of flowers, stretching far into the distance.

When I say a sea of flowers, I really mean that it was like an ocean, and not just because I couldn't see the limit to it. I mean, that was one thing, sure. More importantly, though, was the fact that it was moving.

The blossoms were undulating like waves, building themselves up and rolling toward us, petals spraying everywhere as they crashed at our feet, petering out into a normal, grassy meadow. If this was an ocean, we were standing right at the shore.

"I've heard of the Sea of Blossoms," Maude said. "I've heard of it but . . ."

Her voice trailed off as we all gazed out in something like amazement.

The Sea of Blossoms. It was beautiful. Not just beautiful: it was enchanted. Of everything I had seen since I had come to Oz, this felt the most like the magic that was supposed to be everywhere here. After our near escape from the flying monsters, I knew I should be on edge, but there was something so joyful about the way the flowers were rippling in the breeze that I felt my heart filling with hope.

But then I turned around and saw what was behind us, and I remembered something Nox had once told me: that even in the best of circumstances, every bit of brightness in Oz was balanced out by something dark.

Here was that darkness, right on cue: at our backs, the way was blocked by a thick, black jungle, with trees taller than I'd ever seen before, clustered together so closely that it was hard to see a way through. My body gave an involuntary shiver.

At least they didn't have faces. Still, there was something dangerous about it. Something that said *keep out*.

"Is this where the monkeys live?" I asked, hoping the answer was no.

Ollie gave a rueful little laugh. "Not quite. The Queendom of the Wingless Ones is deep in the forest, high up in the trees. Flying would have been faster, but we still can make it there by nightfall, if we move quickly."

"And if the Fighting Trees decide to let us pass," Maude said darkly. "In the past, they have been friends to the monkeys, but nothing is certain these days. Things are changing quickly in Oz. The Sea of Blossoms was supposed to have dried up years ago. Ozma said the magic was returning. As foolish as she is, she is still deeply attuned to this land. I wonder if something your wicked friends did last night has awakened some of the magic Dorothy and Glinda have been stealing from it for all this time."

"It seems so," Ollie mused. "And what about the rocs? They haven't been spotted in these parts as long as I can remember. I had almost begun to wonder if they were just a legend."

"Do you think someone could have sent them for us?" I wondered aloud.

"Perhaps," Maude said thoughtfully. "But who?"

Ozma, who had been kneeling on the ground nearby, plucked a purple lily and tucked it into her hair. She turned to us and spoke.

"He did it," she said, gathering up a bunch of the flowers and pressing them to her face, inhaling the perfumed scent.

"Who?" I said, still not able to tell if this was just her usual babble or if she somehow knew what she was talking about. I studied her closely.

Ozma greeted my question with a blank stare and tossed the flowers to the ground. Instead of scattering, their stems burrowed right back into the dirt and then they were standing upright again—as if they'd never been picked in the first place.

"It's coming," she said. "He's coming, too. Run and hide!"

Before I could question her further, there was a rustling in the trees and the soft, heavy thump of footsteps. A moment later, a hulking shadow emerged from the forest, and I knew instantly who Ozma had been sensing.

The Lion.

The air went out of everything. The chirping of the birds stopped; the Sea of Blossoms was suddenly still and calm. Or maybe calm was the wrong word. It looked more like it was afraid to move.

Even the sky seemed to know he was here. Just a second ago it had been bright and sunny, but in a flash the sun seemed to dim, casting us in gray and gloomy shadows.

The Lion padded toward us. Where his feet met the earth, the flowers withered instantly into black and shriveled husks. Next to me, I felt Ollie and Maude freeze up with fear.

The Lion circled for a moment and then looked down at me, baring a grotesque mouthful of fangs in what was probably meant to be a smile. "Well, if it isn't little Miss Amy Gumm, Princess Ozma, and their two furry friends," he said. Maude and Ollie shrank back in terror. Ozma stood up and regarded the scene passively. The Lion glanced to my shoulder where Star was still perched, and he raised an eyebrow. "Make that *three* furry friends," he corrected himself.

My hand twitched as I instinctively summoned the magical knife that Nox had given me. The solid handle materialized in my hand and I took a step forward, feeling its heat burning against my palm.

"*You*," I spat.

If the Lion was bothered by the threat in my voice, he didn't show it.

"I thought surely the fall would kill you, but I have to admit

I'm glad it didn't," he said, sinking back on his haunches and surveying us. "This way I get to enjoy you myself. It's been such a long time since I had a nice, square meal. And after that *terrible* brouhaha back in the Emerald City, I'm sure that Dorothy will forgive me if I don't take you back alive."

"Good luck with that, dude," I said. "I'm not as much of a pushover as you might think. I killed your pal the Tin Woodman last night, you know."

A look of surprise registered on the Lion's face, but it was gone as quickly as it had appeared. "The Tin Woodman is a lover, not a fighter," he said.

"Was," I corrected him. "Before I ripped his heart out."

The Lion narrowed his eyes and looked me up and down. He was used to people cowering before him, like Maude and Ollie, who were both quivering with fright, crouched on either side of me, their teeth chattering in terror.

This was the effect the Lion usually had. His courage had somehow been twisted into something dark and sick. Now it was a weapon. Wherever he went, he brought a cloud of terror with him. Just being around him was enough to make most people shrink in fear until it consumed them.

Then the Lion consumed it. He ate fear, literally. It made him stronger. I'd seen him do it—pick up a terrified Munchkin and suck the fright right out of him until the Munchkin was just a lifeless shell and the Lion was supercharged, bursting with power.

And yet, today, standing ten feet from him, I found that for the first time I wasn't afraid. I had already faced down everything that had ever frightened me and I'd come out the other side.

Instead of fear, I felt my body fill with a deep rage. There was something about the anger that seemed to put everything into focus—it was like a pair of glasses I had put on, and I was finally seeing everything clearly.

The Tin Woodman's heart. The Lion's courage. The Scarecrow's brains. According to the Wizard, once I had all of them, Dorothy could finally die the death she deserved. I already had the first item in the bag strapped across my chest: the Tin Woodman's metal, clockwork heart. Now the second thing on my list was within reach—if only I could figure out where the Lion actually *kept* his courage.

No big deal, I thought. I could always figure that out after he was dead.

I wanted to wait for him to make the first move, though. I was counting on him underestimating me, but even on my best day the Lion still had ten times my physical strength.

"Now, let's see," the Lion was saying. "Who should I eat first?" He looked from me, to Ozma, to Ollie, to Maude, raising a gigantic claw and passing it around from one of us to the next.

"Bubble gum, bubble gum in a dish," he rumbled in a low, ominous croon. Maude. Ollie. Me. He paused as he reached Ozma. "You know," he mused, "I've never had much of a taste for bubble gum." The muscles in his hind legs twitched. "Fairies, on the other hand, are delicious."

"You're very bad," Ozma said scornfully. "You can't eat the queen."

I could have cheered, hearing her talking to him, totally unafraid, with such casual, careless haughtiness. You had to give it to her for nerve, even if it was just the kind of nerve that came from not really knowing any better. But the Lion didn't seem to think it was very funny.

I was ready for him when he growled and sprang for her. I moved before he did, slashing my knife through the air in a bright arc of red, searing flame, aiming right for him. Ozma clapped at the display. I was getting better at this magic thing.

But I was also overconfident: my blade barely grazed the Lion's flank. I drew blood, but not enough to slow him down. He simply twisted in annoyance and swiped for me with a powerful forearm. He hit me right in the gut and I went stumbling backward like a mosquito that had just been batted out of the way, landing on the ground on my butt in a burst of petals. I bounced up quickly only to see that Ozma, as it turned out, was perfectly capable of protecting herself.

She hadn't moved an inch, but a shimmering green bubble had somehow appeared up around her. The Lion clawed and poked at it, but wherever the force field had come from, it was impervious to his attacks. Ozma blinked innocently at him.

"Bad kitty!" she said. She scowled and wagged her finger at him. "Naughty cat!"

The Lion growled a low growl, apparently not amused at being called "kitty," and took another swipe at her. Again, though, his attack bounced right off her protective bubble.

While the Lion was distracting himself with the princess, I

was stealthily circling toward him, positioning myself to strike again while charging up my knife with another magical flame.

"You've always been a stupid little thing," the Lion was saying to Ozma. "Nevertheless, I suppose you have your own *irritating* kind of power. It's a good thing there are other ways to teach a fairy a lesson."

He turned from Ozma and reached for Maude, who had curled herself into a ball on the ground, her teeth chattering with terror. She didn't even try to run. "No!" Ollie screamed, hurling himself in front of his sister.

This was my cue: I rushed him.

The Lion sensed me coming. He spun around and gave a furious roar, his jaw practically unhinging.

He lunged for me.

Fake out.

Just as he was about to grab me, I flipped myself backward into the air and blinked myself behind him, my teleportation spell reversing my momentum as I landed on his back. I grabbed a hank of his mane in my fist and pulled hard, yanking his head backward.

"I've been wanting to do this for a while," I said through gritted teeth, using every ounce of strength I had to slash my burning blade across his exposed throat. I cringed at the sound of his flesh hissing under my weapon's white-hot heat, but somewhere, deep down, I found myself surprised at how used to this kind of violence I had already gotten. At how easily it came to me.

As the Lion howled, I felt some small kind of pleasure in his pain. I pushed it aside, but it was there. I felt the tiniest glimmer of a smile at the corner of my lips.

The Lion bucked and shook wildly and I hung on to his mane for dear life, thinking of my mom's friend Bambi Plunkett, who had once won five hundred dollars riding the mechanical bull at the Raging Stallion on Halifax Avenue. Unfortunately, I quickly discovered that I wasn't going to be crowned queen of the rodeo anytime soon.

As the Lion desperately tried to shake me, I felt my hold on his mane begin to slip. He jumped into the air and we landed with a force that shook the ground, flowers flying everywhere. As he gave one last powerful shudder, I lost my grip and tumbled off him, my head cracking against the ground.

My vision blurred. In a flurry of fur and fangs, the Lion pounced, the weight of his body crushing my legs as he pinned my arms with his paws.

"I see you're a courageous little one," he purred, pushing his face just inches from mine. "I must admit, I didn't expect it from you." He licked his chops. "We'll just have to change that, won't we?"

A trickle of blood made its way from his throat, down his fur, and onto my shirt, and I saw that the cut across his throat was really just a surface wound. I'd barely hurt him.

This wasn't going as well as I'd thought it would. I tried to blink myself out from under him, but my head was still throbbing from the fall I'd just taken, and as hard as I tried, I found that I couldn't quite summon the magic for it.

Then, before I could decide what to do next, I heard a squeal. Out of the corner of my eye, I saw something white streak through the grass as Star scurried away, and felt the Lion's weight on my body lighten, as he leaned over and shot a paw out.

"No!" I screamed, suddenly realizing what was coming. But there was nothing I could do. He had grabbed my rat by the tail, and she wriggled and screeched as he held her over my face.

"Dorothy wants *you* alive, brave little Amy," he said. "And while I haven't decided yet whether to let her have her way this time, in the meantime, *this* one will make a nice appetizer."

The Lion snapped his jaw open. Star's final scream sounded almost human as he dangled her over his toothy, gaping maw.

First the fear left her. It went streaming from her trembling body into the Lion's open mouth in a wispy burst like a puff of smoke from a cigarette. Then she was still, looking down at me with wide, placid eyes.

There wasn't much left of her, but at least I knew that she wasn't afraid when she died. The Lion dropped her into his mouth and chomped hard. A trickle of blood made its way down his chin.

"Not very filling," he said with a laugh. "But I hear rats are actually a delicacy in some parts of Oz." He paused and licked a stray bit of my poor dead rat's white fur from his lips. "Now, I've made a decision. On to the main course."

"No," I said as something strange came over me. I felt more lucid than ever, like the volume had been turned up on all of my senses. I felt like I was looking down on myself, watching the scene unfold from somewhere far away. "Wrong. Fucking. Move." With that, I blinked myself out of his clutches.

The Lion lurched in surprise and twisted around to face me where I was now standing, a few yards away, my back to the trees. He pawed at the ground.

Somewhere in my peripheral vision—somewhere on the edge of my consciousness—I saw that Ollie and Maude were both clinging to Ozma under the protection of her bubble. They were safe, but I hardly cared anymore.

I didn't care about them, I didn't care about Oz. I didn't even care about myself. All I cared about was my dead rat.

That stupid little rat was the last connection I had to home. In some ways she was the only friend I had left. She had made it through Dorothy's dungeons with me. She had helped me survive. Now she was gone. The Lion had eaten her as easily as a marshmallow Easter Peep.

Now I was alone for real. But suddenly I knew that it was really no different from before. It was no different from Kansas, even.

I had always been alone and I would always be alone. It had just taken me this long to figure it out.

All I cared about now was revenge.

The Lion bounded for me with a thundering growl so loud it shook the trees. I didn't move to step aside. If the Lion thought eating my rat and creating a racket was going to make me afraid, he couldn't have been more wrong. I was less afraid than ever.

I was ready to kill, and I suddenly had no doubt what the outcome would be.

My heart opened up into an endless pit. I looked over the edge into the void, and then I jumped right in.

Brandishing my knife, I silently called out for more fire—for the white-hot flames of the sun. The Lion was going to burn.

The fire didn't come. Instead, like a glass filling with ink, my blade turned from polished, flashing silver to an obsidian so deep and dark that it seemed to be sucking the light right out of the sky.

It wasn't what I had been expecting, but that was how magic sometimes worked. Magic is tricky. It's not as simple as saying *abracadabra* and waving a wand. When you cast the spell, the magic becomes a part of you. Who you are can change it. And I was different now.

Once, I had been an angry, righteous little ball of fire. Now I was something else.

But what?

THREE

I felt the magic in every pore of my skin, in every hair on the backs of my arms. I felt it in the tips of my eyelashes. I was vibrating with it as the Lion came at me with a roar loud enough to split the world right open.

It was too late for that.

He hurled himself at me in a lithe, powerful cannonball; he clawed and scratched and bit. He wasn't playing around now; there was no taunting and no banter as he hit me with a graceful, animal fury that wouldn't let up. But he couldn't touch me.

When he had killed Star he had unleashed something in me that I hadn't known was even in there. Now the magic was flowing through me like a song and my body was moving to its pulsing, thrumming beat.

I was everywhere at once. I was barely anywhere at all. With every move that he made, I was ahead of him. It was like we were dancing.

I was spinning and dodging and somersaulting, thrusting and parrying, and every time the Lion thought he had me, I found myself melting into the ground, only to rise back up a moment later in the place he least expected to find me.

It was a different kind of teleportation than the kind I did when I blinked myself from one place to the next. It was like I was entering a world of shadows. I wasn't sure how I was doing it, and I wasn't sure where I was going when I disappeared like that—only that wherever it was, it was cold and foreign and deadly silent. From down there, everything was hazy and slow-motion, and I was outside reality, looking up into it from the darkness like gazing up through a layer of black, muddy water.

I may not have known *how* I was doing it, but every time I rose back up, reshaping myself into my own form, I knew *what* I was doing when I was under there. I was touching the darkness.

If I'd had time to think about it, it probably would have frightened me. Somehow, I knew instinctively that I was tapping into some of the blackest kind of magic. Everywhere I slashed and stabbed, my knife left a thick, inky trail behind it. It looked like I was cutting a hole in the atmosphere, and what was on the other side was nothing.

We went on like that for a while. I could tell that the Lion was tiring out. We weren't dancing together anymore. *I* was dancing, but him? He was just going to die.

It was pathetic, really, but I didn't feel sorry for him. Actually, I was having fun. I'd found something in Oz I was *good* at.

Finally, he gave one last valiant effort and sprang up, grabbed a tree branch and swung, barreling down at me feetfirst. I didn't bother dodging. I melted into nothing and rematerialized behind him, wondering how it was that this kind of magic was suddenly coming so easily to me.

The Lion was still scooping himself up from where he had fallen, and I let him flail for a moment in confusion before I swept my leg around in a roundhouse kick that met his face with the satisfying crunch of shattering teeth.

I plunged my knife into his side and a web of inky lines spidered across the surface of his golden, tawny muscles like I was injecting him with poison.

Well, maybe I was.

I twisted my blade. The Lion screamed, collapsing. He had all but surrendered now, but I wasn't done yet. As he lay there howling in pain, I jumped up and found myself moving almost in slow motion, suspended in the air for a moment before I pushed myself forward and launched myself straight for him, sinking my knife into the roof of his gaping mouth, a geyser of blood erupting.

This time he didn't bother screaming.

I tossed the knife aside, letting it disappear to wherever it went when I wasn't holding it. But this time, when I drew my hand back, I pulled a long, dark tendril with it—a black, twisting skein of nothingness.

It was like a tentacle, like an extension of myself. All I had to do was think about it and the blackness twisted out through the air like a snake slithering through the grass. It wrapped itself around the Lion's neck.

The Lion clutched at his throat, gasping and trying to free himself.

All I had to do was want it, and the noose tightened.

"Beg me," I said. The words hung in the air, dripping with venom. It barely sounded like me. If I was a character in a comic book, my dialogue would have been inked in thick, jagged letters. This couldn't be me—could it? I knew what I had to do, but there was no reason to be so cruel about it.

I felt half possessed when I said it again. "Beg me," I repeated, with even more cruelty this time, as the Lion tried to open his mouth.

His eyes widened, but he was barely struggling anymore; he was using everything he had left just to stay alive.

"Never," was all he managed to say.

My knife had returned to me, and when I looked down at it, I saw that its blackness was seeping out of it and up my arm, like I was wearing a glove made of tar. My fist was gripping the hilt so tight that it hurt. It was twitching.

Cut him, I heard a voice in the back of my head telling me. *Punish him for everything he's done.*

I wanted to do it. In my mind's eye, I saw myself slicing him open. His stomach. His throat. Like I was watching a movie, I saw myself stabbing wherever I could, not paying attention to where I was striking, just hacking away as he convulsed and moaned, his hot, sticky blood squirting out in every direction while I kept going.

It was just my imagination. But I wanted it to be real. And it *could* be real. All I had to do was do it.

But then I heard another voice—a real voice this time, not in my head, but from somewhere outside of me. It was soft and lilting, barely more than a whisper.

It was Ozma.

"Come back," she said simply.

With her, you never quite knew if she meant anything by it at all. I couldn't even be sure that she was talking to me. But something about the way she said it brought me down to earth, and when I turned to her, I saw that she had dropped her bubble of protection and was now standing just a few feet away. Her bright eyes were fixed on me plaintively, with a look of deep, almost sisterly concern.

That's when I realized that I wasn't fighting the Lion to punish him. As much as I wanted to let my revenge fantasies play out, I had to remember that there was a larger purpose to everything I was doing. As much as I wanted to kill him—my body was still screaming out for his blood—I knew it wasn't that simple. I needed something from him.

It all came flooding like a dream you've forgotten until something jogs your memory.

The Tin Woodman's heart. The Lion's courage. The Scarecrow's brains.

With the Tin Woodman and the Scarecrow it was obvious. Heart and brains. Duh. But where does a Lion keep his courage?

I looked at him lying there in battered, bloody defeat, toothless and bruised, his mangled tail twitching, the sad little ribbon at the end of it soaked with blood, and then I noticed that there was something strange about it. The tail. It wasn't glowing, exactly, but it had something like a halo around it. A jittery, golden aura so pale that it barely registered.

It made me take a closer look.

I don't know how I'd missed it before, but now I saw it. The tail wasn't even real. It was stuffed and synthetic and made from felt and stuffing, like something that belonged to a doll. At the base, I could see that it was sewn onto the Lion's body in a sloppy cross-stitch. This wasn't the tail that he had been born with. Of course: the Wizard had given it to him.

In one swift, smooth motion, I sliced it off. There was a high-pitched hissing sound, like air being let out of a balloon. The Lion gave a weak, stupid whimper.

I held the tail up, and it twitched in my hands. It was angry. I knew that my instincts had been right.

Looking down at the Lion confirmed it. He was cowering on the ground, covering his face with his hands. He would be out of his misery soon enough. I raised my knife over my head and prepared to finish him off for good.

I thought of everything he had done—all the innocent people he had terrified and tortured as Dorothy's enforcer. I thought of everyone he had killed. Gert. Star. The ones I didn't know—like Nox's family. He had done it for no reason. He had done it just because he liked it. Because it was fun. Because Dorothy told him to.

My hand was poised over my head, my knife bursting with

magic. I realized that, sometime during the fight, the already graying sky overhead had covered itself in an ominous shroud of clouds.

It was like I had caused that. Like my anger and darkness had spilled out into the land around me.

In that moment, I couldn't help being scared of myself.

But my fear was nothing next to the Cowardly Lion's. "Please don't hurt me," he wheezed. He was crying now, curled into a fetal ball and rocking back and forth on the ground, clutching his face.

Seeing him like this it was hard to believe that he had ever been capable of any of the terror he had caused. Without his courage, he was nothing. And I had it now. His tail coiled itself up around my arm like a piece of jewelry. The Lion was less than harmless now. And I felt powerful. Maybe even courageous.

My hands were red with blood; blood had plastered my clothes to my skin. Even my hair was damp with it. Off in the distance, I heard a single bird chirp.

My shoulders loosened. I took a deep, gulping breath. My knife faded from my grip, and as it did, the clouds parted and the sun was shining down on us again. My whole body was shaking as I felt the magic that had filled me during my fight begin to dissipate.

I thought, for a moment, of my mother, and of how fragile she looked when she was coming down from one of her binges. I thought of all the times she'd tried to go clean, and of all the times I'd tried to help her. Of how she'd failed every time.

I stood and turned away from the Lion. "Go," I said, gesturing out into nowhere.

The Lion rose shakily to his feet. He stumbled and fell, then stood again and looked up, his whole face trembling. "Thank you," he sniveled. "How can I ever—"

I cut him off. "Do it, before I change my mind." He flinched, and then went limping off into the forest without looking back, blood trailing his every step.

Two down, one to go. After that, Dorothy would be mine, and one thing was for sure: I wasn't going to let her off the hook as easily as I had the Lion.

Then the world began to come back into focus. In the rolling field of flowers, Maude and Ollie were standing stock-still, staring at me like they barely recognized me. Ozma, though, had a shy little smile on her face. It almost looked like pride.

I wanted to say something to them. *See?* I wanted to say. *I let him go.*

It was true. I *had* let him go. Even so, I knew there was a line that I had almost crossed, and they had watched me walk right up to the edge of it. I opened my mouth and closed it again. I didn't have the words to explain any of it.

I was just standing there, still wondering what had just happened, when I saw the rest of them. They were everywhere. I had been so consumed with the Lion that I hadn't noticed them arrive. Monkeys.

They were sitting in the branches of the trees and crouched in the hillocks of flowers and hiding in the thick shrubbery that blocked the forest. There must have been a hundred of them, monkeys of all shapes and sizes. Too bad I'd never paid much attention in science class; it would have been nice to name all the different types of species that were represented among them.

Like Maude and Ollie, they were just staring at me, unblinking and impassive. Like Maude and Ollie, they all looked scared of me.

FOUR

The Queendom of the Wingless Ones was built high in the trees, just below the thick canopy of leaves that covered the Dark Jungle. The monkeys had known the path through the jungle by heart and commanded enough respect in these woods that we'd been able to pass without being bothered by any of the creatures who shared it with them, but it had still taken us hours to make our way through the dense brush of vines and branches into the heart of the forest where they had their treetop home. We'd paused only once, for me to wash the blood off my body in a stream, before we stopped in front of a big tree.

I looked at Ollie.

"Why are we stopping?"

"This is the human entrance. You can't very well climb up there like the others, can you?"

I looked up to where he was pointing. Most of the monkeys traveling with us had simply scampered up into the branches.

Ollie pressed his palm into a barely visible indentation in the trunk and a door slid open, revealing that the tree had been outfitted with a makeshift contraption kind of like a dumbwaiter. Ollie crawled inside and beckoned for us to follow, and once we were all in, he and Maude and I all took turns pulling on the rope that turned the pulley and raised the platform carrying us up, up, up, into the darkness.

Ollie was completely out of breath and I wasn't doing much better by the time we emerged from the passage onto a narrow platform.

The monkey village was like the world's coolest tree house crossed with something out of a *Swiss Family Robinson* theme party thrown by Martha Stewart. Throughout the village, wooden houses of all shapes and sizes had been built into the treetops, all of them connected by a network of suspended walkways constructed out of roughly hewn planks and twisted vines. Everywhere I looked were monkeys in human clothing. There were monkeys in sharp little three-piece suits, monkeys in sweatpants and T-shirts, monkeys in nurses' uniforms, and even monkeys in tiny little ball gowns who looked like they could be on their way to the monkey Oscars. Most of them weren't using the walkways; instead, the ones with places to be were swinging from vines and scampering across branches, looking perfectly unaware of the fact that we were at least five hundred feet up.

We were greeted by a monkey who seemed not at all self-conscious about the fact that she was wearing a French maid's uniform.

"Welcome back," she said to Ollie in a voice too low and gruff for her tiny size. She gave him a quick pat on the back and a kiss on the cheek before turning to the queen, sinking into a clumsy curtsy as I fought to stifle a giggle. "Greetings, Your Highness," she said to Ozma. "I'm Iris. We are honored to have you join us in our village." After lingering on the queen for a few moments, Iris directed her attention to me. Her smile faded. I was starting to realize that these monkeys didn't quite trust me.

"Hi," I said awkwardly. "I'm Amy."

"Yes," she said. "Queen Lulu has been awaiting your arrival. Ollie will take you to her while I escort Her Majesty to the quarters you'll be sharing." With that, Iris took the wide-eyed Ozma by the hand and led her away.

"I don't think your friends are that into me," I said to Ollie.

He just shrugged. "The Wingless Ones have a bad track record with witches." Before I could protest he was already moving, scampering off across a rope bridge. I followed.

Because the canopy blocked out almost any light from the sun, the village was lit instead by strange, floating lanterns that looked like oversize, translucent lemons. They hung in the air along the walkways and over the tree houses, their glowing light giving the otherwise dim village the feeling of a fancy garden party just about to start. (Not that I've ever been to a fancy garden party, but back in Kansas I did sometimes used to watch HGTV with my mom. When we were getting along, I mean.)

"Sunfruit," Ollie explained, seeing me staring at the lamp-things as we made our way across the walkways. "Try one." He plucked a fruit from where it hovered and expertly shucked a piece of soft, thin rind from the top, revealing a yellowish, glowing goop inside. He handed it to me.

The sunfruit felt warm in my palm and had the rubbery consistency of a gummi bear. I was a little afraid of it, but I didn't want to offend him, so I stuck a finger in, scooped out some of the slime, and tasted it.

I was expecting it to be kind of gross. I wasn't prepared for it to be pretty much the most delicious thing I'd ever eaten. It tasted like ten things at once: like saltwater taffy and pineapples and fruity drinks with little umbrellas. It tasted like summer, and the last day of school, and the beach. I closed my eyes and savored it for a second, suddenly realizing exactly how long it had been since I'd taken the time to actually enjoy something. These days, distractions like that were pretty hard to come by.

I could have spent the next hour trying to separate out all the flavors of the sunfruit, but Ollie was already tugging at my sleeve. "We don't want to keep Queen Lulu waiting. She is a wise ruler, but she gets frustrated easily. You'd rather not see her when she's angry."

I took his word for it, but I continued scooping up more of the sunfruit as we kept walking. A few minutes later, we came to a spiral of stairs that had been built into the outside of a thick-trunked tree. "The queen will see you alone," Ollie said. "When you're done, you can find your chambers near the waterfall."

"A waterfall? Up here? In the trees?"

"Can't miss it," he said, jumping from the path and grabbing on to a vine with his tail. He swung around and hung there upside down, looking me in the eye. "Thank you, Amy," he said, and I knew that he wasn't just thanking me for saving him, or for saving his sister.

Then he was gone into the leaves.

I took a deep breath and began to make my way up the rickety wooden stairs that twisted up toward the canopy. I took each wobbly step carefully, hugging the tree as closely as I possibly could, trying not to think about the fact that I was probably the first fully grown human to use this path in years. You'd think the day I'd just had would have cured me of my fear of heights, but nope.

Look, fear's not always rational, okay? Anyway, there's a difference between being afraid and being a coward. At least there was one thing I could take comfort in: if you're afraid, you must still be a little bit human.

When I finally made it up through the canopy, I discovered that the "palace" wasn't really a palace at all. Just a large, round hut that sat on a spacious platform of planks above the leaves.

Inside, Queen Lulu was sitting on a large throne constructed out of sticks and branches in the middle of a filthy room strewn with banana peels, clothes, and piles upon piles of newspapers, books, toys, and other junk. She wore bright red lipstick, a poufy pink tutu, and pink, rhinestone-encrusted cat-eye sunglasses. She sat there eyeing me, all the while fanning herself with a paper fan.

"Well, well, well," she squeaked from behind her fan. "If it isn't famous Amy Gumm. Welcome to my queendom."

So she was no Kate Middleton. Still, I wasn't sure what to expect from her as I approached her throne, and I figured that even a queen in a tutu expects a certain amount of respect. I bowed. "It's an honor to meet you, Your Highness," I said.

"Charmed, I'm sure," Queen Lulu said. Her voice was squeaky but tough, too. "I hear you're a hero type, the real deal. You and your daring rescues! Oh, sure, we've heard all about those around these parts."

"Uh, thanks," I said. "I don't know. I was just doing what anyone would have done, I guess."

"Well, bless your heart," Lulu said. She set her fan aside and casually scratched her armpit. "Shall we call our debt all settled up here, then?"

"Debt?" I asked.

"Yeah, debt. You saved Ollie and Maude, they saved you. Even-steven. No more monkey business."

"Oh," I said, taken aback. "I mean, okay. It wasn't like I was keeping track or anything."

Queen Lulu lowered her sunglasses and looked out over them. "Let's cut the crap," she said. "You seem like a nice girl, but I want to make sure we have things straight here. I allowed Ollie and Maude to help you out this one little time, but we Wingless Ones aren't going to get involved in whatever nonsense is brewing in Oz these days. What Dorothy and the rest of them do down there? That's someone else's ball of beeswax. We've got a good thing going up here in the trees."

I folded my arms across my chest. "Is that what you wanted to talk to me about? To tell me you're staying out of it?"

"You got it, sweetheart. I know your type. You come around, you stir up trouble, and before you know it I've got all my monkeys wanting a war with the Emerald City. Thanks, but no thanks. You're lucky I let you come here at all."

Um, obviously I hadn't come here trying to get the monkeys to go to war. Come to think of it, I hadn't even asked to be brought here at all. Really, all I wanted in the world was a nap. A really, really, really long nap. And a shower. And maybe some ice cream and some bad TV.

Even so, Queen Lulu's attitude was seriously pissing me off. Without really meaning to, I placed my hands indignantly on my hips. "Seriously? How can you act like what Dorothy does isn't your problem? You may be hidden up here for now, but she'll burn this place to the ground as soon as she gets around to it. Wouldn't you rather live somewhere where you didn't have to hide? Where you didn't have to cut off your wings?"

Lulu picked up a banana from a bunch that was sitting on a table by her throne and peeled it. Royalty or not, she chewed with her mouth open.

"Come on," she snorted. "We monkeys have had the short end of the hot dog for as long as Oz has been Oz. I may be the boss-lady now, but in my day I've hauled more than one witch around like I was a common chauffeur. Dorothy, the Wizard, Mombi, and her stupid little Order—they're all the same to me."

"The Order wants freedom for everyone."

I surprised myself at how strongly I felt about it. The truth is, I'd never totally trusted the Order myself. Because, sure, Dorothy was evil, but who was to say that they weren't *more* evil? They used to be wicked witches, after all. Who's to say they weren't still?

But look. You have to be loyal to *something*, right? I might have my own doubts about Mombi and the rest of them, but I had thrown my lot in with them, and I had to stand by my choices.

Queen Lulu was giving me a dubious, *I've got your number* kind of look.

"Don't give me the babe-in-the-woods act, babe," she said. "Let's just say you and your wicked little friends *do* manage to kill Dorothy. You think I'll be the one resting my hairy heinie on that shiny emerald throne? Not a chance. I've dinged enough dongs in my day to know it'll be the same as it ever was. Maybe worse. Meet the new witch, same as the old witch."

As she'd been talking, Queen Lulu had been working herself up into a frenzy; now she sprang to her feet and bared her teeth, her sunglasses askew.

I knew I should just nod and agree with her. I wasn't going to change her mind, and she looked about one wrong word away from swinging across the room and wrestling me to the ground. But I've always been pretty bad at shutting up and smiling. Come to think of it, that might have been part of how I'd gotten myself into all this in the first place.

"What about Ozma?" I asked. "Things were good when she was in charge, right? Not all leaders are the same."

Lulu cackled uproariously. She laughed until she was wheezing, and then, when she was tired out, she collapsed back into her seat and kicked her legs up. "Sure. Ozma was a doll way back when. But we all know that broad's about six stamps short of first class these days. She's great if you want to hear a whole lot of nonsense, but she's not exactly monarch material, am I right?"

Okay, fine, she was right. But that didn't change my point.

"So what? Should we just be on our way then?"

"Aw, don't get all bent out of shape. You and Miss Princess can stay as long as you want. I do have my principles, after all, and anyway I'm a big softie. But I don't want any trouble—and that means no magic while you're here, got it? We don't go in for that type of thing. And I know the kind of magic you do."

"Fine," I said. "No magic."

Queen Lulu looked pretty much totally unconvinced. "Show me your hands."

"My hands?"

"You think I was born yesterday? For all I know you've got your fingers crossed behind your back. Don't think you can pull one over on me."

I stared at her. Next was she going to knock twice on her throne and call *no take-backs*? But as ridiculous as it all sounded, I could tell from the way she was glaring at me that she meant business.

I dutifully held my hands out to show I was on the up-and-up. Lulu cleared her throat, like, *I'm waiting*.

I sighed. "I promise not to use magic while I'm in the village—"

"*Queendom.*"

"Queendom of the Wingless Ones. No take-backs," I added for good measure.

At that, the queen nodded smugly and picked up her fan again. She fluttered it in front of her face. "Very well," she said. "Now if you please, I must meet with my high council. I'm a very busy majesty, you know."

I turned to leave, and then, with my hand on the door, I thought of something and spun around.

"Have you heard anything about the Order?" I asked.

"Not a peep," she said dismissively. "They're probably all pushing up daisies. Now skedaddle."

"You must have heard *something*," I pleaded. "Mombi told me nothing happens in Oz without the Wingless Ones getting wind of it." When in doubt, lay it on thick.

That was a lie, of course. Mombi had never once mentioned Queen Lulu. But royal types can never resist flattery. Lulu's eyes softened.

"Well," she mused. "It's true that I try to keep up with the latest news. The Order isn't the only one with spies. Even up here, it does pay to have the scoop—and I *am* the queen."

"Please," I pushed. "I just want to know—I *need* to know where they are."

Lulu just sighed. "Sorry, toots," she said. "Only thing I know is that your hag Mombi worked her old abracadabra and went right up in smoke. Took her pals with her. Poof! All I've heard since are the sweetest nothings."

"What about . . . ," I started.

She put a hand up to stop me and checked an imaginary watch at her wrist. "I believe my next appointment is coming up," she said irritably. "Now shoo. I'm a very busy monarch. If you want someone who can sit around making small talk, I'd try the Duchess of Tree People. She's the biggest blabbermouth you'll ever find."

When I still didn't move to leave, Lulu's patience finally decided she was over it. "Begone!" she yelled, picking up a banana and hurling it across the room like a boomerang, aiming right for my face. I ducked just in time for it to bounce off my head.

I was done. I'd heard about the types of things monkeys liked to fling, and I was pretty sure I was getting off easy with just a banana. This was my cue to leave.

But as I was heading out into the night, ready to make my way back down into the jungle, I heard a rustling in the trees, and then the low chirping of monkey voices. The queen's council. I couldn't quite hear what they were saying, but from the tone of their whispers, it sounded important.

I knew I had promised, but I couldn't help myself. It came so easily this time that I barely even thought about what I was doing: I felt myself sinking into the shadows. As four monkeys approached the queen's chambers, I slithered after them. They let the door slam shut behind them, and didn't even notice when I passed right through it.

Everything was different in my shadow world—wherever it was. It was sort of like back home when we tried to steal cable from the trailer next door and everything came out kind of staticky and garbled and sometimes upside down, but you could make it out if you kind of squinted and moved your face really close to the screen.

The queen's throne room flickered and wavered, but I saw four monkeys clustered around at her feet. At first it sounded like they were all speaking some other language, but the longer I listened the more I was able to catch snatches of the conversation until finally I managed to make some sense of it.

"We cannot have her here," a monkey in green corduroy overalls and a propeller beanie was saying. "You didn't see her . . ."

Lulu waved him off. "I wish I had," she said. "You want the truth, I wish she'd finished him right off. The Lion can rot. See if I care."

"You don't understand. She was . . . she was not human. Something overtook her—a darkness unlike anything I have ever encountered."

I jolted. They were talking about me. Even though I had some idea of how I'd looked when I'd been fighting the Lion, I didn't like to hear it described like this.

But it was true. I had touched the dark, and I had liked it. And as much as I wanted to think that it was just a case of getting carried away in the fight, it wasn't so simple. How could it be, when I was watching them through this cold, eerie veil of shadows?

"I must agree, Queen Lulu," said a monkey in a curly red wig. "Princess Ozma is one thing, but the presence of the other one puts all of us in danger."

"She is a—"

"Enough!" Lulu snapped. "I'm the boss, applesauce, and the boss-lady has made up her mind. The little witch stays. The princess stays. I have my reasons. Now tell me what you hear of the rest of Oz. Has Dorothy been found?"

A monkey wearing a pink velour sweat suit rose to her feet. "We believe that Princess Dorothy has fled the city, along with the Scarecrow and the Tin Woodman. No one has seen them since last night."

"Glinda?"

"Glinda was gravely wounded in battle and is thought to have returned to her fortress."

"Oh, of course," Lulu sniffed. "That witch talks a big game, but she couldn't be a bigger candy-ass if she dropped her pink little undies and sat on a pile of gumdrops. Now what about the rest of the witches—what about the Order?"

I held my breath, and then realized I had no breath to hold. When I was a shadow, I didn't have a body.

The monkey council exchanged a look amongst themselves. "We . . . ," the one in the sweat suit began. "We don't know. They may be dead. Or they may be alive. We simply—"

Lulu screeched and gnashed her teeth, waving her fan wildly. "If I wanted a load of baloney, I would've had a cold cut platter brought in!" she screamed. "Are any of you going to tell me something useful?"

Finally the smallest of the monkeys, a tiny marmoset in a

fez and a red bolero who had been silent until now, spoke up. "Funny things are afoot across the land, Your Highness," she said carefully.

Queen Lulu raised an eyebrow, which was strange because until that moment I hadn't even realized that she had eyebrows. "Funny . . . *ha-ha?*" she asked hopefully.

"Not exactly. Funny strange. As we suspected, the magic that Glinda and Dorothy had been siphoning off seems to be coming back—we believe it has something to do with the actions of the Order. They must have destroyed some mechanism that was piping it into the city. It's having some odd effects. We need to be aware of it in case it causes any disruptions to our home."

"More magic," Queen Lulu sighed. "Whoopee. Just what we need."

But my ears perked up. This was the first I had heard of anything like that. I'd thought that last night was just about killing Dorothy. No one had told me about any plan beyond that.

"There's something else," the monkey in the bolero said. "With Dorothy and her allies gone, it's unclear who is occupying the palace—but something is happening there."

"Cut to the chase, please," Lulu said. "I don't know what 'something' means. *What's* happening to the palace?"

The monkey looked nervous. "Well," she said. "For one thing, it seems to be growing."

FIVE

As it turned out, there really *was* a giant waterfall up here in the trees. It was easy to find; I only had to follow a series of signs that led through the maze of walkways in the trees until I heard the sound of rushing water in the distance. Ollie hadn't been kidding around. Even though we were so high up that it was hard to imagine there was anything above us, a bright blue river was raging down from the sky.

It was spilling from somewhere over the treetops and crashing through an opening in the canopy into a series of basins the size of swimming pools, built into the tree trunks like stairs. The water cascaded over the edge of one and into the next, overflowing and spilling off into endlessness as it continued its unstoppable course toward the jungle floor.

In the pools, groups of monkeys were frolicking happily, scrubbing themselves and playing, hooting and doing backflips and cannonballs. They were having fun.

Looking at it like this, Oz didn't seem so bad after all, and I stood there for a minute, just watching them play. It took me a few seconds to figure out why it looked so strange: this was the first time since I'd gotten to Oz that I'd actually felt like I was in the place I'd always known from books and movies. A place with witches and monsters, yes, but a place that was magical and joyful and, in the end, beautiful. A place that was happy.

It was the first time since I'd gotten here that I'd actually seen anyone really having fun.

Then I understood what Queen Lulu had been saying to me. This was why she wanted to stay out of it, why she wanted the monkeys to just keep to themselves and let the rest of Oz fight for power. The monkeys had made a place for themselves, and they wanted to enjoy it.

Would it be so bad to stay up here, I wondered? To just say *screw it* to the promises I'd made—to the war that was going on below us—and never go back down there to fight, and kill, and maybe die?

But it didn't matter. I couldn't stay. Not because I'm such a good person, but because I knew this happy feeling wouldn't last. You can't just cover your eyes and pretend like terrible things aren't happening simply because you can't see them, even if that is something that would seem like a good idea to a monkey.

Evil will always catch up with you. That's why you have to get to it first.

I turned away, and realized that I was standing at the entrance to a tree house with the words "Princess Suite" burned into the door in elaborate but sloppy cursive.

Princess Suite. This had to be my room. I hoped it lived up to its name. After the day I'd had, I was ready for a little royal treatment.

The inside of the so-called Princess Suite wasn't lavish—I'm pretty sure my servant's quarters back in the Emerald Palace had been almost as big—and with only one room it wasn't much of a suite. But it was cozy and welcoming, illuminated by sunfruit that floated along the edge of the ceiling. In opposite corners of the room, situated under tented curtains of gauzy mosquito netting that could be pulled shut for privacy, were hammocks woven from large palm fronds. Ozma was sitting on one of the hammocks. She lit up and waved when she saw me.

"Hey," I said. Ozma smiled and fluttered her eyelashes. She shook out her hair.

It wasn't a surprise that I was tired. Of course I was tired. The surprising part was that I was only feeling it now. I stripped off the servant's dress I'd been wearing for Dorothy's big party, now tattered and blood-crusted from my fight with the Lion, and sank heavily into the free hammock opposite the one in which Ozma was swinging happily back and forth, twirling a lock of hair around her finger.

As I lay down, I realized why she looked so content: the hammock conformed to my body perfectly, and maybe it was just that anything would have felt good at that moment, but it almost seemed to be massaging my aching muscles. It was like one of those vibrating chairs at one of those gadget stores at the mall, except better because it didn't make my butt feel numb.

I closed my eyes. I had a plan, and that plan was to fall asleep.

I wasn't going to think about anything. I wasn't going to dwell on anything that had happened, or on what was going to happen next. I was just going to forget the world.

I'd had trouble sleeping when I was little. I was always worrying about things, and so my mother had taught me a trick to clear my mind that I've used ever since. You close your eyes and relax and try to keep your breathing steady, and every time a stray thought enters your head, you picture it inside a soap bubble. Then you just blow the bubble away, and pretty soon you'll be out like a light. Works every time.

It was a skill that was coming in handy around here. When you don't know what's happening tomorrow, it's important to get your sleep where you can—because who knows the next time you'll have a decent pillow? Or any pillow at all, for that matter.

Tonight I had more than the usual amount of thoughts to fend off. Actually, it was just one thought that kept returning stubbornly, no matter how many times I tried to banish it, of the fantasy I'd had while I'd been fighting the Lion, not just of killing him, but ripping him to shreds. Of the satisfaction I had taken in causing him pain, and the way I had wanted to laugh when I hurt him.

The monkeys were all terrified of me—even Ollie had seemed scared. I was a little scared of *myself*, to tell the truth.

But I had liked it, too. Even now, a part of me wished that

Ozma hadn't stopped me, that I had done all those things to the Lion that I had wanted to.

I could still feel the thrill that had shivered through me when I had looked down to see black magic spilling from my knife and into my body, and I already missed it. I knew I shouldn't, but I couldn't help it. I wanted to feel like that again.

And I'm not even sure if I fell asleep or not. What came next could have been a dream, but it didn't feel like one. It didn't feel like real life either. It felt like I'd taken a wrong turn somewhere on the way to dreaming, and had gotten lost, stuck in between the world of awake and asleep.

It was night and I was walking through a forest dense with thin twisted trees. For some reason I wasn't wearing shoes, and slimy moss squished under my bare feet. I had somewhere to be, and so I was moving quickly, following a path that I somehow knew by heart even though it was too dark to see anything.

I had no idea what I was looking for, but I had the gnawing sense that there was something in these woods that I had lost—something that I had to get to.

So I moved through brambles and leaves and vines, feeling leaves scratching my face, stepping easily over branches and roots without even thinking about it. I was alert for danger, but I wasn't the slightest bit scared. I felt a soft breeze on my face and it felt good.

In the distance, I heard an owl hooting, its call getting louder with every step I took, while at the same time the trees got straighter and taller and closer. I could have used magic to light my way, but I didn't mind the dark, and so I kept on going until finally I found myself in a small and perfectly circular clearing. The full moon hung as big as a pancake in the sky, looking spooky and cartoonish at the same time and illuminating the clearing in a ghostly silver light.

In the middle of the clearing was a dark shape. There was something strange about it: it was both clear and indistinct at the same time, solid and real but blurry at the edges. I couldn't quite judge the shape or size of it. Was it some kind of injured animal? Or something weirder?

Whatever it was, there was something off about it—maybe even evil. Just looking at it made me feel a little light-headed, made the hairs on my arms stand on end.

But it also made me a little excited. And instead of running, or even hesitating, I took a step toward it. As I did, four heads turned toward me.

Because what I'd thought was a single animal was actually four hunching, cloaked figures who were huddled so close together that they appeared to have merged into one being. As they looked up, the moonlight hit their pinched, rotting faces, each one tinted a different shade of green, and I saw that they were each wearing raggedy, pointed hats.

All at once, the four figures opened their mouths and began to hiss.

Witches.

I took another step forward, and then another, feeling more confident the closer I got to them until I was filled with a sensation that was something like joy. Their hissing grew fever-ish and high-pitched, and then, when I had almost reached them, they began to disappear, melting like black candles into the ground. Then they were gone, and I knew that I had found what I was looking for. In the ground, in the place where they had huddled, was a small pool that bubbled in the center. A fountain with water so black that it looked like liquid shadow.

I knelt to examine it, but before I could dip my finger in, something began to emerge from the water; a newer, darker fig-ure that slowly began to take shape. From the dark and glittering mass of shadows, a girl emerged. There, standing in front of me, was Ozma.

It was the same Ozma I knew, except that it wasn't. She had the same emerald green eyes and red poppies in her hair, the same tiny, delicate frame. But her skin was glowing, and her hair was swirling around her face in ropy skeins as thick as snakes. Her pupils were tiny flames.

And from her back sprouted two huge black butterfly wings, twice as big as her body and etched with an elaborate gold pat-tern. As she flapped them gently, they crackled with energy.

She extended a hand in my direction.

"Rise," she said. I felt my feet leave the ground.

SIX

I opened my eyes. I think. Anyway, I was awake, and I was back in my room in the monkeys' tree house village. Ozma was crouched over me, staring into my face with exactly the same look of intensity that she'd worn in my dream. Somewhere behind her pupils, I saw the glowing embers of what had recently been flames. Light streamed through the windows, casting her in an almost silhouette.

She reached out her hand for mine.

"Rise," she said.

That one word startled me so badly that I almost flipped out of the hammock. But then the princess stuck out her tongue and blew me a raspberry, and when she started to laugh I felt my heart slowing back to a normal rate.

I was imagining things. It had only been a dream. Right? I put my hand in Ozma's and let her help me up, trying to quiet my mind. *It was only a dream*, I told myself again.

But what if it had been something more? And what had it meant? Most importantly, why did I feel almost disappointed that it was over now? What did it say about me that I had felt myself approaching something truly evil, and that even though I'd had every opportunity to back away, I'd taken a step closer, and then another?

Some part of me had even wanted it. Maybe. I decided, for now, to just not think about that.

Standing up, I still felt a little unsteady on my feet from the day before, but the sleep had done me good and the soreness in my arms and legs was mostly gone.

Last night, I'd been too tired to really examine our quarters, but now I had a chance to look around. There really wasn't a lot to see: I spotted a folding screen in the corner, the kind people coyly stepped behind in old movies to change. A large wooden bowl sat on a wooden pedestal by the window. It was filled with bubbling water, and a few large, pink blossoms floated on the surface. I walked over and splashed the water across my face gratefully. It tingled in a pleasant way against my skin before evaporating.

I was glad that there was no mirror here—I didn't want to know how terrible I looked. Sure, I'd taken a quick dip in a stream yesterday when we'd been trudging through the forest with the monkeys, just to get the Lion's blood off me, but I had a feeling that I was still a total wreck. How could I not be? Before last night, I hadn't slept since the night before Dorothy's big party.

Still, the water was refreshing, with a vaguely perfumed smell, and it felt good to wash up. I cupped another handful and pulled it through my hair, feeling days' worth of dirt and grime coming off on my hands.

"So what the hell do we do next?" I found myself asking aloud. I wasn't sure if I was talking to Ozma or to myself. I wasn't expecting Ozma to be paying attention or to understand what I was saying, but at least she was someone to talk to. Look, I'd grown up with a mom who was on another planet most of the time, so I was used to having conversations with people who weren't really listening. It was no big deal.

Anyway, after everything Ozma and I had been through together, I was starting to feel weirdly close to her. No, she probably wasn't the friend I would have chosen for myself, but she was something. And with Star gone and Nox missing, friends were in short supply these days.

"We can't stay here forever," I said, taking advantage of her willingness to at least pretend to listen. "But I don't know where to go next either. Do we go back to the city? Do we look for Dorothy? Do I try to find the Scarecrow so I can cut out his brains?" I shuddered a little at the thought of that one. I knew I had to do it eventually, but I *really* didn't feel like it. "Every time I turn around, someone's telling me to do something different; every time I sit down to think, there's another mystery that I can't solve. I just feel stuck."

Ozma looked at me expectantly, and suddenly I found myself saying the thing I hadn't even admitted to myself.

"I have to find Nox," I said. "I know it makes no sense—he's the last one I should be worrying about. But he's the only one I trust."

That's the thing about talking to someone you're not sure is really listening. Sometimes you end up saying stuff you don't know you mean until it just comes spilling out.

But Ozma didn't look surprised. Instead, she gave me a sly wink. "Nox Nox!" Ozma said.

Something about the way she said it piqued my interest. And after all, I was starting to think that maybe I was underestimating her. She had seemed to know that the magic was coming back to Oz. She had known the Lion was coming for us. Underneath all her idiotic chatter, it was becoming clear that she had some hidden depths.

"What about him?" I asked. Ozma just rolled her eyes and scowled at me like I was the dumbest person in the world. "Who's *there?*" she said in frustration.

My shoulders drooped and I let out a groan, suddenly realizing exactly how much I'd hoped she'd been about to say something that was actually useful. "Whatever." I scooped the filthy dress I'd discarded the night before up from the floor, and I was just about to put it on when I noticed that the monkeys had left me a clean outfit, neatly folded on a table by the door. Maybe Queen Lulu liked me more than she had let on, but more likely, she just didn't want me walking around her village looking like a bum.

Thankfully, considering the monkeys' normal fashion sense, they had left me a fairly sensible outfit. Of course, when I say sensible, I mean relatively speaking. As I went through the pile beside the bed, I discovered that they had decided to outfit me in a faded pink T-shirt that read *Kiss My Grits!* in chartreuse script across the chest and a pair of cut-off denim short shorts. Okay, it wasn't quite my style, but at least my hosts hadn't decided I'd look stunning in a nun's habit or an oversize baby's onesie and a pacifier.

Just having a fresh shirt was almost good enough for me, but it wasn't the best part. When I got to the bottom of the stack, I almost jumped for joy. Of all the wondrous things I'd encountered in Oz, this might have been the most miraculous of all: a pair of clean underwear. I didn't even care that they were leopard-print granny panties—I still felt like I'd won the lottery as I stepped behind the screen in the corner to put them on.

"How stupid am I?" I asked myself aloud as I changed. I was still thinking about Nox. "How is it possible that I'm here in the middle of a magical war, supposedly saving the world—or the kingdom, or whatever I'm supposedly saving—and all I can think about is some dumb boy? Tracking him down should be the last thing on my mind."

I stepped out from behind the screen to find Ozma regarding me with amusement.

"What?" I asked indignantly. "You don't like my outfit? Look, not everyone can pull off the nightgown and tiara look as well as you can, okay?"

Ozma gave a little pirouette, sending her flowing white gown billowing, and I giggled. The girl was crazy, no question, but I had to admit that she was growing on me.

"Hey," I said, suddenly curious. "You don't by any chance keep a giant pair of wings somewhere under there, do you?"

She flapped her arms up and down and hopped on one foot, but no wings sprouted.

So much for that idea. "It was worth a shot, right?" I shrugged, then returned to the subject of myself. Because, really, why not? "The thing is that I don't even really *like* him," I mumbled. "I just think he might be able to . . ." I trailed off without finishing my sentence, suddenly embarrassed that I was trying to get away with such an outrageous lie. Of *course* I liked him. I didn't want to find him because he could help; I wanted to find him because I had a crush on him. There, I said it.

I know, I know. How stupid am I?

From the way Ozma was looking at me now, it seemed she wasn't really buying what I was selling either. She was gazing at me with a deep, bemused kindness that was also a little skeptical, and I had to wonder, yet again, if maybe she actually understood what I'd been saying all along. I stepped closer to her.

"What *is* it about you?" I asked. She replied by bobbling her neck and twirling her finger at her temple.

Maybe it was because of my dream, but this time I wasn't quite convinced by her look-how-dumb-I-am act. Was that what the dream had been trying to tell me? That Ozma and her secrets were the key to everything? Or at least the key to *something*?

I looked her up and down carefully, trying to find a clue. This time, I found one.

At first, it was just a glimpse of something overlaid on top of reality. It was like a double vision, another image that was barely there, hovering around the princess's body. It reminded me of what I'd seen, for a moment, when I'd defeated the Lion, just before I'd taken his tail. When that had happened, I hadn't had time to really think about it; I'd been acting totally on instinct. This time I tried to really focus on what I was seeing.

Again, I had to wonder how all this magic was coming so easily to me. Was the fact that Oz was getting its magic back just making it easier to take ahold of, or was I actually finding some kind of power of my own? And if I *was*, was that a good thing or a bad thing?

As I let myself become distracted by questions, I felt the magic slipping through my grasp. I clenched my fists and tried harder, and then it was gone entirely. But I could tell I was on to something—after all, the instinct I'd had about the Lion's tail had been right. I wasn't about to give up now. I narrowed my eyes and tried again.

One of the first lessons Gert had taught me about magic, in the long series of barely successful lessons she'd given me before she'd died, is that it's hard to hold. Magic is tricky; it will do what it wants to, but not if you boss it around. You have to ask nicely. You have to think it's the magic's idea instead of yours. Kind of like Sandie Charlemagne, my old manager at Dusty's Diner back in Kansas.

It was a funny connection to make, but thinking of Sandie made me think of quicksand, and how the more you struggle the

faster you sink, and that made me think about those Chinese finger traps you get when you're a little kid—the ones you can only
get out of if you stop trying. Then I thought of the soap bubble
trick from my mother that had helped me fall asleep last night.

I decided to just let all my thoughts drift away, and as my
mind began to clear, the glowing aura around Ozma got brighter
and clearer while, at the same time, the princess herself became
more and more vague.

It wasn't just Ozma either. Everything in the room was coming in and out, like when you're driving and the radio reception
changes depending on whether you're going up or down a hill.
Why not try adjusting the dial? I thought. And it worked.

When I shifted my attention in one direction, the glowing
got stronger while everything else faded away. Everything that
had been in the room was still there, except that it was made out
of a strange, glittering thread. The screen, the wash basin, the
sleeping hammocks, Ozma. Even my own body. All of it was just
energy, and all of it was connected to each other.

I knew, on some level, that what I was seeing was the *real* Oz.
I had pulled back the curtain and stepped through it, but instead
of finding a humbug wizard, I'd found the controls to the whole
operation—and it turned out the whole operation was made out
of what appeared to be magical silly string.

Well, that makes it sound kind of lame. It wasn't lame. It was
literally the most beautiful thing I'd ever seen. So beautiful that
I had to try to touch it: I just reached out in front of me and
tried to grasp one of the stray filaments floating randomly in the

air. It swayed a little, but it didn't really move, and my fingers passed right through it. When I tried to grab a fistful of them, I came up empty. But I found that if I sort of brushed my fingers against them, they responded to my touch as long as I didn't push too hard. And if I was patient enough, I was able to move them around.

It was weird and very cool, but I didn't really see the point until I noticed that the wayward strings of magic that had seemed to be floating randomly through the air—the ones I'd been playing with—were actually slowly gravitating toward something. And that something was Ozma.

They were flowing into her, sort of, but they were also twisting around her body, which was the brightest thing in the whole room. When I looked closely, I saw that she was just one big knot of magic.

And what do you do with knots? Well, duh. You untie them.

I didn't want to hurt her. I just wanted to see what would happen. And so I hovered my fingers around Ozma, trying to see if I could get the jumbled lines of magic to untangle themselves.

At first, it seemed like it wasn't doing anything, but after a few minutes, I noticed that one tiny thread was now twisting out from her elbow, and I managed to catch it on my finger, and I tugged on it, feeling just the slightest bit of give.

I bit my lip in concentration, careful not to pull too hard. And, just like I was tugging on a loose string on an old sweater from the thrift store, Ozma began to unravel.

No—it wasn't her that was unraveling, exactly. It was more

like I was unraveling some kind of spell. Meanwhile, Ozma herself was changing shape. She was getting bigger. Taller. Her
shoulders broadened into a man's. Well, a boy's, I guess. And
I could tell from his slouch and the tilt of his head that it was a
boy I knew.

"Pete," I muttered under my breath.

As soon as I spoke, it all slipped away. I was back in the real
world, Ozma was gone, and Pete was standing right in front of
me, wide-eyed in surprise. He took a step backward toward the
door and held up his hands, looking as guilty and sheepish as
someone who has just been caught shoplifting a Hostess Twinkie
from the Piggly Wiggly.

"Um, hey?" he said. "So, uh, that was pretty weird, huh?"
He scanned me up and down. "Nice outfit," he said, grinning.

I didn't know what to think. All I knew was that Pete had
played me one too many times already, even if I didn't know
why, and I wasn't going to let him do it again.

Still, I couldn't help it if I was just a little bit happy to see him.
Because it was Pete, who had saved my life about five minutes
after I'd first arrived in Oz. Pete, who had kept me from going
crazy when I'd been trapped in Dorothy's dungeons. Pete, who
had been the only person I could talk to when I had been posing
as a servant in the Emerald Palace.

"Forget the outfit," I said shortly. I took a step back and felt a
sizzle of heat in my palm as my knife appeared without me even
calling for it. "I think it's time for you to do some talking."

He brushed his dark hair from his green eyes. The same

exact eyes that belonged to Ozma. He looked away and took a deep breath. When our eyes met again, I suddenly saw a sadness in him that I recognized from somewhere. "It's kind of a long story," he said. "Don't we have better things to talk about?"

"Dude," I said. I took a step toward him, and I saw him glance at my knife. I didn't want to fight him, but I would, if it came to it. "I've known you longer than anyone else in this whole messed-up fairyland, and I still don't know you at all. All you've done is lie to me. So yeah," I spat. "I like you. I think. But I think you'd better start giving me some explanations."

Pete just nodded with resigned understanding. He took a deep breath and slumped against the wall, folding his tense, sinewy arms across his chest. "Okay," he said. "But you might as well have a seat, 'cause I wasn't kidding when I said it was a long story. And I don't even know the whole thing."

I considered it, and then sat back down in the hammock I'd slept in, leaving my bare feet firm on the ground to steady myself. For now, I kept my knife in my hand. I didn't think I would need it, but you could never be too safe around here.

"Let's hear it," I said. "Just tell me everything you do know."

"Where should I start?"

"The beginning."

So Pete started at the beginning. "Once upon a time . . . ," he said.

SEVEN

"Once upon a time," Pete began, "there was a little girl—a fairy, actually, but who knows what a fairy really even is? I've always been sort of fuzzy on that. Anyway. She was a princess. Or, well, really she wasn't a princess at all, because she had no parents, so technically she was the queen. But everyone thought it seemed dumb to call her a queen, because she was just a baby. I mean, she couldn't even walk. So they called her Princess Ozma."

"How can a baby be queen?" I asked. "Was she just crawling around the palace by herself? Who was taking care of her? And, like, who was ruling Oz?"

"She had a nursemaid," Pete explained. "A winged monkey named Lulu whose family had worked for the royal family for ages. She took care of Ozma, and after a time, Lulu came to think of Ozma as her own."

I did a double take. "Wait a minute," I said. "*Queen* Lulu?"

"I guess that's what she's calling herself these days," Pete said with a rueful smile. "Everyone and their babysitter's got a crown in this stupid fairyland, huh?"

"Actually, Queen Lulu wears a tutu and cat-eye sunglasses," I pointed out.

Pete snickered. "I meant, like, a metaphorical crown," he said. "Because, look, the thing about Oz that you have to understand is there's only one true queen. It didn't matter that Ozma was a baby or whatever. She's the only living descendant of the fairy Lurline, so that makes her the one in charge. It's like the law or something. They call it Old Magic. Look, I don't totally understand it either, but I don't have to. Everything sort of depends on it, you know?"

"Not really," I said. "But keep going. Maybe I'll get it later."

"The point is that basically no one was in charge. So when the Wizard showed up from god knows where, well—let's just say the people of Oz were ready for some real leadership. Didn't even really matter that he wasn't a wizard at all. So he sets himself up in the palace, takes the baby Ozma, sells her to Mombi, and—"

"Hold up," I interjected. This story was getting more confusing by the second. "He just *takes* the baby?"

Pete raised his eyebrows in consternation. "If I have to give you every little detail it's going to take all day."

"But what about Lulu?" I asked. "If she was supposed to be taking care of Ozma, why didn't she stop him?"

Pete shook his head sadly. "He found this magic hat thing. If you have the hat, you control the monkeys. This was a long time ago, remember—Dorothy must still have the hat lying around somewhere nowadays. Anyway, the Wizard gave the magic hat to the Wicked Witch of the West in exchange for her help, and she made all the monkeys into her slaves. So that got rid of Lulu, and then the Wizard could do what he wanted."

"I never realized the Wizard was such a total dick," I said. "Although, I guess by now I should know better." Pete just gave me a look, annoyed.

I settled back in my seat and willed myself to shut up. I was sort of glad I did, because it was a good story. Crazy, but good. This is what he told me:

Once upon a time and long ago (but not that long ago), in the land that may by now be familiar to you, there lived a fairy princess who, like every fairy queen before her, had been born from a flower that grew from the center of an ancient fountain that sat in the center of a maze where the land's magic was at its strongest. Because of certain unbendable principles of this very magic, the kingdom was the girl's to protect and rule.

Her name was Ozma, and, the fact is, she was far too small to be much of a leader.

Despite this deficit, the princess was beloved by all, and most of all by her loyal nanny, a flying monkey by the name of Lulu. Lulu doted on Ozma and cared for her fiercely in the absence of parents, governing Oz herself as Ozma's proxy until the day that the little princess was old enough to take over the job.

Lulu was pragmatic and fair, and although all was not per-
fect, all should have at least been well. But it was not, for there
were other forces at work. Yes, there were witches involved—if
there's something to be involved in, you can be sure that witches
will always be lurking nearby. But in this case, the witches
were not the real problem. The real problem was a newcomer
to the kingdom who had arrived in a strange, colorful flying
machine and took to falsely calling himself a wizard.

At first, this false Wizard went unnoticed as he traveled
through the wondrous kingdom, exploring its customs, its out-
lands, and, naturally, its magic. And when he had decided
that the time was right, he journeyed to a city made of emer-
alds to seek an audience with the queen.

It wasn't until he saw Ozma that he realized she wasn't
much of a queen at all. He had heard she was young, but this,
he thought, was ridiculous.

The Wizard could see that Oz was in desperate need of a
true leader. With no one minding the shop except a monkey and
an infant, he was certain that the kingdom would quickly fall
into disrepair. So he considered it his solemn duty—perhaps
his destiny?—to save this strange and beautiful fairyland
from itself.

Why shouldn't he be king? he wondered. (Never mind that,
in all its history, Oz had only had queens. The Wizard was
from a place called America, and to him, a female ruler was
a strange and unsettling notion.) Other than the witches, who
were too consumed with squabbling with each other to be in

charge of anything, no one seemed much interested in leader-
ship, least of all baby Ozma.

So the Wizard hatched a scheme.

Before we get to that scheme, let us return, for a moment,
to the witches. There were four of them. Two were evil, two
were good (supposedly), and all of them were silly and petty,
if fearsome. The wickedest of them, the Western Witch, was
also somewhat less silly than the rest, and so it was she with
whom the Wizard chose to conspire. Through this conspiracy,
the Wizard snatched Princess Ozma from the monkey Lulu,
and conscripted the poor beast, along with her winged brothers
and sisters, into the Western Witch's enslavement.

Then, because the Wizard knew that the people of Oz
would never accept him as their king so long as they believed
the princess was alive, and because the Old Magic that courses
through everything in the land would not allow him to kill the
princess outright, he sent her north, to the hag Mombi, who
had her own motives for taking the baby in. To ensure that
Ozma would remain safely hidden, it was decided that old
Mombi would enchant the child and keep her far away from
the eyes of the world.

And so many years passed. Meanwhile, changes were
afoot in Oz, brought on once again by a visitor from the Other
Place: not the Wizard, this time, but a plucky and plainspoken
farm girl named Dorothy Gale. Within weeks of her arrival,
Dorothy made short work of killing two witches and, finally,
exposing the Wizard himself and banishing him.

With the Wizard deposed, Dorothy could have held the crown herself. But being of sentimental and truly generous spirit, Dorothy was of the belief that there was No Place Like Home. Thus, she chose to forgo a seat on the emerald throne in order to return to the place your people call Kansas. So again, there was a vacuum of power.

This time it was filled by Dorothy's companion the Scarecrow—who, even having been blessed by the Wizard with a set of artificial brains, was a few bales short of a haystack and was not much up to the task of kingship. Chaos ran rampant.

During all these goings-on, Tippetarius, the princess formerly known as Ozma, who by now had come to be known simply as Tip, was in Gillikin Country, far away from the tumult and intrigue of the Emerald City.

Tip had grown weary of his lot in life. And so he left Mombi, and set out to seek his fortune.

Remember this: Old Magic runs deep. It finds a way to prevail. Perhaps it was Old Magic that compelled Tip to leave the only home he'd ever known. Either way, Tip wound his way down a strange and treacherous path through Oz, surviving trial after trial, until he finally found himself in the Emerald City.

There, Tip came face-to-face with the sorceress Glinda, who was easily able to see through Mombi's shoddy enchantment. Tippetarius was revealed as Ozma, and with that, the rightful queen was restored to her throne, and for the first time in many years, Oz was a truly happy place.

But with all the turmoil in the land, Glinda's hold on power had been dwindling, and she had thought that young and inexperienced Ozma would make a suitable pawn. She was incorrect. And so, being unable to rid herself of the princess, Glinda arranged for Dorothy's return.

At first, the kingdom was overjoyed to have their beloved heroine back, and Ozma welcomed the girl into the palace. Soon, though, the princess discovered that Dorothy was no longer the bright-eyed, kindhearted girl that she had been on her first voyage. Something had changed. Like the Wizard before her, she lusted for power, fame, and, above all, magic. Soon, Ozma decided that it would be better for all if Dorothy returned to Kansas.

This displeased Dorothy greatly. In fact, it drove her into a wild fury. In a fit of rage, Dorothy—who had great power but little experience with magic—cast a wild and unpredictable spell on Ozma that left the princess in the dim-witted state in which she can now be found. And Dorothy got the thing that she had come to desire most: Oz.

Which, of course, brings us to the moment in Oz's history in which you find yourself, save for one final detail that very few people know, including Dorothy herself. And this is where it gets weird:

When Mombi transformed the baby Ozma into Tippetarius, she was out of her depth. Remember this was many years ago. Mombi was a bit second-rate as a spell caster in those days, and not even skilled enough to call herself a true witch. She had meant to simply disguise Ozma's physical form. Instead, in creating Tip, she split Ozma's soul. Tippetarius was not just a new name for a made-over Ozma. He was an entirely different person, with his own thoughts, feelings, and personality. And although Dorothy's spell had erased Ozma's mind—or, at least, turned it off—it had not erased Tip's.

Which is why, in certain moments, Tip, who had been in Ozma somewhere, all along, was able to emerge, both in body and in spirit. In those moments, Tip was able to carve out a certain kind of half-life for himself. Now that he finally knew who he was, he was able to understand everything that he wasn't—everything that had been taken away from him, and everything that he had never been allowed to be.

He no longer felt like Tip. So he decided to call himself Pete.

With that, Pete looked up at me, his dark, messy hair falling in front of his eyes, a self-conscious half smile on his lips. In that moment, he looked vulnerable and unsure of himself. I wanted to get up and give him a hug, or something, but I wasn't sure if that would be weird. I had a million things I wanted to ask him—my head was spinning with them—but it seemed like now wasn't the right time. So I didn't say anything for a minute.

And then, when the silence just started being awkward, I said, "Let's go for a walk. I could use some air, I think."

Pete looked relieved. "You think *you* could use some fresh air. Think about *me*," he laughed. "I've been cooped up in a teeny tiny little corner of a fairy princess's brain for god knows how long." He paused. "How long *have* I been cooped up in there, this time?"

"Not that long, actually," I said. "Just like a couple of days. But it felt like a lot longer."

"Well, it's Oz," he said. "The whole concept of time lost its meaning ages ago."

"You're telling me," I said. "Now let's go. I think I know a good spot." With that, Pete grabbed my hand, hoisted me up, and we headed out into the sun.

It was a perfect day out, and the whole world looked gilded in golden-green. Monkeys were everywhere, out strolling, bounding through the tree branches, and frolicking in the pools under the waterfall, just enjoying the weather.

"Wow," Pete said, watching them playing. "At least *someone* in Oz is having fun these days."

"Yeah," I said. "Lucky them."

Pete gave me a sly glance. "You know," he said. "We could take an hour off ourselves. Wanna go for a swim?"

It took me a second to agree, but in the end, it was too tempting to resist. "Sounds like a plan," I said.

So we made our way across a rope bridge and down a set of wooden stairs to the entrance of the monkey baths. From here, they looked even more impressive—it was like the world's most exotic water park, complete with a giant waterslide that started at the top pool and spiraled to the bottom in a series of death-defying drops and hairpin turns that made me shudder.

We found a smallish pool that was mostly hidden from sight by leaves but was still sunny enough to be warm. Pete stripped off his shirt and his loose-fitting pants, then jumped into the water in just his undershorts.

A few seconds later, he emerged, grinning. He climbed back up onto the edge of the pool and shook himself off like a dog, flexing every muscle in his white, slender torso. I tried not to stare.

"You have to come in," he said. "The water's incredible."

"I don't have a bathing suit," I said. I was suddenly feeling shy.

Pete gave me a *whatever* look. "Who cares? Anyway, can't you just magic yourself something else?" he asked. "I thought you'd gone all witch now."

"The Order's training camp isn't exactly fashion school," I said. "If you need me to incinerate someone, though, I'm your girl." Then I thought of something. "Hey," I said, with a sly, sidelong glance in his direction, hoping I wasn't hitting on a touchy subject. "What about *you*? Aren't you a fairy or what-ever?"

Pete grimaced like I'd just insulted him. "Um, no," he said. Then he caught himself. "I mean, not exactly," he said, more calmly. He paused and looked at the ground. "Well, maybe, I guess. Maybe technically? But I can't do magic," he said. "Not even a simple spell. I don't really know why. I wish I could."

This time, when he jumped in, he did it in a huge cannonball, purposely drenching me with the splash. "Come on," he said.

"I won't look. I promise. Anyway, I hate to tell you, but I've already seen you in your underwear."

"What? When?"

"Um, try this morning?" Pete said. Then he screwed his face up and started talking in a squeaky voice. "I *have* to find Nox," he said. "He's the *only* one I trust."

It took me a beat to realize that he was mimicking me.

"You heard that?" I asked, my stomach dropping as I realized exactly what he was saying. Trying to remember everything I'd said and done around Ozma with no idea that I'd had an audience beyond one catatonic princess. "What else did you hear?" I asked, not sure I wanted to know the answer.

"I don't know." He shrugged. "Not everything. When Ozma's in charge, things are sort of fuzzy. Sometimes I miss days at a time; other times it's like I'm seeing through her eyes. But don't worry—I try to be a gentleman about it. Anyway, now we're even. You've seen me in my underwear, and you know all my secrets. Plus, I don't care about your crush on Nox. Is it supposed to be surprising? Who can resist an angry, tortured rebel type? Especially when he's—you know . . . extremely attractive."

He dove back under the water without waiting for my answer, and I watched his pale figure disappear as he went deeper and deeper below the surface. I was basically dying to go in myself.

Screw it, I thought. I couldn't remember the last time I'd gone for a real swim. It would be a total waste to pass up the opportunity now. So without thinking about it anymore, I stripped down to my bra and my leopard print granny panties and jumped in.

The water felt better than I'd imagined was possible. It was cool, but not freezing, and there was something about it that gave my skin a minty tingle. I stayed under as long as I could, just letting it seep into me.

Finally, I had to come up for air, and when I did, Pete was waiting. He grabbed me around my waist and lifted me into his arms, both of us laughing, then tossed me across the pool.

"You suck!" I shouted at him after I recovered myself. He was still laughing, but then his laughing stopped and his smile turned into something more serious. "I'll tell you one other thing I saw," he said. His tone wasn't mean, just concerned or something. "I saw you fighting the Lion. I'm glad you did what you did, but . . ."

He didn't seem to be able to put it into words. But he didn't have to. I'd been trying to put it out of my mind ever since it had happened.

"I know," was all I said.

He wasn't going to let it go quite that easily. "It's just like . . . Dorothy was good once upon a time, too, you know? Not just good. She was the *best*. Until the magic got ahold of her."

"I know," I said. He didn't look away. "I know," I repeated.

"You know what that means, right?"

But before I could reply, there was a crashing sound, a burst of purple smoke, and Mombi was sprawled out on a bamboo platform next to the water, right between where Pete stood and I sat.

Her face was bruised and swollen. Her cloak was in tatters.

She looked from me to Pete and back. "Well," she said in a strained voice. "I'm glad to see you two are getting along."

Then her eyes rolled back in her head, and she crumpled to the ground.

EIGHT

Later that afternoon, I once again found myself in Queen Lulu's chambers, which the monkeys had transformed into a makeshift courtroom. Mombi was on trial.

In addition to being queen of the monkeys, it turned out that Lulu was also the chief justice of their supreme court, and she was presiding in a long black robe and a crooked white judge's wig, clutching an oversize gavel in her paw. All around the room, the members of the monkey council were perched in whatever spots they could find, all of them outfitted in somber courtroom garb, monkey style.

The hours following Mombi's surprise arrival had been a blur. We had no idea where she'd been or how she'd found us. Within seconds of her collapse, a retinue of monkey guards in beefeater uniforms had swept in—apparently her teleportation spell had tripped their alarms. The Wingless Ones had not been amused to have yet another witch in their presence, and as they'd hauled her motionless body off to the monkey slammer, it was unclear whether she was even still alive.

If she *was* dead, it was even more unclear how I felt about it. Of all the members of the Order whom I'd met, Mombi was the one I trusted the least. She had lied to me more than once, and she had always seemed to have the most right to call herself *wicked*.

But, for better or worse, I had bound myself to her, in more ways than one. And, on top of that, I had questions I needed to ask her.

Queen Lulu had declared that the trial be held as soon as Mombi woke up. *If* she woke up. And while Pete—who Lulu, oddly, had been unsurprised to see instead of Ozma—had been barred from entering the queen's chamber, *I* had been chosen to act as Mombi's lawyer, for reasons I couldn't make sense of.

Now, here we were. I'd heard of kangaroo courts and even monkey trials, but this was taking it to a whole new level. Not that it mattered much anyway—I'd been in Oz long enough to know that courtroom procedure around here didn't have much in common with what I knew from watching *SVU* reruns. In Oz—in my experience at least—there was no due process, no Fifth Amendment to plead, and if the judges were sassy, it wasn't usually in a well-meaning, salt-of-the-earth kind of way. It was usually more like sassy-psychotic.

For Mombi's sake, I could only hope that Lulu was a more evenhanded judge than Dorothy had been when *I'd* been put on trial.

"This court will now come to order!" Lulu barked from the

bench, which was really just her throne. "The despicable crone known as Mombi stands accused of high witchery, gross dishonesty, untold crimes against monkeys, *outrageous* trespassing, and general unpleasantness. Also, she is extremely unattractive. Miss Amy, do you speak for the witch?"

I was standing behind a long, wooden table that had been set up in the middle of the chamber.

"Uh, I'm not exactly a lawyer," I said, addressing Lulu and the rest of the monkeys. "But do you really think she's fit to be put on trial? Look at her—she can barely stand up at all."

It was true. On her best day, Mombi was haggard and withered, but you only had to spend a minute or two with her to realize how tough she was despite her old age. Today was the first time she'd ever truly appeared fragile. There was something about it that was unsettling, and I was reminded of the first time I had ever really understood that when my mom was "relaxing," she was high as a kite and not taking a funny kind of nap.

It was that feeling you get when you realize that the person you've always looked to for protection can't help you at all—that she, not you, is the one who needs taking care of.

Mombi was leaning heavily on the table, hunched over, her shoulders trembling as she strained under every breath. It was no secret to anyone in the room that she was in serious pain. She had a stool next to her if she wanted it, but she was standing. You had to give her credit for poise.

I had to get her out of here and make her get better, if for no other reason than because she was my best chance of figuring out what was going on. Not to mention my best hope for finding Nox.

"Your honor," I said, addressing the queen as politely as I could.

"Your *royal* honor," Lulu corrected me in her high-pitched, nasal singsong.

"Sorry, your royal honor," I said. "But I think we need to get Mombi to someone who can help her. It's—"

"Zip-zip!" Queen Lulu barked, pulling her fingers across her lips. Suddenly I realized who she reminded me of: Judge Judy. Now *this* was a version of the law I recognized. Back home, *Judge Judy* was my mother's favorite show—Mom was always coming up with enemies she wanted to face off against in Judy's courtroom. You know, like our landlord, the lady in the next trailer over with the annoying dog, the bartender at Paddy O'Hooligan's who wouldn't serve her a third drink. She was always sure she would win. Big surprise, she never quite got around to filling out all the applications to get Judge Judy to take her cases.

The good news was that if this was Judge Judy, I knew how to deal with it. Basically, I just had to suck up. "It's an honor to appear before you today," I said to Lulu, smiling smarmily. She seemed pleased at my deference, and as she shuffled some papers around in front of her, I looked over at Mombi. "Are you okay?" I whispered.

"I'll be fine," she muttered through gritted teeth. But she didn't look fine.

"How should I say you plead?" I asked.

Mombi wheezed. "Guilty!" she cackled to the room at large, doubling over at the effort it took just to laugh.

"Miss Gumm," Lulu said sternly. For some reason—procedure?—she was refusing to speak to Mombi. "Please remind your witch friend that the sentence for her crimes is *death*."

"I'm sorry," I said. "But can you remind me exactly what her crimes *are*?"

My words were lost in the pandemonium that had broken loose as Lulu had announced the penalty and the rest of monkeys began hooting and chattering and jumping up and down.

"Kill the witch!" screeched a monkey—the one who had looked so cute in his little green overalls just yesterday.

"Burn her!" a smaller monkey shouted.

Then they were all yelling at once:

"Melt her with water!"

"Make her pay!"

"Witches get stitches!"

Queen Lulu let the pandemonium go on for a long spell, looking extremely pleased at the scene she'd created. Finally, when things were threatening to get truly out of hand, she hopped up in her seat and waved her tiny, furry fists.

"Shut up!" she screeched. She didn't really seem angry, just excited. "All of you! I'm in charge here!" The room snapped to silence as I heard Mombi clear her throat. All eyes turned back to her.

"Monkeys of the court," she said. Her voice was measured and quiet, but had a commanding edge to it. "If I may speak." Mombi gathered herself up and stood tall, clearly trying to summon as much dignity as she could. You know, given the situation.

"I stand before you bruised and bloodied," she said, laboring over each word. If this were *Judge Judy* I'd probably have assumed it was all a show, and that she was playing the victim card. But Mombi looked like she was in real pain. "My comrades, the Revolutionary Order of the Wicked, are lost, scattered to the four corners of Oz—an Oz whose future has never been more in doubt. My magical abilities are almost completely drained. In short, I am a shadow of myself. Why? Because I have been fighting a war for many years. I have done this not for power, not for glory, but for Oz. I fight not just for myself, but for the Munchkins, and the Nomes, and yes, for the monkeys—for winged and wingless alike. You ask me how I plead. If I am accused of fighting for those who cannot fight, then I refuse to pretend at anything other than the truth. Of that crime, I am guilty."

As she rolled along, I could see a fearsome glimmer of the Mombi I knew returning as she marshaled the little strength she had left to make her plea. She was building up steam.

"But what of those who can fight, and choose not to? Wingless Ones, while you cavort mindlessly in the trees, far from the troubles below, your brothers and sisters are in chains, forced to serve their mistress's cruel whims. You turn your backs on them simply because you think that they are not as brave as you. Need I remind you what those backs look like now? Did you deform yourselves—pay the ultimate price—just so you could cover your eyes and ears to the truth? Is *this* bravery?"

She fluttered a quivering hand around the room dismissively and went on. "But I am not a young witch, and I know very well that monkeys do not learn new tricks easily. So I do not stand here asking you to fight. I only ask that you grant me safe harbor so that I might continue to do battle on your behalf."

I was impressed—even after all the time I'd spent with her in the Order's headquarters, I'd never been completely convinced that she was *really* the freedom fighter she claimed to be. As much as Nox had always sworn otherwise, I'd always had a nagging suspicion that maybe she was just an opportunist, eager to get rid of Dorothy so that she could be in power for herself.

Now, listening to her speech, I saw the true passion she had for what she believed in. It was hard not to admire it.

The monkeys of the council all looked convinced, too, and were exchanging nervous, thoughtful glances. The only one who didn't seem to be buying it was Queen Lulu, whose eyes were fiery with anger.

"Save me the sob story, sister," Lulu said. "You talk a good game, but I wouldn't call bingo just yet. We all know who you are. We all know what you've done. If it weren't for you, Oz might not be in this mess in the first place. Or are you forgetting the little deal you cut with the Wizard way back when?"

There was murmuring among the monkeys, but Mombi cut in.

"What do you want me to say?" she bellowed, suddenly

full-throated in her rage. "That I'm nothing but a common bush hag like Glinda the Supposedly Good? You want me to say it? Yes, I've been wicked, and I regret my crimes! You want more blood? Well, if it's blood you want, you'll have that, too, I promise. Just let it be Dorothy's blood—and mine, if it comes to it—rather than your own and the blood of your people. Persecute me not, Wingless Ones. Instead, let me rest here safely to recover my strength so that I can help destroy our oppressor before she destroys us all."

With that, Mombi collapsed breathlessly onto the stool at her side, and there was silence again. Queen Lulu stroked the hairs on her chin in contemplation, and then, finally, climbed up onto the back of her throne. She slammed her gavel against the wall of the royal tree hut with so much force that the whole structure shook.

"The court has reached its decision!" she said. I took a step back in surprise. Wait, that was *it*? "Mombi, as not even you yourself dispute the charges against you, you have been found guilty on every count."

There was a murmur throughout the room, and I held my breath, waiting to see what came next. Was I going to have to fight to save her? The Tin Woodman, fine. The Lion, okay. They were both monsters. But I hadn't signed up to kill any monkeys. And I also wasn't going to let them just kill Mombi for no reason.

Luckily, I didn't have to make that choice. Because Lulu wasn't done:

"However," the queen went on. "In my role as monarch of the monkeys, I have chosen to overrule the decision of the court. There can be no doubt that Mombi is as guilty as a nun dancing the hoochie coochie on Sunday morning. Even she admits it. But for now, witch, out of the goodness of my heart, I'm reducing your sentence and placing you under house arrest."

She banged her gavel again. She liked that gavel. "Justice has been served!" she proclaimed. "Miss Gumm, you may escort the convict back to the Princess Suite, where she will be allowed to contemplate her crimes while she recuperates. But I remind you once again: *no magic. Capisce?*"

"*Capisce*, your royal honor," I said.

The court broke out into applause, and Mombi nodded solemnly. She stood, and slowly began hobbling to the door. When she got there, she stopped and looked over her shoulder, glaring at me. "Well?" she asked impatiently. "Are you going to escort me or not?"

I looked at Lulu, who nodded, dismissing me, and then followed the witch. I still wasn't sure what had just happened. I was just glad it was all over.

NINE

"Monkeys," Mombi muttered as soon as we were outside and out of earshot. "Winged, wingless, makes no difference. They're *all* a damn pain in the ass. Now let's get out of here before they change their minds. I could use a good foot massage after a day like this."

She flashed me a sly grin, baring two crooked, slimy rows of teeth the color of moldy corn chips.

"You were amazing in there," I said. "I've never heard you talk like that. All this time, I was never totally sure that you really cared."

Mombi replied with a guffaw that turned into a hacking cough. "Oh, please," she croaked when she'd recovered herself. "You really bought all that? I doubt even the queen herself believed a word of it. But, you know, Lulu and I go way back. This is at least the third time I've had to go before the monkey court, and it's always exactly the same. In the end, she's nothing but a puffed-up scullery maid at heart. You have to make her feel powerful—let her have her little trial; drum up some tears to show you respect her."

I looked at her incredulously, kicking myself for being taken in by her load of bullshit in front of the monkey court. But *had* it been bullshit? With Mombi, you never really knew.

"But . . . ," I started, and then stopped. Whether or not Mombi had actually been sincere was the least of what I cared about right now, and I didn't have the patience to play games anymore. "Just tell me what's going on," I said. "After everything I've done for you, I deserve some honesty."

We had come to the twisting, narrow staircase that led down to the rest of the village. She took a deep breath when she realized that she had to get down there somehow.

"Well, isn't *this* nice," she said. She looked totally humiliated as I put an arm around her waist to steady her. I clutched her frail body tightly, worried that if I didn't drop her I might break her, and we made a slow, careful descent into the trees.

"Where were you?" I asked her. "What happened?" I was desperate to know what was going on, and at the same time, I wasn't sure if I wanted to hear the answer. "After I . . ." I trailed off.

What I couldn't say: *after I failed.* After I abandoned everyone. After I let Dorothy get away with her life. I knew it wasn't my fault. Nothing I could have done would have changed anything. According to the Wizard, the only way to kill Dorothy was to remove the Tin Woodman's heart, steal the Scarecrow's brain, and take the Lion's courage—something Mombi and the Order had failed to mention. But it didn't matter what I knew now. The fact that I'd been given a job, failed, and ran away had been eating away at me ever since I'd left the Emerald City.

"Let's just say it didn't go exactly as planned," Mombi said. "Then again, I suppose you know that already." She glanced at me ruefully.

"It was fine at first. Better than fine, actually. While you tried to deal with Dorothy, and I worked to place a field around the palace to block her from using her magic, Glamora and Annabel led several of the Order's other members on a mission to destroy the devices that Glinda had placed around the city to store and convert the magical energy they had been mining from Munchkin Country. Their success is the reason you may have noticed a sudden resurgence of enchantment throughout the kingdom."

I nodded. I'd already figured most of that out, but I would have liked to have known about it from the start. "And then?" I asked.

"Then? What do you *think* happened then? You failed, and we did what we've always done. We kept fighting so you could have a running start without anyone following. Wanted to give you the best chance of escaping that we could."

"Thank you," I said simply.

Mombi reacted by rolling her eyes. "We weren't doing it to be nice," she said. "We were doing it because we need you. Personally, I would have given you right up, if I didn't know how important you are. Lucky you. It wasn't a fun fight, or a fair one. There were too many of them. Glinda, the Lion's beasts, the Tin Soldiers. It felt like it went on for days—maybe it did. By the end, I don't even know who we were fighting. Some of them were Dorothy's people but others . . ." She shook her head. "Hell, maybe we were fighting our damn selves by the end. I just don't know."

With that, she sighed a creaky, defeated sigh. I felt like someone had stepped on my heart. She hadn't answered the only question I really cared about.

"What about the others?" I asked.

"It was chaos. Nox, Glamora, and I were separated from the rest of the Order. We were surrounded. Cornered. There were just too many of them. You see the shape I'm in now. I didn't look any better back there, and neither did they. Let me tell you, it's going to take a mighty long trip to the hair salon for Glamora to get herself all clean and pretty again. We weren't going to make it. Simple as that. So I zapped us out of there. It was the only thing to be done. Tried to get us back to headquarters. But teleporting's tricky stuff even on a good day, and with more than one person? Over that kind of distance?" She let out a long whistle. "That wasn't a good day, and I was in no shape for spelling around. Didn't go so well."

I couldn't stand it. "What happened to Nox?" I asked more urgently. "Just tell me."

Mombi squinted at me. "Let me explain it this way. When I teleport, I travel through another place. A kind of limbo, I guess you'd call it. It's not very pleasant but you move through it so quick you barely even know you were there. Not this time. I lost my anchoring point—the part of the spell that takes us where we're going. Lost my hold on the others, too. Before you know it, I'm stuck in limbo, and they're gone. They're not teleporters really, don't have much of a feel for it. They could be anywhere. For all I know, they're still in the in-between trying to get out."

I let out a breath I didn't even know I'd been holding. It wasn't great news, but at least it meant that Nox was still alive. Probably. Maybe. "We have to find them," I said.

We had finally reached the bottom of our descent through the trees, and Mombi gingerly stepped onto a platform. She wriggled free from my grip and fixed me with a withering glare.

"Don't you think I know that? How do you propose we do it?"

"We have to go back in and get them. Into the in-between or whatever."

"Go back? It doesn't work that way. It's not like taking a weekend in the country—you can't go in without fixing your out first. *That's* how you get stuck. And speaking as someone who was stuck in there for longer than I care to think about, I'm not willing to take that risk. Especially since we don't even know that's where they are. Just as likely, they never got stuck in the first place—could have been spit out the moment I lost them; could be anywhere in Oz. You just can't say."

I wasn't happy with her answer, but I could see that she was right. Still, I wasn't going to give up on finding Nox. I kept that to myself, though. I had a feeling Mombi wouldn't be happy with my priorities.

"How did *you* get out?" I asked instead. "And how did you know to come here?"

"My, my, aren't *you* full of questions? Don't you think I've got a few of my own to ask you?" Mombi countered tartly. Then she paused, and sighed. "The truth is, I don't know," she said with a grimace, like it pained her to admit there was something she didn't know. Or maybe she was just in actual pain.

"It's like being underwater in there. Like under the mud, really. It's dark, it's cold as a fairy's ta-ta, and you can't see past your own two fingers. There are *things* in there, too—and I don't mean kitty cats. Evil, slimy things. Things you'd run away from if you saw them caged up in a zoo—not that you can see them anyway. They just hiss in your ear, drool on you, rub up against you in the dark. I'm a tough old witch, but even I have my limits. You want the truth? I was about to call it a day, just flip the off switch on this old bag of bones. There's a spell for that, you know, and I was ready to cast it. To just give up for good. And that's when I saw you."

I stepped back in surprise. "Me?"

"No, I'm just pulling your braids. Yes, *you*. Now, don't get confused—you're no favorite of mine, but seeing you in there, out of nowhere, lit up bright as day in all that darkness, you were a sight for sore eyes. So I followed you. You disappeared before too long, but by then it didn't matter—I had myself a new anchor point, and it was you. Had to sniff it out some, but I kept at it, and then I was here. Would have preferred somewhere with less monkeys, sure, but beggars can't be choosers, can they?"

I tried to sort it all out as we walked, with Mombi staggering along behind me. What did it mean that she had seen me? Had I sent a signal to her somehow, without meaning to?

I was still thinking about the question of how to find Nox and the others when we were finally back at our hut. It had taken forever for Mombi to drag her battered body across the rope bridges and suspended platforms of the monkey village and now the sun was beginning to set. It occurred to me that time had been passing with a surprising regularity. I wondered who was turning the Great Clock—Dorothy sometimes forgot to do it until it felt like it had been the same day for a year. I put my hand on the door and then stopped.

"I'm sorry," I said quietly.

"Sorry? Sorry for what?"

"For leaving you guys. For screwing up. If it weren't for me . . ."

Mombi rolled her eyes and shook her head dismissively.

"Look, you did good, kid. Didn't kill Dorothy, but the way I hear it, she's on the run now, and that's a start. Heard about what you did to the Tin Woodman, too. Good for you. We got the magic back, for now at least, and that's not nothing. We tore the whole damn city down while we were at it, too, just to show Dorothy we could. Got that princess out of the palace, hopefully for good. Plus"—she wiggled her eyebrows—"we weren't the only ones who got beat up. I had the pleasure of taking a big chunk out of Glinda's pretty face. Been waiting a while to do that. So buck up, girl. Could be worse."

Mombi gave me a weak little swat on my arm. I knew that my guilt wouldn't disappear completely until I saw with my own two eyes that Nox was safe—and that he didn't hate me leaving him when I should have stayed behind to fight—but knowing that Mombi had forgiven me made me feel a little bit better. I gave her a thin smile and opened the door, eager to tell Pete about everything that I'd learned.

I felt a surge of disappointment when I realized I wasn't about to get my wish. Pete wasn't there. Instead, Ozma sat cross-legged on the floor, amusing herself with a game of cat's cradle using an old string she'd found somewhere. She was so engrossed with her private game that she didn't even notice us come in.

"Oh," Mombi said sourly. "It's *you*. Did the boy go back into his hidey-hole?"

That got Ozma's attention. She looked up and stuck her tongue out at Mombi. "Go away, witch," she said. "You're not my mother."

I should have been proud of her, but I was too busy being annoyed for the umpteenth time to learn yet another thing that had been kept from me. "So how long have you known about him?" I asked.

"*Known* about him? I created him, didn't I? Wasn't until more recently that I learned he could still come out to play, but I wasn't too surprised. Doesn't matter much, in the end, does it?"

"Obviously it matters. I'm sick of being in the dark about

everything," I said. "You should have told me. It could have been useful to know."

Mombi gave a little chuckle. "You still have a lot to learn, don't you?" she said. "In a war, here's how it works: we tell you what you need to know to do your job, and you don't ask questions. That way, when they torture you, you can't give up anything important."

I put my face right up against Mombi's.

"That changes now," I said. "If I'm going to be a part of your little revolution, it's going to be as an equal, not as your stupid pawn. From now on, you tell me everything, and I'll decide whether I listen or not."

Mombi looked at me like she didn't get what the big deal was. "Sure," she said. "Not many secrets left to tell anyway, but if I come up with something I'll be sure to let you know right away. Until then, I need to rest these old bones."

She flopped into my hammock and stretched her arms. "At least I've got a nice place to heal up. Those monkeys may *say* they hate magic, but if there isn't something magical about these beds then I'm no witch. Pity though"—she gestured toward Ozma—"I was so looking forward to letting the boy give me a foot massage, just like old times. He was *so* good at them."

I didn't understand Mombi. Sometimes she seemed *almost* human, and then sometimes, like now, she . . . didn't. She had practically raised Pete. No. Scratch the *practically*. She *had* raised Pete. Maybe she'd done it under unusual circumstances, but still. She was basically his mom, she hadn't seen him in years, and now, when she'd almost had her chance, she didn't seem to care at all that she'd missed it.

The last time I'd seen my mother she'd been in the passenger seat of Tawny Lingondorff's beat-up red Camaro, riding away from the home we'd shared together, knowing the cyclone was just about to hit. She hadn't even looked back.

"Is that all Pete was to you?" I asked Mombi, feeling my face flush. "Just someone who rubbed your feet? Don't you care about him at all? I guess it figures. He told me all about what it was like growing up with you. He said you treated him like shit."

"Oh, not *that* old sob story again," Mombi moaned. She looked perfectly relaxed in the hammock, her eyes closed, her head thrown back. It made it all the more infuriating. "You try to do a good deed for a child in need and all you get for it is bellyaching. Do me a favor and save the soul-searching for a day when there's not a revolution happening." Her eyes snapped open, and she looked me up and down carefully. "In the meantime, you and I have other things to talk about. First of all, I believe that *a certain item* has come into your possession?"

I nodded. I was still pissed off at her—but I knew this was important.

I unstrapped my bag and pulled out my first trophy: the Tin Woodman's mechanical heart, which was still beating like a watch that didn't know time had stopped.

Mombi plucked it from my hand and cradled it at her chest. She ran her fingers over the surface and squinted carefully at it from every possible angle.

"You did good, getting this," she said.

"Not *just* that," I said. I tried not to let my pride show as I pulled out the Lion's tail. "I had a run-in with the Lion after we left the Emerald City. One to go."

Mombi's eyes widened. "I guess we trained you well," she said, as she took the tail and compared the two items. She stretched the tail to see if it had a breaking point and tapped the metal heart against her teeth as if trying to judge exactly what it was made of. I just stood there, antsy and eager to get them back.

"Fascinating," she mused. "The Wizard wasn't lying about one thing—they're magic all right. But I can't read the spells on them, and I don't sense any special tie to Dorothy. And who enchanted them? The Wizard didn't have the power to put any spell on anything back then—especially not spells this strange."

She scrunched her eyebrows together. "I wonder . . ."

"What?" I asked.

"Oh, who knows. Good for you, getting them. That takes some kind of gumption."

I put my hand out, and Mombi raised an eyebrow at me, then handed them back. "Someone's awfully attached," she said. "Be careful with those. We don't know what they do, and I don't trust the Wizard past the length of his pinkie finger."

I was barely listening as I placed the objects back into my bag.

"Now," Mombi said. "Do you have anything else to gather up?"

"Gather up?"

"Of course. Belongings. What, you thought you were

staying here? The pool party's over, sweetie." She jerked her head toward Ozma. "Wouldn't be much fun anymore now that your plaything's packed himself back up in the toy box anyway, am I right?"

I didn't tell her I was pretty sure I could turn Ozma back into Pete whenever I wanted to. A girl's got to have a few secrets here and there.

"You're in no shape to travel," I said.

"Me?" Mombi laughed. "Who said anything about me? We both know I'm no good to anyone right now. I'm going to stay right where I am until I'm feeling better."

"I'm not going to just leave you like this," I said.

Mombi gave a wry, weak chuckle. "Oh, yes you are," she said. "And don't think I'm not going to enjoy myself. I deserve a little R & R. If I do say so myself. *You've* got work to do, though. I want you to seek out Polychrome, the Daughter of the Rainbow. She's never been much of a joiner, but she's helped the Order before and she'll help us again. She wants Dorothy gone as much as anyone, and she has power. Wouldn't be surprised if other members of the Order were on their way to find her, too."

I considered it. I had decided a while back that I was done taking orders from Mombi, and I wasn't sure I wanted to leave the comfort and relative safety of the monkeys quite yet. On the other hand, if Nox was headed to find this rainbow lady, that was where I wanted to be, too. "How do I get there?" I finally asked. I hadn't made up my mind, but I would hear her out.

"Ahh, now *there's* the rub. The Rainbow Citadel is no easy

place to find. The way it usually works, Polychrome only opens up a door when she wants you there. Unfortunately, I don't have a way to get in touch with her at the moment. So you'll have to find the back way in."

"Okay, fine. So how do I do it?"

"It moves around," Mombi explained. "That's what makes the Rainbow Citadel so safe—and it's how Polychrome gets away with having as much power as she does. Only way to get in uninvited is to find the back door. And no one finds the back door. Dorothy spent a year looking for it a while back. Tore apart half the kingdom, offered up a reward to anyone who could give her a clue, but no cigar. Eventually she gave up—wasn't worth the hassle, I guess."

"If Dorothy can't find it after all that, then how am *I* going to?" I asked.

"You won't," Mombi said. "But I have a feeling *she* can."

The witch crooked a finger at Ozma. "Come to dear old Mombi," she cooed sweetly. When Ozma kept her distance, Mombi rolled her eyes. "Bring the little darling over here," she snapped.

I gingerly took the reluctant princess's hand, eyeing Mombi warily. Ozma didn't look pleased, but she didn't resist.

"You're not going to hurt her, are you?" I asked.

"No, no, no. We *need* her," Mombi said, looking Ozma up and down wolfishly. "As stupid as she looks, there's still power in there. Somewhere. She's a fairy, you know. She's connected to Oz's lifeblood in a way that none of the rest of us ever could be. If anyone can find the Rainbow Citadel, it's her. It's magic, she's magic, it's the way these things work. She just has to *want* to find it."

"Yeah, good luck with that," I said. "I don't think Ozma wants anything. Except maybe to play patty-cake."

Mombi ignored me and placed her hands on Ozma's cheeks. Ozma looked like she was going to run away, but the witch held her firm. "Don't be afraid," she said. "I'm just an old woman. Wouldn't hurt a fly, would I?"

Mombi stared deep into Ozma's eyes and bit her lip in a look of mild concentration. A small, purple dot of light began to form in the center of the witch's forehead. Mombi plucked it off like she was removing a piece of dirt and placed it in her palm, closing a tight fist around it.

"Just hold still and close your eyes, my darling." As if in a trance, Ozma obeyed.

I watched the whole scene with a slightly sick feeling in my stomach. "Ozma's shielded from most magic," Mombi explained nonchalantly. "But when you're dumb as a brick like she is, certain spells can get through well enough."

She opened her hand, revealing that the pinprick of energy had taken the form of a glowing indigo spider the size of a nickel. She plucked its wriggling body up and placed it on Ozma's temple, where it sat for a second and then crawled down, across her cheekbone and onto her earlobe, finally skittering into her ear canal and disappearing.

"Yuck." I shuddered.

"Oh, don't be a ninny," Mombi scoffed. "It's just a little spell of intention. She won't even feel it. Barely does anything except give her a little push in the right direction. Think of it like this: if I whispered *I want doughnuts* in your ear while you were asleep, you'd wake up craving doughnuts, isn't that so? This isn't much different, except that I'm too old a woman to stay up all night muttering in Ozma's ear, especially with those enormous flower earmuffs she loves to wear. Just wait—she'll be able to guide you to the Rainbow Citadel now. Just follow where she leads, and keep an eye on her along the way. Make sure she doesn't walk off any cliffs or into any glass doors. And for god's sake don't let her get captured. She's more important than she looks, you know."

I folded my arms across my chest. "So let's say I agree to go looking for this Polly character?" I asked. "What do I do once I find her?" I asked.

"You ask her to help you find Nox and Glamora, not to mention any other stray Order members she can get a line on. You show her those little trinkets you've got in your goody bag, and see what she makes of them. You have her point you in the direction of Dorothy, who, may I remind you, still needs to be disposed of. You ask her to return the shawl she borrowed from me last time she paid me a visit. Oh, and have her take a look at Princess Dumbbell. Polychrome knows a fair bit of fairy magic. Now that we've finally got Ozma out from Dorothy's watch, maybe we can fix whatever spell Dorothy used to turn our beloved monarch's brains into royal scrambled eggs."

"Oh, *that's* all?"

"Should I give you a list, or will you remember?"

I didn't say anything.

I looked from Mombi to Ozma and back. I weighed my options. I could stay here. I could go off looking for Nox on my own. I could look for the Scarecrow and Dorothy without any clue where either of them were. Or I could just take a nap.

Call me stubborn, but I didn't really feel like obeying Mombi just for the sake of following orders. On the other hand, what if *orders* were, in this case, also the right thing to do?

"Fine," I said. "I'll go. But I'm not doing it for you. I'm doing it for Ozma." I looked over at her. If there was a chance of fixing her, I wanted to give her that chance. I was doing it for Nox, too, but Mombi didn't need to know that.

"I don't care why you're doing it," Mombi said. "Just go! I'll find you when I'm myself again."

"Now?" I asked. "Can't we wait till the morning?"

"Certainly not. Leave in the middle of the night and no one will notice or ask questions. Secrecy, my dove! Even up here, you never know who's watching. Anyway"—Mombi looked around pointedly—"I only see two hammocks, and three of us. What would you propose to sleep on?"

"Can I at least say good-bye to Ollie and Maude?"

"Can't you see I'm too weak and weary for all this tiresome chitchat? Tell no one! And if you encounter anyone on your journey, keep your trap shut. Or, better yet, kill them."

I wasn't prepared for this. I'd been looking forward to *one* more comfortable night's sleep, at the very least. But Nox was out there somewhere, needing my help. And the bug Mombi had dropped in Ozma's ear must already have been working, because she was making for the door.

I knew it was no use. I took a look at my dirty clothes heaped in the corner and decided I was better off traveling without them. I turned to Mombi, but she had already fallen asleep, and was now loudly emitting an unpleasant combination of a snore and a moan.

It was time to get moving. I followed Ozma out of the Princess Suite. This time, I took a page from my mother's book and didn't look back.

TEN

It was the dead of night, and Ozma and I were making our way through the jungle. Yet again, I was reminded of the dream I'd had that wasn't quite a dream. The feeling of déjà vu was so visceral, tingling in my pores, setting the hairs on my arms on end. I ignored it and pushed ahead, following Ozma, and tried not to let it get to me.

I was holding a tiny orb of flame in my palm, just bright enough to light our way. But still, the woods around us were black, and we were moving more quickly than I thought possible. Ozma walked ahead of me with a strange purpose, not seeming to even need my light to see by. She didn't hesitate with a single step, but she didn't seem to be following any particular path either; she was weaving and zigzagging through the thick clusters of trees, sometimes doubling back on herself, sometimes groping oddly at the air as if feeling for something. In her flowing white dress, with her luminous ivory skin flickering in the glow of my flame, she looked like a teenaged ghost.

I just hoped she knew what she was doing, because I thought there was a distinct possibility that she was leading me in a circle.

With every step we took, I second-guessed myself. Was I doing the right thing? It didn't feel like it. I couldn't remember the last time I'd felt so alone. I wished I had Star. I wished I had Indigo, or Ollie, or anyone. I wished I had Nox.

Ozma didn't count. Tomorrow I would try to summon Pete back—at least he would be someone to talk to—but for now, I just wanted to get out of the woods, find a place to rest, and take stock of things in the daylight.

So I walked, letting Ozma lead the way. My hand was clenched hard around my knife, which had appeared in my hand without even being summoned, the way it always did when I sensed danger or felt out of my element. The knife was beginning to feel so much like a part of me—like an extension of my body—that it was easy to forget Nox was the one who had given it to me, had spent hours carving the bird-shaped hilt himself not just because he wanted me to be able to protect myself, but because he wanted me to have something that he had made; something that was just mine.

I felt a pang of loneliness at the thought, but instead of getting sad, I tried to take that feeling and use it, to shape the pointless emotion into something more like determination. It felt almost like working with magic—the way you could take it and mold it into something different from what it had started as. Into something you could actually use.

The thing about Nox was that I didn't even know him that well. I really didn't.

We had kissed, what—twice? Three times? And most of the time that we *hadn't* been kissing, it wasn't even obvious that we were friends. Much less anything more than that.

Look, it didn't matter *what* we were to each other. It didn't matter whether I really knew him or not. I just knew that I wanted to find him.

But Nox wasn't why I was roaming through the dark forest in the middle of the night. I wasn't doing it for Mombi either, or for the Order, or for Ozma, although I had to admit I was starting to feel a certain amount of protectiveness toward her. I wasn't doing it for Oz, or for justice. Some of those things were part of it, but they weren't the main reason.

For some reason, I had kept it from myself, because it had made me feel somehow selfish, but isn't everyone allowed to be selfish sometimes?

The real person I was doing this for was me.

In my old life, I had been picked on by Madison Pendleton, taken advantage of by my mother, and ignored by pretty much everyone else. Because I had never been special. I had never been powerful.

When I'd dreamed of getting away from Kansas, what I'd really wanted was to find a place I could *matter*. Where I could be someone, and have a purpose.

Now I had found the place where I belonged. Yeah, it might have been nice if it had been a fairyland with fewer problems—someplace a little harder to mistake for a nightmare—but on the other hand, the more I settled into this nightmare, the more I began to realize that the insanity of the place was what gave me this feeling of purpose that I'd never had before.

Before Oz, I'd never been needed by anyone other than my mother, and apparently I wasn't even much of a help to her. Oz, though, I could try to fix, and I was going to.

Some people spend their whole lives searching for the one thing that they can do to say, *I changed the world*. I had found that thing. I might not be able to accomplish it, but I was going to die trying. So call me selfish.

But that didn't mean I wasn't scared. I tried not to think about what else was out there in the woods, in the dark, beyond the glow cast by my fire. The jungle might not have been the Lion's domain anymore, but there were still monsters who lived here, and they didn't need the King of Beasts to tell them I would make a delicious snack.

Lions, tigers, bears. None of those really bothered me. It was the thought of things I wouldn't even be able to put a name to.

It wasn't just an abstract fear of creepy-crawlies. Ever since we'd left the monkeys' treetop village, I'd had the sensation that we weren't alone. I couldn't quite place the feeling, or give any evidence to prove my suspicion was right. But I could feel a lurking, heavy presence somewhere just over my shoulder, creeping behind me through the trees, almost close enough to reach out and grab me.

At first, I told myself it was just my imagination, but after an hour of walking, I heard a telltale crunch of branches and a faint, wheezing grunt.

I spun around and shone my flame up and down in the dark, but the only movement I saw was a giant spider half skittering up the trunk of a tree to take cover from the light.

There was a time when just *that* would have been enough to have me running for my life. Now it was nothing.

I knew in my gut that there was something else, though. Call it magical insight or just good old Kansas intuition. There was something bigger, badder, something dangerous. It had been stalking us this whole time.

I tried to shift my focus, the way I'd done earlier in the day, trying to see if whatever was out there was using magic to hide. But nothing revealed itself except for the vague shimmer of energy that coated everything in Oz. And considering how jumpy I was feeling right now, I couldn't be sure that even *that* was anything other than my overactive imagination.

Ozma had noticed that I was hanging back, and had looped around to join me. She looked at me curiously and gazed out at the forest.

"Mommy," she said. A slow smile spread across her face. And then, more urgently, she repeated it: *"Mommy!"*

Between her demented smile and the flickering light on her face, she looked like a horrible, beautiful jack-o'-lantern.

Mommy. Was she talking to me? Was she trying to say *Mombi?* Or was it something else? None of the options really reassured me. I put a finger to my lips, and Ozma narrowed her eyes and nodded as if she understood.

Without any further warning, I let the flame in my hand extinguish. Everything went black, and I was already a shadow, effortlessly sinking into the in-between place I'd somehow learned to unlock over the past few days, then I was back, myself again, ten paces behind the place where I'd started.

I couldn't waste any time; I had to move before our pursuer figured out what I was doing. In one swift motion, I stabbed my knife into the air and brought it down in a crackling arc that lit the whole forest for a split second, as if I'd just set off a flashbulb.

But that split second was enough: I saw it. The thing that had been following us was crouched menacingly behind a tree, its shoulders heavy and muscular. It spun its head toward me, and I saw its yellow eyes staring back at me in two thin, yellow slits.

A chill went up my spine as I thought of the cloaked figures I'd seen in my dream last night.

But those had been witches, and when this thing rose up onto its hind legs, I knew that it was not a witch. It was a monster.

An enormous ball of orange fire was already bursting forth from my outstretched palm, and before I could see my flame hit the target, I was teleporting straight for where I'd seen it hiding.

When I reappeared, I expected to hear whatever it was screaming as it burned. But I'd gotten cocky. When I materialized, there were no screams, my fire had already extinguished itself, and I couldn't see anything in the blackness.

Hopefully that meant it couldn't see me either. Instead of trying to light things up, I decided I would try to use the dark to my advantage, and I mumbled a few words to cast a simple amplification spell. This way, even if I couldn't see my attacker, I'd be able to hear it.

I listened, turning in a careful, clockwise circle, until I had picked out the creature's thumping heartbeat and labored breathing.

I came up with nothing and stumbled forward.

Suddenly, before I'd recovered my balance, a flying ball of muscle hit me out of nowhere like a bag of bricks. I grunted loudly and, instead of falling, let my body roll into a sideways somersault, and then flipped easily back to my feet.

I was fast, but the thing was faster. It had ricocheted away from me before I'd even managed to get a look at it, back into the trees where, even with my magically heightened senses, I could barely make out the sound it made as it crawled from branch to branch.

Just a few minutes ago, I had been feeling lonely and a little helpless. In other words, I could use a good fight.

"Come and get me!" I shouted, brandishing my knife, knowing I barely needed it. Once again, my loneliness had turned, like magic, into fury. I would kill this thing with my bare hands if I had to. "C'mon, asshole!" I screamed, my voice reverberating through the trees. "I don't care who you are. Mess with me again. I dare you."

I stopped, picking through all the sounds around me until I heard a soft heartbeat, a few feet away, behind a tree. But when I listened more closely, I realized that it didn't belong to my stalker.

From its steady, even pace, I knew it could only be Ozma—no one but her could remain so calm in the midst of all this.

So I tuned it out, glad she was safe, and then focused on all the other sounds.

I scanned through all of it, casting aside the noises that weren't relevant—the crickets and owls in the trees, the snakes slithering through the grass, the wind in the leaves—building a picture of my surroundings in my head. When I listened hard, it was almost like being able to see again.

It only took me a minute but then I found it. *Thump. Thump. Thump.*

The noise wasn't coming from anywhere near where I'd been looking for it, but once I found it, it was unmistakable. The beast's heart was racing from adrenaline; its breathing was heavy and hungry.

But I didn't want to use the same trick twice, and so instead of throwing another fireball, I decided to try something new. I called down a bolt of lightning from the sky to fry my mystery attacker before it knew what hit it.

There was a sizzle, and the electrical smell of ozone, as a blue bolt zigzagged in through the leaves, striking at the place where I'd guessed my target to be hiding. The creature shrieked as my spell connected.

But if I'd thought that would be enough to kill my enemy, I was wrong again. There was a whistling sound of a vine swooping through the air, and then the creature was on top of me, its legs wrapped around my midsection as it scratched at my face with giant, almost human hands.

I felt its claws drawing blood, but I spun on my heel, using the thing's momentum against it, tackling it to the jungle floor. We landed together, me on top, and I pressed my forearm to its chest, pinning it—whatever it was—to the ground.

"Game over," I said. It had been easier than I'd expected, and I found myself almost disappointed that my workout had been cut short. I was getting pretty good at this.

I raised my knife to go in for the kill. I didn't even really care *what* it was that I was killing, I just wanted the fight to be over.

But then it spoke in a voice I recognized. A surprisingly *squeaky* voice.

"No! Uncle! Uncle! I give up already!"

It couldn't be. But who else sounded like that?

I willed my knife to glow, illuminating my now captive enemy.

"You!" I exclaimed. Looking up at me in shamefaced, pathetic defeat was none other than Queen Lulu of the Wingless Ones. One second ago, I'd been ready and eager to kill. Now I wasn't sure what to do.

I looked over to Ozma, who was leaning against a tree a few feet away, observing the whole scene with a kind of birdbrained calm. After a moment's pause, she gave the monkey a dopey, sad little wave.

Under me, Lulu blanched at the sight of Ozma.

"What do you want?" I demanded slowly, debating whether

to put my knife away. "Why were you following us? Don't lie to me."

"Didn't mean to scare you . . . ," my captive wheezed. "Wasn't gonna hurt anyone. I just wanted to see her. I didn't . . ." She stopped herself, seemingly overcome by something she couldn't say.

"*See* her? You could have seen her whenever you wanted. You wouldn't even let her into your throne room. Now you expect me to believe you just wanted to *see* her? Do you think I'm stupid? And why do you even care?"

She wriggled under my weight, trying to crane her neck toward where the princess was hanging back. Lulu blinked. I would have thought she was fighting tears, if I hadn't known she wasn't the type for sentimentality.

"I was afraid she'd remember," she finally said.

"Remember *what?*"

"She was so little when it happened but . . . you never know with fairies. What if she remembered?" She sounded almost frantic.

I looked at her quizzically. I had no idea what she meant. Then I remembered, and with a jolt, I suddenly understood what Ozma had meant by *Mommy*.

"She was mine. I was supposed to protect her. I was all she had, and she was happy anyway. She loved me. Trusted me. I left her, see? Left her all alone. When she came to the village . . . I couldn't look her in the eye, not after all I did. How could I? But I didn't want her to leave like that either. Barely there a day.

And not even a simple sayonara?" Queen Lulu bit her lip and clenched her eyes shut. "My spies told me you were trying to dip out, and I knew I had to say good-bye. I had to see her. Just once, that's all. I wasn't going to hurt anyone."

Lulu was quiet but almost panicking, too, so different from the imperious, fast-talking dame who had haughtily held court at Mombi's trial. Her brassy bluster had faded in the bright, searing light of her own memories, leaving only regret.

Maybe I was being stupid—weak, a pushover—but I believed her. I lifted myself off the monkey queen and stood, now holding on to my knife only for the light it was casting.

Lulu breathed deep in relief.

"Thank you," she said. She didn't stand; instead she crawled forward on her haunches in a crouch, just looking Ozma up and down.

Now that the monkey's attention was on her, Ozma's calm demeanor melted away, and she began to shake her head manically. She clenched her fists to her temples, yanking frantically at her hair. "No, no, no," she chanted to herself. But she didn't back away.

Lulu hardly paid attention to the way Ozma was freaking out. It was like she had expected it.

"She's so different now," the monkey queen murmured, half to herself and half to me. "You should have seen her before, witch girl. When she was born, she was so tiny I could hold her in the palm of my hand. Now look at her, all grown up and pretty as a penny fresh from the mint. Powerful, too. So I hear."

"She is," I said. It might have been a lie. Or it might not have been.

"And she was a good queen, when she had to be. I wish I'd visited, but I didn't know what to say. Still, I knew. She was one of the best. I'm an awfully good queen myself, so I should know."

"You are," I said.

Lulu seemed very far away now. "I didn't expect any of this," she said. "Didn't ask for it, didn't want it, it just happened. I was just a monkey. Don't know why I was the one to stumble into all this. I just was. Stranger things happen." She glanced at me sheepishly. "But not that much stranger."

Lulu bowed her head to the dirt and didn't say anything else. Her shoulders were trembling now, and she took her sunglasses out and put them on again to hide her face as she wept.

Somehow it made everything even sadder that she was so proud of Ozma—the girl she'd loved as her own—and sadder still when you thought about everything that she wasn't saying. About what had been done to her, what had been done to Ozma. About everything that can go wrong even when you have every best intention.

Lulu was a monkey queen and I was a girlfrom Kansas, but we were the same in a few ways. I wondered what it was like for her, how it must feel to see Ozma again now in a place and time as strange as this, with both of them so changed. I wondered if I'd ever find out the answer for myself.

Okay, so I was crying, too. Only a little bit. Even a wicked witch like me has a heart, you know?

The confusing show of emotion must have been what got Ozma's attention. She was now looking back and forth from me to Lulu, thinking god knows what.

Lulu was still stooped over, but she had recovered herself and lifted her head with a graceful, stubborn pride.

Ozma bit her thumb nervously, and her eyes locked with Lulu's for the first time. The fairy queen took a tentative step forward, looking a little frightened and a little curious and maybe—I mean, *maybe*—like something was coming back to her.

Just that tiny move, that small show of familiarity, was enough to make Lulu brighten. But when Lulu stood up and began to open her arms, the princess jolted and backed away again. Lulu looked like she understood.

"I'm sorry, honey pie," Lulu said softly. "It's only me. Good old Nursey Lu." At that, Ozma just turned her back to us, facing out into the darkness beyond my magical ring of light.

"Lulu—" I said.

"No," she interrupted. "It's what I expected. I understand." With that, it was like we were making a silent agreement to pretend we hadn't noticed what had just happened.

"I'm sorry," she said.

I wiped my eyes and shook my head. "It wasn't your fault. You didn't even have a choice. They made you a slave. It's demented."

She made a loud buzzer noise, like the sound on a game show when someone messes up. "Wrong! I could have done something.

Maybe I couldn't have done anything about the deal the Wizard made with the Western Witch, but I could have stopped Dorothy from . . ."

Instead of finishing her thought, Lulu fluttered her oversize paw halfheartedly in the air. I understood. It was too much to talk about.

The silence was heavy but something she had said snagged my attention. "The *Wizard*. He's the one who made the deal with the witch. He sold you out."

"Sure did, toots. No use thinking about it. That's yesterday's news and I canceled my subscription to *that* paper a year ago anyway."

I was confused. "But you've worked with him. He's the one who gave Ollie and Maude their paper wings. I thought he was your friend."

"Nah, not a friend, but not an enemy either. Not anymore. He made his mistakes a long time ago. Time might move slow around here, but everything else changes fast. It wasn't his fault anyway, not really, and Mr. Wiz paid the price. Got himself right with me and mine. I can't say I ever know what the hell is going on underneath those dinky little hats of his, and I won't be picking his nits for him anytime soon, but he's okay by me until he messes with the monkeys again. Or with her."

Lulu jerked a thumb toward Ozma.

"Seriously? How can you forgive him?" I couldn't decide if I admired her willingness to put the past behind her or if I thought it just made her seem a little bit weak.

"Forgive him? I didn't say I forgave him. Didn't say I didn't either, though. It's not the point. Don't worry about *me*, hon. No need to go poking your beak into my birdseed. But I want to tell *you* something and I want you to listen like I'm talking *real* quiet. You need to be worried about yourself. I heard all about what you did with the Lion. Heard you scared the fur off half the monkeys."

"I did what I had to do," I said. "He was a monster. He's lucky I didn't kill him. I probably should have."

"It's not what you did. It's how you did it. Something came over you. Something not quite kosher. You have to be careful— magic doesn't always sit well with people from the Other Place. You think you're the one using it, then one day you wake up and realize it's using you."

"That won't happen to me," I said emphatically. "I'm careful."

"Most of the monkeys didn't want to let you in, to tell the truth," Lulu went on. "Too dangerous, they said. Someone like you—too unpredictable. Just the unsavory type of broad we don't want to get involved with. Lots of people around here think you're like *her*. Meet the new witch, same as the old bitch. We monkeys have dinged enough dongs to know. But I saw what you did for Ollie and Maude, and I had a feeling. I went out on a limb for you. Me, I said, *Nah, she's different*. I said *We'll give her a chance*. Just a feeling, like I told you. I trust my gut."

"I'm not like her," I said, feeling my spine straighten. "I'm nothing like her. I could never become her."

"Prove me right, okay? Keep ahold of yourself. People are on your side. I hope you're on theirs."

"You don't have to worry about that," I said firmly, wishing as I said it that I could be as sure as I was trying to sound. "Come with us," I said, on impulse. "You know this part of Oz better than anyone. You can keep us safe."

But she was already shaking her head. "No can do, babe," she said. "Whether I like it or not, I'm not a nursemaid anymore. I'm the queen, string bean. I have my subjects to take care of. I need to stick around with them for whatever's coming down. Anyway, the kid's better off with you than she would be with me. I'm no one, really. I'm brave, but I'm just a monkey. Not much use unless you need someone to peel a banana with their feet. You? You're something else—it's just too soon to say *what*. But I know you can keep her safe. Because you *want* to."

Lulu reached into the black bustier that I guess counted as undercover gear among the monkeys and pulled out a pink, lacy handkerchief. I thought she was going to use it to wipe her still-lingering tears, but instead, she folded it neatly into a little square and handed it to me. "Here," she said gruffly. "Take it."

I took the cloth from her and looked down at it. "Um," I said. "Thanks?" I was a little confused about why she was giving me a hanky. I mean, I had been crying, but if anyone needed it, it was her.

"Magic is against the laws of the Wingless Ones," Lulu explained, "but when you're the queen, you have to have a *few* tricks up your sleeve, don't you think? I 'borrowed' that one from Glinda way back when; it comes in handy sometimes. Throw it on the ground when you need to rest. It will keep you safe—hidden." She paused. "Well, *mostly* hidden. Cozy, too. Glinda travels in style."

I didn't ask any questions. It didn't seem like the right time for it. "Thanks," I said again.

Lulu made a move like she was turning to go, and then stopped. Ozma still had her back to us, but Lulu decided to talk to her anyway.

"I know you don't really understand what's happening, hon. You don't even understand what I'm saying, most likely. Maybe it's better that you don't. If you did—if you could—you'd probably give me a piece of your mind. I don't even know you, really, do I? When you were in diapers doesn't count. I wish I'd gotten a chance to see you grow up. Get to find out what you're like. First I let you get kidnapped, then, when you were back where you belonged, I missed my chance. Coulda come back and visited when you were living it up in the palace, if I hadn't been too proud. Maybe it will make sense to you someday."

Slowly, Ozma turned around to face us, casting her eyes to the ground. I could see Queen Lulu struggling; I could see that all she wanted was to reach out and hold the girl she'd once thought of as a daughter. But she held back.

"Somewhere inside you, I hope you know who you are. I hope you know what you are. I hope you know that you're powerful. We need you."

Ozma looked up.

"And I want you to know that I love you, even if I haven't done the grandest job of showing it. Somewhere in there, I hope you can hear me."

Ozma's shoulders twitched. Was she listening? Could she understand what Lulu was saying?

Lulu turned to me. "Keep her safe. I don't care how. It's the least you could do, dollface. Help her get better. Help all of us."

At that, Her Highness Queen Lulu of the Monkeys, royal nanny and loyal protector to the rightful queen of the Land of Oz, born a scullery maid and an outcast, now a wise, and only slightly silly ruler, grabbed on to a thick vine and shimmied up, into the vast, unknowable wild, and out of sight.

Just as I was wondering if I would ever see her again, I heard her funny, foolish cartoon voice echoing down from somewhere high above us: "Remember—don't be wicked. Unless you really have to!" Parting words, I guess. It was good advice. I promised myself that I would try to follow it.

ELEVEN

I smiled to myself and glanced at Ozma out of the corner of my eye. Through the darkness, I could see that she was looking at me, too. We were alone again.

We just stood there for a minute, catching our breath together. Somehow I knew that she had heard everything Lulu had said. Somehow I could tell that it had mattered, too. That, in some small way, Ozma was different now than she had been yesterday.

I put my knife away, and cast a flame again to light the dark. "Are you okay?" I asked. Not necessarily because I thought Ozma would answer me, but only because it seemed important to say.

But she did answer. "No, thank you," she said. I got the gist: she didn't want to talk about it.

She started walking again. This time, she moved forward in a straight, undeviating line, carelessly pushing aside anything in her way. I followed after her, and then she started running, throwing herself through the brush.

I ran, too. After all my training with the Order, I'm in pretty decent shape. When you've spent several months of your life in twenty-four-hour training to be a witch assassin it's hard not to be. I don't tire out easily, but now, after a few minutes of trying to keep up with Ozma, my feet flying over everything in my way, I was struggling. Ozma, meanwhile, seemed to have totally forgotten about me and was getting farther and farther ahead, her white dress streaming behind her. She was going so fast that I was starting to lose sight of her.

I couldn't let her get away. I was panting and sweating, and my legs felt like they could give out from under me at any second. I wanted to stop and catch my breath, but I couldn't. I didn't have a choice except to dig deep.

So I dug deep. I pushed past the pain and exhaustion, just kept my legs moving as fast as I possibly could, and then faster. I wasn't even trying to use magic. It just sort of happened. My body began to course with a tingling, now familiar warmth, and the trees were blurring by faster and faster until it was like they weren't even there at all. The only thing that stayed in focus was Ozma ahead of me, the bright red flowers that she always wore at her temples glowing in the dark and leaving a smudgy crimson streak in her wake.

We ran, and everything melted away: the pain in my legs, the ache in my chest. Home, and Oz, and the rest of the world. Even the sadness and loneliness that had been with me for as long as I remembered—not just since I'd come to Oz, but before that, too, for most of my life. It was just gone. All that was left was the wind on my face and in my hair, my feet thumping in the dirt, the magic rippling through my veins.

I felt more like an animal than like a person. Like a dog chasing a ball that had been tossed out into a field, or a wild horse that runs for no reason at all, except because it can. I understood why Ozma had started running in the first place. Because it was a relief.

I had no idea how far we ran, but when I finally broke through the trees, I stopped.

The sun was rising on the horizon, peeking up over a hazy, faraway mountain range. I was standing at the edge of a purple field, and Ozma was alone in the middle of it, her arms across her chest, staring at the sky.

We had made it out of the woods.

I didn't care that it was technically morning, or that there might be people nearby. Lulu had told me that the handkerchief she'd given me would protect us while we rested, and rest was exactly what I needed.

I tossed it in the grass in front of me, just like she'd told me to do, and watched to see what would happen. Before my eyes, it began to unfold itself into a huge sheet. The sheet floated up into the air and the gauzy material began to thicken, changing color, and it began to take on a shape.

A minute later, l was standing next to a modest canvas camping tent, festooned in jaunty pink and white stripes. At its peak, a miniature flag bearing the royal insignia of Oz—a golden, ornate *Z* inside a larger *O*—fluttered in the breeze.

After spending some time in a fairy kingdom, it's not hard to get a little jaded about the whole magic thing, especially when most people, including you, are basically just using it to try to kill each other. But then it impresses you when you least expect it. And when I crawled inside, I remembered, with a gasp, that appearances in Oz are often deceptive.

From the outside the tent had looked like a normal camping tent, barely big enough for two people in sleeping bags, and only if they didn't mind getting a little cozy. But the inside was easily twice as big as the rooms at the Best Western that my mom and I had sometimes stayed in when we'd gone on vacation—back when we sometimes used to go on vacation.

Several lanterns hung from the peaked ceiling, burning with soft, pink flames and lighting the space with a rosy, homey glow. On either side of the room were two impeccably made-up beds that looked straight out of a department store display; in the corner, a small sitting area housed an armchair and ottoman upholstered in pink and gold brocade. In the middle of the room, a table with crisp, white linens, flickering votive candles, and an arrangement of pink roses had been laid out for us with a lavish spread and two bubbling flutes of champagne. The remainder of the bottle was chilling in a standing ice bucket next to the table.

Well, Lulu *had* mentioned that she had "borrowed" the handkerchief from Glinda. And it *figured* that Glinda wasn't going to sleep in the dirt in some ratty old sleeping bag.

Ozma had crept in behind me, and made a beeline for the

champagne, which she downed in one gulp before moving on to some cheese.

The delicious-looking spread was tempting, but even more tempting were the beds. I was out before I could even crawl under the covers.

I woke up to the smell of freshly cooked bacon. And . . . wait. Was that coffee? Mom must have been in a great mood. Maybe she'd won bingo night with Tawny down at the bar. No, it was more likely I was dreaming.

I rolled over, rubbed the sleep from my eyes, and then remembered: I wasn't in Kansas anymore. I was in a plush bed in a magical tent in the Land of Oz. I blinked away the sleep and pushed away the sudden, raw feeling in my chest from believing for half a second that my mom might have cooked me break-fast. That's when I saw that the table that had welcomed me and Ozma the night before delicious food and champagne was now overflowing with a truly sumptuous breakfast feast. Bacon, scrambled eggs, fresh fruit, glass carafes of juice and sparkling water—I'd barely had a decent meal the entire time I'd been in Oz, and now I was looking at a World Series-winning grand slam breakfast.

I had seen a lot of incredible things in Oz, but this took the coffee cake. My mouth dropped open.

Just as I was about to jump from the bed to pig out, I saw a small movement out of the corner of my eye, in the tent's sit-ting area. I turned, expecting to see Ozma already awake and wandering around the way she always did.

It wasn't Ozma.

Instead, sitting in the armchair was none other than Doro-thy's coconspirator and right-hand woman, Glinda the Good.

TWELVE

"Well, someone's a sleepyhead," Glinda said brightly. For a split second, I wondered if it could be Glamora, Glinda's twin sister. But no: I'd spent enough time with Glamora when I'd been training with the Order to know that this wasn't her. The differences were subtle and obvious at the same time. The tightness of her chignon, the shade of her lipstick, the way her eyebrows were overplucked until they were barely there. The hardness in her gaze and the muscles twitching in her clenched jaw.

But it was also the fact that she had a thick, jagged scar stretching from her chin to the bridge of her nose—the chunk that Mombi had talked about taking out of her face had been stitched up, but the evidence was there to stay.

I jolted straight up, and felt my knife materialize in my hand, which was under the covers and out of sight.

My head was spinning, still numb and heavy from sleep. Was it too much to ask to wait until *after* I'd had my first cup of coffee in ages to tangle with a psychotic sorceress? I inched backward in bed as I tried to size up the situation.

"Oh, darling, *relax*," she said. "I come in peace. Really." She raised her perfectly manicured hands in the air as if to say *See?*

In a pale pink linen pantsuit with a large diamond pendant dangling at her just-this-side-of-tasteful décolletage, she looked fresh, perky, and utterly nonchalant, the perfect picture of kindness, poise, and sophistication. Other than the scar. I hoped she was embarrassed about it.

Even now, after everything I knew about her, I had to remind myself that *this* Glinda was nothing like the kind, generous sorceress I'd grown up reading about. *This* Glinda was a cold, calculating psychopath who probably ate babies for dinner. The only thing the one had in common with the other was a true passion for all things pink.

It was tempting to try to rush her right there—to jump up and take her out once and for all. But I had to play this carefully. With someone like the Lion, you could stab first and ask questions later. Glinda was too smart for that. She wouldn't just waltz in here and expect me *not* to attack her, and as casual and vulnerable as she appeared, she had to be ready for a fight.

Oh, she would get a fight all right. But I wasn't going to play straight into her hands. I had to be sneaky. I decided to bide my time until I had a real plan.

Unless she attacked first. Then I would fight her with everything I had.

"I hope I didn't wake you," she said airily. "You looked so

peaceful sleeping. The beds are glorious, aren't they? I had them special ordered from a group of Nomes in Ev who've been making them for centuries. Best sleep you'll ever get outside of the Emerald City. Even Dorothy's jealous. I daresay you must have been tired, though—you slept all morning, afternoon, and then clear past the night again. Not that I blame you after all you've been through."

I looked her straight in her luminous blue eyes. "What do you want?" I asked coldly.

"Oh, I just wanted to check in and see how you were doing. Maybe clear a few things up. You and I got off on the wrong foot, and I've been hoping you, Her Royal Highness, and I could all try a do-over. There's really no point in fighting, is there?"

Shit, I thought. *Ozma*. I'd been so startled at the sorceress's sudden, unexpected appearance that I'd forgotten all about the princess. I glanced over to her bed, hoping she was safe, and saw that it was empty. *Double-shit*.

Glinda shook her head with a smile, reading my mind. I mean, maybe she really *was* reading my mind. If Gert could do it, why not Glinda?

"Don't worry about her, she's been up for hours," Glinda said, gesturing to the far corner, where Ozma was standing with her back pressed to the wall, half hidden by a large potted fern. She was white-faced and silent, watching us. "We had a nice long chat. Of course, I was doing most of the talking. She *is* a quiet one, isn't she? A shame, really—she used to have such spirit! All Dorothy's fault, of course." She sighed. "I don't know what

I was thinking, bringing that spoiled little brat back here from Kansas. What can I say?" She shrugged. "It seemed like a good idea at the time. Who knew that a simple farm girl could go and make such a hash of things?"

I barely heard what she was saying—I was too busy calculating my options. I couldn't help being annoyed that I had been put in charge of protecting a fairy princess who probably had more raw magical power in her pinkie finger than I would ever be able to wield, even with years of practice, but didn't know how to use it. Ozma should have been a valuable ally, but she was really no use in her current state. Even Pete—who couldn't use magic at all—would have been of *some* help.

As soon as his name entered my mind, an idea came to me. Pete. I hoped that wherever he was, he was paying attention right now. I hoped he was ready to think on his feet.

I let my knife vanish from my hand and stood up, just to see how Glinda would react. I felt her eyes following me, sizing me up as I walked casually to the breakfast table. She didn't move from her seat.

I took my time as I poured myself a cup of coffee and took a sip. I won't lie: even under these circumstances, it tasted pretty incredible.

"See?" Glinda said, registering my obvious pleasure. "Don't you feel better now? Finest coffee in all of Oz."

How dumb did this witch think I was? Did she really think that she was going to win me over with some coffee and this Little Miss Sunshine routine? Was she *trying* to win me over, or was she just messing with me? As crazy as it sounded, I actually got the feeling that she thought she was a lot slicker than she was—that she was so used to people falling for her bullshit that she seriously thought I would fall for it, too.

I filed that away as a potential weak point I might be able to use against her someday.

For now, I just had to keep her talking. "How'd you find me?" I asked. I had already figured out the answer to that question, but I figured she didn't know that.

Glinda gave a lilting, melodic laugh.

"Oh, Amy," she said. "This tent belongs to *me*. I may not know exactly where it is, even now, but I can tell when it's being used. That silly monkey who stole it from me has no idea that I can see everything that goes on inside it. And, my word, she *does* have some horrifying personal habits. Still, I try to check up when I see that someone's in here, and as soon as I sensed that you and Little Miss Ozma had set up camp, I figured it was high time I pay you both a visit. It seemed like it might be good for us to talk woman-to-woman without Dorothy listening in. She can be *so* meddlesome, you know."

Glinda prattled on while I was busy attuning my consciousness to the magical web that glimmered just under the surface of reality. It came easily now, and I realized that, in this state, I didn't even need to be facing Ozma to see her. I just had to shift my mental perspective until I found where she was standing, behind the plant.

When I looked carefully, I could see Pete's energy-form, too, hovering somewhere just behind her. I had an idea of what to do.

"Can you even fathom the nerve of her?" Glinda was

babbling, enchanted by the sound of her own voice. "I said, 'My dear, you simply *must* have an audience with the Nome King. It's only proper.' But does she listen to me? Of course not. She"— *oh, shut up*, I thought, tuning her out and focusing back on the web of magic around me.

Without wasting any more time, I reached out toward Ozma with a magical hand and yanked hard, and in one quick burst, Pete emerged from the princess's body like a snake shedding its skin. I was getting good at this.

Glinda's neck snapped toward him like an owl's, seemingly disconnected from her body. Her eyebrows shot up into a confused arch; her lips formed a tiny *O*. Pete didn't miss a beat. He handled it as perfectly as if we'd planned it out together ahead of time, and I knew that I'd gotten lucky—while Ozma had been standing there half catatonic, he must have been paying attention. He knew exactly what he had to do.

Without even the slightest hesitation, he dove forward and grabbed a glass bottle of water from the breakfast spread, then slammed it against the edge of the table with a crack. The bottle shattered, water spilling everywhere, and Pete spun around with more hatred in his eyes than I was prepared for. He leapt for Glinda, who hadn't moved in her chair.

I only had a split second to act while he had her distracted. I called my knife back to my hand, blinked myself behind her, and as Pete came dashing forward brandishing a giant shard of jagged glass, I drew my blade—now slick with the darkest magic—across her throat.

Instead of slitting her throat open, all I did was ruin the

upholstery of the chair. My knife slipped past the witch like she wasn't there at all.

A look of surprise crossed Pete's face, and he hurled the broken glass across the room. It whipped neatly through the air toward Glinda's face in what should have been a perfect shot to take out her left eye.

No dice. The glass bounced easily off the back of the chair while she just sat there, completely unharmed.

"Oh, you *two*," she said in a chiding tone. "There's really no need to get so hot under the collar. Amy, I have to say I'm surprised at you. All that time at that little witch academy Mombi runs, and they didn't even teach you to recognize astral projection when you see it?"

I moved slowly back around to face her. She raised an eyebrow and pressed her hand to her cheek in mock surprise. "You *do* know what astral projection is, don't you?"

I didn't answer the question. I felt dumb for not knowing what she was talking about and double-dumb that I had given her the opportunity to lecture me like a disappointing pupil rather than treating me as her most-feared enemy.

"My word. Well, I just don't know where to begin. No, my physical body is not with you right now. Currently, my corporeal form is comfortably back in Quadling Country, deep in a mystical trance in my own lovely four-poster bed, where I am being carefully protected by my most trusted bodyguard. *You*, on the other hand, are speaking to my spirit form. In other words"—she gave me a look of incredulous disapproval as she swiped her hand back and forth to demonstrate that her fingers could pass right through her skull—"put the knife away, Amy. It's not going to do you a lick of good."

I was pretty sure she was telling the truth, for once, but I kept the knife out anyway, just to get on her nerves.

Glinda rolled her eyes. "Oh, for heaven's sake, Amy, don't be a *child*. I came here to give you a simple message. A *nice* message. I don't want to be your enemy. I'm done with Dorothy. I believe your goals and mine are more similar than you might think, and that we can work together. If nothing else, perhaps I might be able to teach you some actual sorcery rather than the bargain basement hoodoo that Mombi's apparently been tutoring you in."

"She was busy teaching me other things. Like how to kill witches," I said.

"Well, how perfectly violent! As for *you*—" She pointed to Pete. "Remind me of your name again?"

"None of your business," I said at the same time that Pete replied, "Pete."

"Yes, of course. Pete. Imagine my surprise when I saw the Wizard transform you the other night. I spent a good several hours puzzling that out. A real head scratcher! I had a good laugh when I untangled it all. How could I have forgotten that I'd met you before, when you were an enchanted little boy with a little princess inside just *bursting* to get out. Of course, I thought I'd gotten rid of you when I disenchanted you all those years ago—didn't imagine that you would hang around like this." She tossed her hair. "No one's perfect, even me. I think we can all agree on one thing at least: mistakes were made."

"Get to the point, Glinda," I said. She paid me no attention.

"And now, *Pete*, take a look at yourself. A handsome, virile young man with all the promise in the world, forced to live out his days trapped inside the thick skull of a nincompoop princess, while with every passing moment the delicate flower of your youth is losing its petals one by one. It's just plain tragic. To grow old without ever getting to *live*?

"Rest assured now that Amy's witch friends have been reminded of your existence, they won't let it continue for much longer. Trust me. They'll be looking to do away with you lickety-split, and won't that be a disappointment for everyone?"

"The witches would never hurt Pete," I said. "Mombi *raised* him."

"You go ahead and think that, Amy," Glinda said. "It's sweet, really, the way you trust them. Never lose that sense of innocence, dear, it *is* so charming." She stood and smoothed out her suit. "At any rate, I can see I'm getting absolutely nowhere with you two at the moment. My offer of peace stands, though. If either of you would ever have a yen to speak to me in the future—even if you just find yourself with a hankering for some company and a fine cup of coffee—you know where to find me."

Her body—her "astral form," I guess—flickered into transparency and then she was gone.

Pete and I just stood there. We looked at each other. It was obvious we were both thinking the same thing: *what the hell was that about?*

THIRTEEN

"She's getting more powerful," Pete said.

We were sitting in the grass in the field, next to Glinda's tent, chowing down on scrambled eggs and bacon. With the likelihood that she could hear everything that we said in the tent, it seemed safer to eat outside. So we were having a nice little picnic while everything else went to hell.

"Who?" I asked. "Glinda? She was pretty powerful to start with. I didn't notice anything different today."

"Not Glinda," Pete said grimly. "*Her.* Ozma."

I paused. What good is all the magical prowess in the world if you can't—or won't—actually use it? So far, I hadn't seen much evidence at all of Ozma's so-called power. But from the expression on Pete's face, I could see that, whatever he was talking about, he wasn't happy. "What do you mean?" I asked.

Pete scarfed his last piece of bacon and set his plate aside in the grass. As soon as he did, it disappeared in a poof of glitter.

"I mean that, like, I'm not going to be able to stick around much longer," he said. He stood and stared wistfully off at the mountain range in the distance. "It used to be that when I took the wheel from Ozma, I had a good six hours at least—sometimes even longer—before she came back out. I never quite knew why it sometimes lasted longer than other times, but I think it had something to do with Dorothy. She never knew about me, but for some reason, when she was distracted, or not nearby, it made things easier. But now Dorothy's gone and Ozma seems stronger than ever. It doesn't make a lot of sense."

I didn't say it, but it actually made some sense to me. If Oz was getting stronger since the witches had broken down the pipelines that were sucking the magic from the land, it stood to reason that Ozma would be getting stronger, too. That would explain why, lately, she had also seemed more present.

"I wish we didn't have to worry about her," I said, trying to lighten the mood. "You're not as much of a pain in the ass as she is. Plus, you come in handy in a fight. Ozma just kinda stands there, you know?"

What I didn't mention was that it was probably for the best if Ozma came popping back in soon. In fact, if she *didn't*, I would probably have to make it happen myself, like it or not. It was Ozma, not Pete, who was supposedly locked on to the scent that Mombi had given her and was going to take me to Polychrome.

It was Ozma who I needed, not him. But this was nice. I could wait a few minutes.

"Do you think Glinda was right?" Pete asked. "That the

Order wants to restore Ozma to her real self? I can see why they would, I guess. She's the queen; putting her back in power is a step toward getting rid of Dorothy. But what happens to me when Ozma gets better? Does that mean I'll be trapped in there for good, like I was before Dorothy came back? What if, this time, I just stop existing?"

"No!" I blurted. "It's Glinda, remember? You can't trust a word she says. She's just trying to get in your head. She wants you to go running to her so she can send you straight back to Dorothy."

"I guess," he said, but he sounded doubtful. "But how do you know for sure?"

"Because she lies," I said. "That's what she does."

As I said it, I found myself wondering if I was really being honest. With Pete, with myself. I mean, yeah, I knew I was right about Glinda—she was a nasty, manipulative piece of work, willing to play on any insecurity she could think of to worm her way in. On the other hand, that didn't *always* mean she was lying, and until this moment, I hadn't considered any of the questions Pete was asking. It was hard not to wonder if there was something to what he was saying.

"It will be fine," I reassured him, trying not to feel guilty about it.

"You won't let them do that, though, right? You'll watch out for me?" Pete searched me as if he could sense every one of my doubts.

"Of course," I said. I wanted to mean it.

"Look, I know Glinda's a liar," Pete said. "But part of what she said was true, you know. About what a waste it is, and how much it sucks. I've already missed out on so much. You have no idea how good you have it."

"Oh, sure," I said. "I'm *really* lucky. Just look at me, living the good life here."

There was a slight, warm breeze, and it ruffled Pete's hair. He gave me a wistful frown with a million responses wrapped in it. Among them: *girl, please* and *you really have no clue.*

"I never stop appreciating it," he said, tilting his chin into the sun and closing his eyes to soak it in. "Just being able to stand outside like this and breathe the air. You should remember it, too. Think of all the things you've already gotten to do; all the things you'll still get to do. Okay, so maybe things could be better. But you have this *life* that's just sitting there, waiting for you to take it. It could be worse."

I realized too late how selfish I must seem. "You're right," I said, standing up, too. "I'm sorry." As I placed my own dish aside and watched it disappear like his, it occurred to me to wonder where it had disappeared to. Had it gone off into some magical dishwashing dimension to be cleaned or had it just ceased to exist? The more I learned about magic, the more questions I had about it, but for now, I put them out of my head. I took Pete's hand.

We both just stood there, looking out at everything Oz had to offer. For all the evil that was part of this place, there was so much that was good about it, too. Despite everything, Oz was a place of light and magic, and we had found our way to the center of it.

I don't know where the next thing came from. I guess it was just something about the wildflowers all around us in the meadow and the mountains off in the distance. The breeze, the sun, the unexpected, unreasonable feeling that everything was going to be okay. Maybe it was what Pete had said about appreciating everything you had in the moment that you had it, or maybe it was the fact that I had no idea where the future was going to lead. What was I waiting for anymore? Why had I ever waited for anything?

Okay, so maybe I was just wired from the first caffeine I'd had in months. Whatever it was, I was just kind of like, *oh, screw it.*

So I kissed him. Because why not?

Pete's skin smelled like sandalwood and soap. His lips were soft. His eyes widened in surprise as he pulled away.

My cheeks began to flush. Crap. "I'm sorry," I said, backing away in embarrassment.

"No, it's fine," he said. "It's just . . ." Out of nowhere, he started laughing.

"I . . . I just thought," I stuttered. "I mean, uh, I guess I just thought, you know . . . since you said you'd never . . ."

"Amy," he said. He collapsed back into the grass and pushed his hair from his face with a manic and astonished grin, like he sort of couldn't believe it. When he laughed again, I started to feel a little insulted. "Well, I don't think it was *that* ridiculous," I said.

He just laughed harder. "No, it's not that. It would be totally nice to kiss someone. It would be nice to kiss *you*, if things were different. But I don't want to kiss someone just to kiss them, you know? I'm probably not going to get too many chances, see? It's like, when I do it, I want to make it count. I guess I just thought you knew."

"Wait," I said. "Knew what?"

"Listen. I get you. You're *trouble*. If I were into girls, I'd be so into you. But I'm not. Even girls as awesome as you."

"You mean . . ." I'm pretty sure gears were visibly turning in my head.

Pete shrugged. "I guess," he said. "I mean, I don't know, but basically."

"Oh," I said.

Okay, so I was kind of dumbstruck. The idea that Pete was gay just wasn't something I'd ever considered as a possibility. "I don't know why I thought you knew. I mean, it's not like I told you or anything. There's no reason you should have known."

I hadn't really ever thought about it one way or the other. But as soon as he'd said it, it made perfect sense. As handsome as he was, and as much time as we'd spent together, there had always been something missing—a distance between us that had always been hard to pin down. Now I knew what it was.

"And even if I wasn't," he said. "Would it matter? I kinda get the feeling you're into someone else anyway. So it's probably just as well, right?"

"I guess," I said. "Just do me a favor, okay?"

"Sure," he said. "What?"

"When you're in there . . . keep an eye on me. When you can see me, I mean."

He tilted his head, and his hair fell in his face. "What do you mean?"

"I mean . . ." I paused, not wanting to admit what I was really afraid of. "I mean, if you think I'm about to do something, you know. Scary. If you're in there somewhere, and you see me not being myself. Try to give me a signal. Or stop me. Or whatever."

Pete nodded, understanding. "Fine," he said. "If I can, I will. But you have to look out for me, too. Don't let them do anything to me."

"I promise," I said. I hoped it was a promise I would actually be able to keep.

I had a bunch more stuff I wanted to ask him, but it was too late. Pete's body began to shudder. He winced in pain and jerked his head back. He swallowed hard.

"Told you," he said. "She wants control again. Here I go. Hopefully I'll see you again soon. We'll have plenty to talk about. But I don't know. I'm not sure it's going to be as easy after this. She's different now. She's going to fight hard from now on. I can tell."

As if on cue, his face began to change. It was like the two of them were wrestling each other to occupy the exact same square foot of space. Pete's skin rippled as the princess struggled to get out; his arms and legs began lengthening and contracting. His face was flipping back and forth between his own and Ozma's and something in between.

Pete screamed. He clutched his head. Then he was gone and Ozma was standing in his place, looking steely and hard. She gave me the once-over, cocked her head, and raised her eyebrows, her lips pursed. It was kind of intimidating.

Was she mad at me? Did she blame me for bringing Pete out again?

It didn't matter. As nice a respite as the last hour had been, it was time to go. I wasn't sure exactly how I was supposed to pack up the tent, but it turned out I didn't need to worry about it. As soon as I decided it was time to get moving, the tent seemed to understand. It collapsed in on itself like I had issued a command out loud, and folded itself back up into a small, neat square of cloth that I placed in my back pocket. I knew that it was dangerous to use again, but I couldn't quite bring myself to leave it behind.

Ozma turned in a circle, getting her new bearings, and then she began to walk. If nothing else, she certainly was single-minded. That spider spell really worked.

She moved carefully and deliberately, but slowly. For every few steps she took, she'd back up a few times and then change direction. Finally, when she had found a spot in the meadow a few paces from where we'd started, she stopped, paced around as if judging it, and knelt to the ground as I looked on from a respectful distance.

On her knees, the princess ran her hands carefully through the grass, letting her fingertips graze each blade. Next, she turned her attention to the flowers and began to examine them.

I moved in closer, trying to see exactly what she was doing. All of the flowers I'd seen in the field were one shade of purple or another, but as Ozma searched, she managed to find an assortment, which she began to pluck up as she settled on the ones she wanted: first a tiny red one, then an odd royal blue flower with thin, spiraling petals, and a purple crocus and a yellow buttercup until, finally, she was holding a tiny bouquet representing the four colors of Oz.

She rose, holding the flowers to her chest, and, with her other hand, licked her index finger and held it up. She turned clockwise, then counterclockwise, gauging the wind, and then stopped. I felt a prickle on the back of my neck as a gust came from behind me, out of nowhere. As the wind blew around us, Ozma tossed the flowers into the air and watched as the current caught them up and carried them, flying, into the distance.

Ozma was still. A second later, a brick appeared in the grass at her feet. Then another, and another, each one of them blooming in front of her like flowers in a time-lapse video.

They popped up slowly and then quickly, and while they appeared scattered at first, a pattern began to emerge. It was a road. And it was yellow.

Ozma stepped onto the path to begin the next part of the journey. "Follow," Ozma said.

So I followed: not Ozma, but the road itself. Now the princess and I walked together, side by side, in a looping, meandering path that I knew was taking us into the mountains.

FOURTEEN

We spent the morning walking, following the Road of Yellow Brick as it took us through pastures and meadows and an orchard of squat trees whose branches hung heavy with luscious plums that I was still too full from breakfast to eat; it led us across babbling streams and over rolling hills, into and then out of lush, vibrant valleys.

A few times, way off in the distance, I noticed clusters of domed buildings that looked like villages, but whenever they popped up in my peripheral vision, the road always veered off in the opposite direction. I was familiar enough with Oz to get that it wasn't just luck—the road knew that we wanted to be stealthy, and it was helping us.

Was this the same road that, once upon a time, had led both me and Dorothy from Munchkin Country to the Emerald City? That was a hard question to wrap my head around. That road had a fixed beginning and ending, but I knew from experience that it was also known to move around, depending on traveling conditions. I'd been told more than once that it had a mind of its own. It was possible that Ozma had summoned it with Old Magic, and it had veered off course to help us find our way.

The sun was still out, the walk was peaceful, and I was actually making some headway teaching Ozma to sing "Ninety-Nine Bottles of Beer on the Wall." The only problem was that she didn't really know how to count, and kept mixing up the numbers.

After a while, I gave up on correcting her and just let her keep on singing. Even though the song didn't make any sense at all anymore, her voice was actually nice, and I let my mind wander.

This morning's conversation with Glinda had been unsettling, although I guess it could have been worse. But what did she want from me? Why had she changed her tune so drastically? She had to be trying to trick me . . . but trick me into what?

I was reminded of Lulu's warning in the forest, to *keep ahold of yourself.* If Lulu was worried that Oz was corrupting me, did that mean that Glinda thought so, too? Had she come to me this morning because she thought she'd be able to take advantage of that?

Glinda had made it sound like, out of nowhere, she had no more use for Dorothy. I wondered what could have caused such a huge rift between them in just the few days since the battle in the Emerald City—unless their alliance had never been as solid as it had appeared. And where did that leave me? Did Glinda think that the fact that I was from the Other Place meant that I would be able to pick up the slack now that her favorite little despot had fallen out of her favor?

It was frustrating that everyone was so convinced that I had this great potential to be evil, when all I'd done was show up, get thrown in the dungeon by Dorothy, and then follow the Order's instructions pretty much exactly. I'd fought for what I thought was right. For what I believed in. And now even people like Lulu—people who were supposed to be on the same side as me—seemed suspicious of me because of it. It all felt a little unfair.

Anyway, I had a hard time thinking of myself as a ticking time bomb waiting to explode in a burst of evil when I was in such a good mood. Yeah, the morning had been a little dicey, but ever since Ozma and I had started walking, it had been a pretty perfect day.

The whole time we walked, the mountains stayed fixed in the distance. They were a jagged set of purple teeth on the horizon, rising higher and higher as we moved closer. Based on the deep indigo hue of everything around us, as well as the little I remembered of Oz geography, I was pretty sure these mountains had to be the Gillikins—the treacherous, sprawling range that stretched all the way across Oz's northern territory, separating *wild* from *wilder*.

We'd seen no monsters since we'd left the forest—not counting Glinda—so I was guessing things were still basically civilized for now. But the landscape was slowly changing, and even without crossing the Gillikins, I wasn't sure that we were going to stay in civilized territory for much longer. As morning faded to afternoon—in a way that felt pretty normal by Oz standards—the sunny fields and groves of trees gave way to muddy swampland dotted with intermittent patches of brush, milkweed, and the occasional stunted, tired-out-looking tree. The sun had disappeared behind a dense, rolling cloud cover, leaving everything around us a gloomy gray that was only barely tinted with a washed-out lavender. Everything looked as though the life had been sucked out of it. The world had lost its color.

The air had changed, too. It had thickened, turned sticky and cold, until I felt like I was draped in a used, mildewy towel like the ones my mom had always had a penchant for leaving strewn all over our trailer.

Ozma had stopped singing.

Only the path we were walking on lent any bit of cheeriness to the landscape. The road had brightened in contrast and now cut a curling swath into the distance, no longer yellow but a glittering, pulsating gold.

Then even the road began to lose some of its fight against the gloom. This morning it had been a wide and open boulevard, but as the terrain grew rocky, it narrowed and snarled to weave its way through the obstacles that had begun to pop up.

Meanwhile, though it didn't feel like we were getting any higher, the sky appeared to be getting much closer. The clouds were now so low over our heads that I could practically reach up and touch them, and then I didn't need to reach at all: the road curled sharply, leading us into a corridor of boulders barely wide enough to lift your arms, and I saw the clouds scraping the bricks just ahead of us, swallowing the path.

Sitting at the edge of the fog was a lone figure: it was a woman, wearing a long, hooded cloak of midnight blue feathers, each one tipped with gold. Her skin was smooth and unlined, but there was a sharp wisdom in her eyes too. She looked both very young and very ancient. When she saw us coming she let out a long, stuttering howl that bounced against the rocks, echoing in a chorus like there were twenty of it instead of just one. And she began to change. She spread out her arms, and her cape became a set of enormous wings; her nose and mouth joined together and stretched themselves into a long, thin beak. Finally, the creature blocking our path was no longer a woman at all, but a giant bird.

I took a step backward. This thing—whatever it was—didn't look like it was going to attack, but there was something spooky about it, and my previous experience with giant birds hadn't exactly been fun.

"Amy Gumm," the bird said, in a wispy, whistling voice that was kind, but with an edge of fierceness to it. "I have waited here many months for the day that you would pass through here. I see that your transformation has begun. But only just. I wonder: When you claim your name, what will it be?"

Something about its words jogged a place deep in my memory, and suddenly I recognized the creature. This wasn't a roc. It was the same bird that Nox had carved into the hilt of my knife, the bird that he said reminded him of me, because of the way it transformed itself. The same bird I carried with me into every fight.

"Yes," it said, laughing softly at my recognition. "I am the Magril. I see that you know me. Just as I know you. Just as I have always known you, since long before you came to this place."

My shoulders tensed. "How——" I began to ask.

"Those like me do not concern ourselves with *how*," the Magril said, "We are creatures of magic and transformation. We only ask to find the shape that is ours. I have found mine. You have yet to find yours. But you are on the path."

My head was swirling with so many questions that I didn't know where to start. I couldn't find the right way to say any of them.

"I understand," the bird said, even though I hadn't said a word. "But beware. I guard the Fog of Doubt. Think carefully before entering. Only those with unshakable faith may pass. Many have failed. You need not. I give you a choice: if you choose to turn back, I will send you home."

"Home?" I asked.

"It is within my power, yes."

"But . . ." I started. I didn't know where home was. Did *home* mean Kansas? Dusty Acres? It had never felt like home when I had lived there, and now it felt as far away as something out of a storybook.

The Magril gazed at me like it could see right into my soul. "I cannot tell you where your home is," it whispered. "That is for you to discover. I can only offer you the choice. Will you continue? Or will you return to where you belong?"

"I . . ." I started to say. And I understood I didn't have a choice at all. "This is where I belong," I said quietly. For better or worse, it was the truth.

The Magril ruffled its feathers. "As you wish," she said. "I must leave you. But I offer you a final warning: To survive the fog, you must be willing to become yourself."

Then, without waiting for a response, the Magril took off, soaring into the white expanse of nothingness above and beyond us. I looked at Ozma, who blinked back at me and twisted her lip uncertainly. I took her hand, squeezing it for reassurance—I just wasn't sure if I was reassuring myself or her.

"Who are you?" she asked me. Another question I couldn't answer. But I didn't have to, not for now. For now, all I had to do was step forward. So I took a deep breath, and Ozma and I walked into the mist.

It turns out that pitch black is not the scariest thing in the world. Bright, blinding *white*—the kind of white that makes you wonder if the whole world around you has been erased—can be just as scary.

That was where we had found ourselves. The fog we had entered was so thick that when I held my hand out in front of me, I couldn't see it. I wiggled my fingers just to make sure they were still there. Well, I could *feel* them, so that had to count for something. Right?

With my other hand, I was still gripping Ozma's, tighter than ever now, but when I looked to see her reaction to all of this, she might as well have not even been there.

The only thing I could make out at all was the road, and even that was just a faded, ghostly after-impression, like the floaters you get in your vision when you stare at a light bulb and then look away. Still, it was there: pale and thin, spinning out ahead of us, up and out into the blankness.

From behind the shroud of thick fog, it was impossible to tell what lay on either side of the road's edges. Were we a thousand feet in the air, with only the clouds separating us from a heart-rending plunge to our doom? Or were we strolling through a peaceful meadow without even realizing it? All I could do was put one foot in front of the other and try to keep the faith that we would make it through.

Faith: everyone knows it's something you're supposed to have, but it's harder to put that into practice when your senses are telling you all hope is lost.

And the fog was just getting started on me. We had been walking for probably five minutes when there was a soft, sinister whispering in my ear. It sent me jumping out of my skin. The voice was slimy and reptilian, neither male nor female. It was so close that I could feel breath tickling my earlobe.

"Turn back," it said. "You're weak. You'll never make it. You've never been ready. You've never been brave enough, or strong enough. You shouldn't have bothered. You should never have come here."

I shuddered, and tried to remember the giant bird's warning. This was the Fog of Doubt. Whatever was speaking to me probably wasn't even real—it was just magical trickery playing off my natural fears and insecurities. If I was going to let a little

DANIELLE PAIGE   161

ghostly torment get to me, I had no right to be here in the first place. I was tougher than that. I just had to ignore it.

The next voice I heard was one I recognized, even if it wasn't the one I had expected. It was Madison Pendleton, who had made my life back home hell from the day that my father left us, who had turned all of my friends against me, just for fun, and who had gotten me kicked out of school—the same day that I'd been carried away to Oz on a cyclone.

"Well, look who it is," she was saying. Just the sound of her called up a feeling I thought I'd left behind for good, of being both angry and powerless at the same time. It was that horrible feeling that no matter how hard you tried, you were making things worse for yourself, and the best thing to do was give up.

"Salvation Amy. Haven't changed much, have you? Still just a piece of worthless, stupid trailer trash. I didn't ruin your birthday party. No one was going to come to it, anyway. And *what* are you wearing?"

"Go to hell, Madison," I muttered. I wasn't very impressed. Honestly, Madison had usually been more cutting than this in real life. If anything, she was just making me realize how far I'd come since the days when she could ruin my day just by sneering at me.

I wasn't that girl anymore. I wasn't a victim anymore. But as soon as I dismissed her, her voice changed seamlessly into Nox's.

"So, I hear you have a crush on me, huh? Come on. Look, we kissed, okay, but I hope you didn't get the wrong idea. I know messed up when I see it, and I don't waste my time with it."

Another voice chimed in on top of his. It was my mother. "Children are just vampires, sucking the life out of you. If I didn't have you, Amy, I might never have started drinking. You drove me to it. You made your father leave me. You drove me out into that storm. You ruined my life, and then you just left. Did you even think of what you put me through?"

And a voice from so long ago that I was surprised at how familiar it was. A man's.

"The best thing I ever did was leave," my father said. Unlike the rest of the voices, his didn't sound vindictive, or angry. He sounded just like I remembered him: gentle and easygoing. "I'm happy now, you know. I have a new life. A new family. I made things right for myself."

"No!" I screamed. "You're lying!" But I couldn't hear myself, because suddenly there were so many voices shouting at me that I was drowned out. So many that I couldn't separate them all. Glinda, Mombi, Lulu, Indigo, all of them reminding me of how I had messed up and worse, of all the things that had been wrong with me from the start. It was like that old show *This Is Your Life*, except this version was called *This Is Why You Suck*.

"Shut up!" I screamed, dropping Ozma's hand to cover my ears and stopping in my tracks. "Just leave me alone! You're lying!"

I'd yelled it so loudly that my throat was sore, but I barely heard myself—my screams were lost in the nothingness. Meanwhile, the other voices just got louder, now an indistinguishable chorus that shook my skull.

Selfish bitch. Loser. Damaged goods. Even when you win, you lose.

No one wants to come to your birthday party. Boyfriend? Who could ever love you? Who could you ever love?

All you know how to do is kill. And you couldn't even kill her. You failed. Again. Just like you'll fail next time.

You're weak. You don't belong here, and you don't belong there.

My heart was racing; my breathing was shallow. I sank to my knees and took deep breaths, squeezing my eyes shut tight as I bit my lip, trying to hold back my rage and despair. I tasted blood.

It's not real. It's not real. I kept repeating that to myself.

It wasn't. And the voices were wrong. Even if some of the things they were saying might have been true, they were still wrong.

Because I didn't care what Madison Pendleton thought of me.

Because I knew what I had done for my mother—all the sacrifices that I had made for her, and that she had left *me*, not the other way around.

Because my father was no kind of father at all.

"Who are you?" Ozma had asked, just before we'd entered the fog. I had ignored the question, but now I knew that she had been trying to help me. It didn't matter what Nox thought of me, or didn't think of me. All that mattered was that I knew who I was.

And I did. For all the ways I had changed since I'd come to Oz, I was still the same person I'd been back in Kansas. Yes I might have been quiet and shy, the kind of person who did my best to keep my head down just to get through the day. But even then, I had never let people walk all over me. Even in the days when I didn't know a left hook from a karate kick, I'd still always found my own ways of fighting for the things I believed in.

I had never been selfish or disloyal: I'd spent more time thinking about my mother than about myself, I'd put myself in the line of Madison Pendleton's fire more times than I could count, because I saw her picking on someone even weaker than I was. I'd never given up, even when it might have been the smartest thing to do.

Oz hadn't changed any of that. It had just made me stronger. Now I had the power to win any fight I took on. I had a knife that could cut through anything, if I wanted it to. And I knew it.

Slowly, I opened my eyes. The clouds around me seemed to have lifted a little bit. And I couldn't be sure that it wasn't my imagination, but I knew that in a place like this, imagination and reality were pretty much the same thing.

Even without Ozma's hand in mine, and even without seeing her, I knew that she was next to me. I knew that she, in her stupid, nonsense way, was the one who had helped me through this. What had the Fog of Doubt showed *her*?

"Who's next?" I shouted to the nothingness. "Any more ghosts out there?"

When I got my answer, I kind of wished I'd kept the question to myself. The fog had saved its biggest gun for last: Dorothy.

And not just her voice. She was there in the flesh, hovering a few feet above the road, right in the middle of my path, haughty and imperious, her red shoes crackling with magic.

At first, she didn't seem to notice me, but when she did, her face softened into a disarmingly kind expression that bordered on sympathy. Instead of screaming or insulting me or telling me what a loser I was, she smiled.

"I knew you'd be here before long," she said. "The Scarecrow didn't believe me, but I told him you were too smart to listen to the Fantasms. They're liars. Figments. I know you better than they do, that's for sure. You and I are alike, you know."

"Yeah, people keep saying that," I said.

I moved toward her slowly, not sure what I was supposed to do next. She wasn't any different from the rest of them, except that I could see her. But if she was a figment of my imagination, would she go away if I ignored her or did I still have to fight her?

She *was* a figment of my imagination, right?

Dorothy shrugged. "Aw, c'mon," she said. "Don't make it like that. We're two of a kind. Two good old farm girls a long way from home. We could practically be sisters."

"First off," I said, still advancing on my probably imaginary enemy, "all I know about farms is that they stink when you pass them on the highway. Second, I don't have a sister. If I did, and she was anything like you, I would have drowned her before she'd learned to walk."

"Back home, they call that kind of spirit *gumption*," she said, curling a beckoning, red-nailed fingertip in my direction. "And I like a girl with gumption. I *am* a girl with gumption, after all. Join me. It's lonely at the top, you know? Plus, ruling this place is a lot of work. Between the two of us, though, we could really turn this dump upside down. Make it a place actually worth living in, and have some fun in the meantime."

I shot off a fireball, aiming for the center of her chest. It went right through her, just as I'd known it would, but at least it had been enough to annoy her: Dorothy's smile curdled.

"Fine," she said sourly. "I didn't really expect anything different. Hoped, maybe. Go ahead, keep on fighting, if that's what you want. Like it even makes a difference? If you think you're really doing any good, think again. You're just winging it anyway, aren't you? You have no idea what you're doing unless someone else is telling you to do it. Guess what, none of the witches you let boss you around know shit either. Every brilliant move you make just makes me stronger."

"Oh yeah? Maybe we should test that," I said, faking confidence.

"You know why? Because you'll never kill me, and the harder you try, the closer you get to becoming just *like* me. Pretty soon, you'll be knocking on my door, just begging for me to clear off a throne for you. You know I'm right. I can see it in your face."

Claim yourself, the Magril had said. I suddenly understood. Dorothy and Glinda both thought they had my number. They both thought I was what Dorothy herself had been: a good little girl from the prairie who hadn't meant any of it, who had never *dreamed* that she would turn out evil but just needed a little help—a little temptation, a few empty promises—to get there.

"Maybe you're right," I said. "Everyone else seems to think so. But there's one important difference between us."

"What's that?" Dorothy asked sweetly.

"I know who I am," I said. I thought I'd said it quietly, but when the words came out they weren't quiet at all. They reverberated like I was whispering into a microphone.

Dorothy took a step backward.

I felt my knife itching to come to me, but I willed it away, just to prove a point to myself: that I didn't need it. It was just a knife. It had a few magical bells and whistles, sure, not to mention a really nice hand-carved Magril on its hilt, but I wasn't powerful because of the knife. The knife was powerful because of me.

So instead of summoning it, I just summoned myself. I thought of every doubt I'd ever had, of every time I'd had to eat the crap sandwich that my mother, and Madison Pendleton, and Dorothy had served me. Those days were gone.

"I. Know. Who. I. AM," I said again, more confidently this time with each word bringing forth every bit of the power, the rage, and—yeah—the *wickedness*, that had been building inside of me since I was just a little girl. "And I'm willing to fight for it."

My hands began to vibrate, and I clenched them into fists, then thrust them forward and brought them together with a thunderclap as a bolt of black lightning came down from the sky, cutting through the fog.

Everything went dark, and then slowly, the darkness lifted. The fog was gone, the voices were gone, Dorothy was gone, and I could see again. I had passed the test.

Ozma and I were standing on a narrow, pebbly beach in a basin in the mountains where the road had led us. When I turned around, I saw the road curving up through a narrow gap in a ridge of rocky peaks so high that I could barely see the tops when I craned my neck. Ahead of us was a vast, glassy lake, and beyond that, on the other side—it was impossible to tell how far away—were more mountains, even taller than the ones we had just come through.

As the road wended down the shore toward the water's edge, it petered out until all that was left of it were a few scattered, moss-covered yellowish bricks. Wedged into the gaps sat a small, wooden canoe so weathered by age and wind and rain that it looked ready to fall apart at the slightest touch. Next to it, staked into the muddy bank, was a hand-lettered sign.

This way to the Island of Lost Things, it read.

The Island of Lost Things. That sounded at least slightly better than the Fog of Doubt. Actually, it sounded like it had possibilities. I kicked the side of the canoe and found it surprisingly sturdy, and as Ozma and I exchanged a glance, I sensed that we were both wondering the same thing.

If we were headed for the Island of Lost Things, was it to find something that had gone missing, or did it mean we, too, were lost?

No. I felt, for the first time, like I was found.

FIFTEEN

I rowed until my arms felt like they were about to fall off and then rowed some more while Ozma mostly dozed, every now and then waking up just long enough to look around, see that nothing much had changed, and slide back into a blissed-out nap.

I had started out paddling toward the mountains on the other side of the water, under the assumption if I just kept going in one direction long enough, I'd find the island eventually. But the mountains—which had loomed so huge in the distance from the beach—were now somehow growing smaller as I moved toward them, sinking into the horizon line until they had disappeared.

Even with a paddle, that left me pretty much up a creek. I was sitting in the middle of a smooth, almost motionless plate of water that reflected the sky to the point where it was hard to tell which was which. I couldn't even head back to where I'd started: with nothing in any direction except water, it was impossible to tell where I'd come from.

I felt like I had rowed out to the end of the world and found myself right back at the beginning of it.

The only thing I had to guide me was the sun—not that *it* seemed very trustworthy at the moment either. While the mountains had been busy doing their amazing disappearing act, the sun's movement in the sky had been speeding up, and now it was rising and sinking and rising and sinking over and over, like a time-lapse animation brought to life.

I guess it was possible that someone was going crazy with the Great Clock back in the Emerald City, but somehow I didn't think so. When I was little, and my mom had told me about the International Date Line, I'd imagined it as a real line, painted down the middle of the world, and that if you stood with your feet on either side of it and looked at your watch, it would get so confused that the hands would start spinning around, out of whack. This felt something like that—like we were trapped in a place where time didn't know which way was up anymore.

"I thought *you* were supposed to be the one leading the way," I snapped at Ozma, who was still oblivious in her slumber, her hand dangling out of the boat, her fingers dragging in the water. "How about waking up and helping me out here?"

She sighed in her sleep and turned the other way.

Out of ideas, I tried casting a pathfinder spell, but when I conjured up the usually trusty ball of energy to guide us, all it did was flutter around in confusion, then sputter out.

I stared out at the water in frustration. "At least it's not telling me what a loser I am," I mused aloud. Secretly, I kind of wished it *would*, if only for the change of pace. A few Fantasms might not have been pleasant, but they would have given me someone to talk to other than myself and Sleeping Beauty over here.

The sound of my own voice made me feel giddy to the point of near drunkenness, and I began to giggle. "I guess I should have known that the Island of Lost Things wouldn't be easy to find," I said. "It would almost be funny, right? I mean, if we weren't so totally, completely, *utterly* lost."

Then my giggles became hysterical laughter. I wasn't laughing at my joke (which wasn't really a joke even) but from sheer joy. Because at the exact moment that my words escaped my mouth, I saw it: against the hot-pink silver dollar of the plunging sun, a tiny, crescent-shaped sliver of land had made itself suddenly apparent. Roused by my whooping, Ozma yawned, stretched, and rubbed her eyes, sitting up and cracking her neck from one side to the next.

"Finders keepers," she said groggily.

I was too overjoyed to be annoyed at her nonsense. Now that I had spotted it, I began to paddle again in earnest and the island was approaching rapidly, rising up out of the water like some reverse Atlantis.

It made such perfect sense that I felt stupid for not thinking of it earlier. *Duh*. You couldn't find the Island of Lost Things until you had gotten yourself lost beyond any hope of finding. If I'd given up an hour, or a day ago, it would have appeared that much quicker. So much for *quitters never win*.

But the sight of a destination—any destination!—had

energized me, and I pushed myself as hard as I could, gaping when I realized that the island, while small, was actually something like a city, complete with a cluster of tall, boxy, and downright *American*-looking high-rises shooting up into the sky.

As the island grew nearer and nearer, I noticed all sorts of detritus floating in the water. There were old, soggy books, loose papers, pieces of clothing, wooden toys, and other stuff I didn't recognize. Soon, there was so much of it that you couldn't see the water at all.

The boat began to drag, so I jumped overboard, into the muck, and began pulling it, behind me, with Ozma still in it, trying not to think about what I was wading through. Before long, I was crawling ashore onto blessed, wonderful, dry land.

I mean, there must have been land *somewhere* underneath all the junk strewn about. This beach was in serious need of a caretaker, considering that the whole shoreline was heaped with piles upon piles of what appeared to be trash. It struck me that maybe there *wasn't* any land underneath it. Maybe the island was just one big landfill.

Upon closer inspection, I realized that it wasn't exactly trash. Some of it might as well have been, but there seemed to be some kind of method to the way it was organized. There were heaps of old coins and silverware and laundry and magazines as well as other stuff I didn't recognize, all of it piled on top of more piles up and down the coast. The only thing natural that lay in sight was a thin barrier of palm trees that marked the end of the beach. Beyond those, the buildings I'd seen from the water loomed.

By now, Ozma had made it ashore, and she seemed just as intrigued by the island as I was. She looked around, made a beeline for what seemed to me to be a random mound of metallic scraps, and began to dig through it.

After only a few minutes of tossing stuff aside, she came back up, triumphantly holding a golden, jewel-encrusted scepter almost as tall as she was, topped with Oz's insignia. She held it forth, beaming with pride, and banged it against the ground as if to remind me not to forget that she *was* the queen, after all.

I would have been more impressed if I hadn't been distracted by something I'd spotted out of the corner of my eye. Something pastel and Argyle.

I gasped when I got a good look at it. It was a sock. It was *my* sock; the long-lost half of my favorite pair. How had it made it all the way here from Kansas? Had it shaken loose somehow when I'd been carried over in the tornado?

No. I was positive I'd lost it at the laundromat.

Oh, so what. It didn't matter where it had come from. I leaned down and scooped it up. It didn't do me a hell of a lot of good with its unmissing match still safely back in Kansas, but I was glad to see it, if only for the unexpected reminder of home. I held it to my face to find that it was warm from the sun and still smelled like the off-brand fabric softener I used to buy out of an old-fashioned coin-op dispenser.

Ozma was rooting around on the ground like a pig searching out truffles, and I felt a surge of unreasonable glee as I joined her in the hunt for who knows what. Pretty soon, I had unearthed the final page of my tenth grade state government term paper, which I'd dropped somewhere between arriving at school and getting to class—earning myself a B minus for the quarter in the process—along with an old door key (I knew it was mine because of the battered, plastic SpongeBob key chain), a French textbook I'd had to shell out forty bucks to replace, and, most astonishingly, the beloved silver chain that my grandmother had given me for my tenth birthday just before she'd died. When I'd realized it was missing a few years later, I'd just assumed it was because my mom had pawned it for cash.

I rolled the chain over and over in my hand, admiring it, then hung it carefully around my neck. There was a satisfying click as I locked the clasp, and something about that sound, and the feeling of the metal against my collarbone, gave me a pang of regret.

Things had gotten insane so quickly since I'd arrived in Oz that I'd never really stopped to think about all the things I'd lost in coming here. Not the big things: of course I'd thought about my mother, and I'd even missed my room back in my old trailer every now and then. It was the other stuff that I hadn't thought about that came back to me now. The books I'd loved that I'd never read again—books that had nothing to do with Oz—and my favorite sweater, and the birthday cards from my father that I'd kept saved in a shoebox in the back of my closet.

Even my old self. She had been ordinary, but she had been someone, and now she was gone. I'd never taken the time to say good-bye to her.

I was so caught up in the feeling that I didn't notice at first that Ozma and I were no longer alone on the beach.

But then I had the sense that I was being watched, and when I looked up and saw the lanky, wild-haired figure who was gazing at me, my heart practically burst open with joy.

This had to have been Pete's doing. When he'd promised to try to help, I hadn't dared to think he would actually be able to make good on it, but apparently I should have given him more credit. He had led me right where I'd asked him to, and done it in what had to be record time.

Standing there, atop a hill of ballpoint pens, looking as beautiful as I'd ever seen him, was Nox.

"I was wondering when you'd make it here," he said. "I figured it only had to be a matter of time, but damn, you sure know how to keep a guy waiting."

SIXTEEN

I jumped to my feet and flung myself into Nox's arms, practically knocking him over in the process.

If it had been a movie, the camera would have rotated around us as the orchestra swelled and Nox swept me up in his arms. Young lovers, reunited at last, happily ever after—you know the drill. If it were a movie, the strings would have come in at the very moment that our lips met in a passionate, do-or-die kiss.

But it wasn't a movie. Instead, we held each other for a few seconds before awkwardly breaking apart and standing there, not quite looking at each other.

"Hi," I said.

"Hi," Nox replied.

"So," I said.

"Yeah," he said.

Seeing him again, just when I least expected it, I was reminded of how little I knew him. We had fought against each other, and fought at each other's sides. When he was gone, I missed him—I knew that much—but did it actually mean anything?

"So," Nox said. "I guess we have a lot to talk about."

"I guess so," I mumbled. "So where do we start?"

Nox ran a hand through his hair. He looked up at the sky, where the sun was setting again. "Look," he said. "I don't even know how long I've been stuck here. Long enough to think about some stuff. And . . ."

He clenched his eyes shut, like he was in pain. "Oh, screw it," he muttered to himself.

So *here's* where the strings come in. And, more importantly, the kiss. It wasn't a kiss from a movie. It was just a kiss: sloppy and grateful and a little awkward, as we found our footing and tried to figure out exactly how we were supposed to fit together and then settled into something that was both new and familiar at the same time.

When it was over, the credits didn't roll. There definitely was no happily ever after. But I felt happy anyway.

We both stood there looking at each other like, *what was that?*, neither of us with any idea what we were supposed to say.

Then every question I had came spilling out in one breath. "How'd you get here?" I asked. "Do you know where Glamora is? Are you okay? Did you take that stupid boat, too?"

Nox tried to speak over me, answering my questions and asking his own, but I didn't leave him any room. It was too much of a relief just to get to talk to him. After all this time. I would shut up when I was ready.

"What about the fog?" I asked. "What did *you* see in there?"

Nox shook his head blankly. He didn't know what I was talking about. "Fog?"

"Didn't you come through the Fog of Doubt?" I asked. "To get here, I mean."

"I don't actually know how I got here. I just kind of, uh, showed up," he said. "One minute Mombi was teleporting us out of the Emerald City, the next minute things got all screwed up. And then I was here. Guess I got lost."

"It sort of makes sense," I said, rolling it over in my head. "I mean, kinda. How long have you been here?"

"No idea. Days at least. Weeks? Who knows. Time's even screwier than normal here, I think."

"What have you been doing?"

"Nothing, really. Just sifting through all this stuff, hoping I'd find something useful. Mostly I was just trying not to go crazy. I probably would have, if I hadn't known you would show up eventually."

"Wait. How did you know I was coming? Even *I* didn't know I was coming."

"I just had a feeling telling me I should sit tight. That you were on the way." He wiggled his fingers and made a spooky warbling sound. "I'm psychic, I guess."

"Ha," I said, giving him a funny look.

He gave me the exact same look right back. "No, really. I *am* a little psychic. You knew that, right?"

"Somehow I missed it."

He raised his eyebrows in surprise.

"You're serious?" I said.

"Oh. It's really no big thing. The sixth sense comes in handy in fights, so I can figure out my opponent's next move. Basically when my gut talks, I listen. It's just that my gut has a lot to say. Been that way since I was a little kid. Since before I even learned magic. What, you think Mombi rescued me out of the kindness of her heart?"

"Kinda, yeah," I said. "I guess that *is* what I thought."

"Nah. I mean, she probably would have rescued me anyway, but I doubt she would have taken me under her wing the way she did. Mombi only does *that* when she thinks someone might be useful. Anyway, I'm half-kidding. I mean, I *am* a little psychic, sometimes, but I don't think that's how I knew you were coming. I think I just . . ." He paused. "I mean, I guess it was less like I *knew* you were coming and more like, I had to hope for something. Otherwise I really would have lost my mind. I'm serious."

"Oh," I said, taken aback. I was flattered, yes, but this was way more sincerity than I was used to from him. It was more *talking* than I was used to from him too. The Nox I knew wasn't exactly what you would call an open book. He was more like a tightly locked safe.

"Sorry," he said. "Forget it. And forget the questions, too. I don't have any of the answers. I've been stuck on this island. You're the one who's been out in the world. Tell me what I've been missing."

So I took a deep breath and then started at the beginning. Nox listened in rapt fascination.

Then he went in a direction I hadn't expected. "You met a Magril, huh?"

"Yeah," I said. "Why?"

"No reason," he said. "It's just that I've never heard of anyone actually seeing one before. The Magril's more like a legend or something. I didn't even know they were real."

I let out a little laugh. "Come on. This is Oz. Witches are real. Fairies are real. Everything's real here."

"Yeah," he said. "Everything except the Magril. That's why it's kind of strange that you saw one. That you talked to it. Especially since . . ."

He trailed off, but I knew what he was talking about, and I pulled my knife down from the air and held it in my open palm so that we could both look at it. On the hilt, just as Nox had carved it, was the very same bird I had encountered.

"What do you think it means?" I asked.

He shook his head. "Means something," he said. "But anyway. What happened next?"

"Oh," I said, realizing that there were some parts of the story I wanted to keep to myself. "You know. Fog. Doubt. A really dumb boat. Then I was here."

Nox raised an eyebrow, but he didn't press any further. "So here we are," he said. "I guess it would have been too easy for you to show up and tell me that Dorothy was dead, the kingdom was restored, and all wrongs had been reversed, huh?"

I gave him an *in your dreams* look. "Yeah," I said. "Maybe you *did* go crazy out here."

"Maybe," he said. Then something struck him. "Hey," he said with a touch of excitement in his voice. "I want to show you something."

I nodded, figuring that it would be something useful. Something to lead us where we were going. Instead, Nox pulled a piece of paper from his pocket and unfolded it, carefully smoothing the creases.

"I searched this island up and down. Didn't find anything. Except this." He handed me the paper with a cockeyed expression that was both proud and bashful.

It was a photograph. In it, a chubby kid—really just a baby—sat wedged between two handsome grown-ups. On the left, the man was stern-mouthed, but his eyes were twinkling like he was laughing inwardly at a secret joke. The woman, on the right, was beautiful, but with a certain goofiness to her, which was accentuated by the fact that her hair, like Nox's, was so wild that it looked like she'd just stuck her finger in an electrical socket. Meanwhile, the kid looked like he would never in his life be able to take anything in the world seriously. His face was all scrunched up like he couldn't stop laughing long enough for the shutter to snap. If it weren't for the full head of hair so black that it was almost purple, I would never have guessed.

"It's you," I said.

Nox nodded, blushing furiously. I didn't think I had ever seen Nox blush before. It was basically adorable.

"Are those your parents?"

"Yeah," he said. "I didn't even really remember what they looked like, until I found it. It must have gotten lost when our village got ransacked."

I looked at the picture again, this time trying to imagine another life for Nox. In the picture, he was just a little kid who couldn't stop laughing, who had two parents who loved him, and all the opportunity in the world to look forward to. It broke my heart, a little bit, to see him like this, knowing what was in store for him—knowing how the picture would have been different if it had been taken just a few years later.

I wondered who he would have become if Dorothy had never come back to Oz. If his parents hadn't been murdered when Dorothy's soldiers had raided his village, if he hadn't had to be rescued by Mombi and raised to fight, if he'd been able to make his own choices about what he wanted for his life, rather than having them all made for him.

"Things should have been different for you," I said quietly. I wasn't sure he would know what I meant, but he did.

"We're the same like that," he said. "Aren't we?"

I had never thought of it that way, but I realized that he was right, sort of. I hadn't grown up in Oz or had my life ripped apart by a monster like Dorothy Gale, but it's not like things had gone the way they could have for me either.

Once upon a time, my mother, my father, and I had all lived together in a house that was full of sunlight. On Sunday mornings, I would wake up to the smell of pancakes and bacon and the country station turned up loud to George and Tammy singing a duet, and even when things hadn't been completely perfect, it had always felt a little bit like the world was just waiting for me to step out into it.

That was before my dad lost his job, before he'd left, before we'd lost the house. It was before my mom's accident, and the drugs that took her away, too. Before the tornado that brought me to Oz, whether I wanted it to or not.

If those things hadn't happened, would I have grown up into someone happier and easier, with a smile, someone who could just laugh things off? Someone prettier, more popular, someone who didn't always feel a little uncomfortable in my own skin?

Would I still have had this angry thing always coiled up inside of me like a rattlesnake itching to strike?

I looked at Nox.

"Sometimes I wish things had been easier for me," I said. "But in the weirdest way, I'm kind of glad for it, too. Because I don't think I would have wanted to be anything else."

"I know," he said. "Same." We didn't have to say anything else. He put a hand on mine and let it rest there for a while.

In its own way, I realized, the island was beautiful. Like us.

It was messed up to think it, but it felt like everything—for now at least—was perfect.

"Do you think Glamora's somewhere on the island, too?" I wondered aloud.

"Not likely," Nox said. "I've pretty much covered the whole place. There's no one here. The city is just past the trees. It's unbelievable; I've never seen anything like it."

"I saw the skyscrapers from the water," I said. "I didn't realize there was a whole *city* though. I wonder how it got here. You don't think there's anyone hiding out in there?"

"I guess you never know, but if there is, they're hiding pretty good. Anyway, Glamora's got to be okay. She's second to Mombi when it comes to sorcery. Sometimes first. I'm sure she found her way out of the in-between just fine. She's probably biding her time, resting up until she gets her power back. Like Mombi."

I hoped he was right.

"So what do you think we do next?" I wondered, casting my eyes across the terrain, trying to see where Ozma had gone. She was still digging through the piles of lost objects, but she was doing it aimlessly, like she had lost whatever trail she'd been following all this time.

"Well," he said, "we should probably find Polychrome, right? If that's what Mombi Dearest says."

"Yeah," I sighed. "I guess so. Ozma should be leading us, but ever since we got in that boat, it's like her radar's been jammed. Something about this place is messing with her, I guess."

"Or maybe she wasn't bringing you to Polychrome at all," he said. "Maybe she's not as suggestible as Mombi thinks."

We sat there for a minute quietly. When I looked at him, I realized he was looking at me in this intense, serious way.

"What?" I asked.

Instead of answering me, he touched my cheek softly.

"We can change things," he said. "Forget Mombi, forget

Glamora, forget the Order. We don't need to do it for anyone else. Let's just do it for us."

I didn't quite understand what he meant, and then I did. He meant that we had both been through some terrible shit, but that the credits weren't rolling yet. There was still time for us to write ourselves a happy ending.

He leaned toward me, and I leaned in to meet him halfway.

This kiss was different than the first one. It was slower, and longer, and still awkward, but in a different way. It was a kiss that felt right.

If I hadn't felt a persistent tugging at my sleeve, we probably could have kept going for another hour. But the tugging didn't stop, and I broke away to see what was up. It was Ozma.

"Come *on*," I groaned.

She was pointing to the line of trees, drawing my attention to a rustling in the leaves as another figure stepped into view.

"I thought you said there was no one else here," I said to Nox.

"There wasn't. Must be a new arrival. You ready?"

"I guess," I said. "When am I not?"

Ready or not wasn't the point. I was always ready. But now, this time, and especially after a kiss like that, I was nervous. I had finally been reunited with Nox, and I didn't think I could handle losing him again.

Luckily, the stranger looked friendly as he shambled toward us. Or, if not exactly friendly, then at least like he wouldn't be much of a threat unless you ran into his elbow in a mosh pit.

"Hey," he shouted, looking utterly unconcerned when he

spotted us. "You guys come here often?"

He was wiry but muscular at the same time, and was wearing a pair of faded black skinny jeans with a loose, tunic-like tank top that revealed his rail-thin physique.

The best way to describe him was *pretty*. He wasn't just cute, or handsome, or sexy, although if you thought about it, he was all of those things, too. Mostly, though, he was just pretty, with sharp, high cheekbones, pale, deep-set eyes, and a halo of perfectly unkempt white-blond ringlets framing a chiseled, angular face. He had pillowy, apple-red lips that made me think of one of Madison Pendleton's prized Madame Alexander dolls. Like the dolls, this guy looked like he belonged in a glass case.

"Well, well, well," he said when he'd had the chance to really check us out. "I see you've got a princess on your hands." He bowed toward Ozma. I was a little surprised he knew her, but then again, she *was* the rightful whatever. "Who are you guys? Is this, like, some kind of diplomatic mission?"

"Who wants to know?" Nox asked, eyeing the guy with suspicion.

"Uh . . . I do. That's why I asked, you know?"

"I've been here for weeks," Nox said. "The whole island's been totally empty. Wanna tell us how you got here?"

If the guy noticed how hostile Nox was being, he didn't much care. "Same as you, I figure," he said affably. "I got lost. But I'm always lost, pretty much. Actually I kind of like being lost. When you're lost, you don't have to be responsible for anything. I'm Bright, by the way."

"I'm Amy," I said.

"Nice to meet you, Amy," Bright said. He turned to Nox, who looked him over with one eyebrow frozen in a skeptical arch.

The two of them eyed each other carefully, sizing each other up in that way that guys do. I could have told them to just skip it. So they weren't going to get along. Fine. Why waste time making it official?

"Is Bright your real name?" I asked, just trying to move on. Totally dumb question—I was just trying to break the tension.

"I don't *think* so," Bright said. "But who can remember?" He sighed. "My parents always said I was *bright* as a button. I can't ask them, though. They're dead. Dorothy, you know. Whatever." He swatted a careless hand at the air. I couldn't tell if he was sad, bored, or just really, really spacey. If he was the kind of guy who got lost on the regular and couldn't remember what his real name was, it was probably the latter.

His eyes lit up as he spotted something on the ground.

"Ah! *Here* it is. Been looking all over for this. Knew it had to be around here somewhere."

Bright knelt to the ground and plucked up a cigarette case made from some kind of metal that I couldn't identify. In the few seconds it took him to pick it up, flip it open, and pull out a cigarette, the case must have changed colors at least six times in the light.

He shoved it into his pocket and lit up with a heavy silver lighter, inhaling deeply before letting out a thick puff of smoke that I waved away without thinking about it.

I wasn't actually trying to be rude. It was just a habit from the long, ongoing battle I'd had with my mother about smoking in our tiny trailer without bothering to crack a window.

"Oh, relax," Bright said. "It's not even tobacco—that stuff will kill you, plus it makes you stink. These are good for you. " He took another drag, and this time when he exhaled I noticed that the smoke was vaguely multicolored. It smelled pretty good, too, kind of like the fresh smell of pavement right after a rainstorm.

"What? " he said, registering my curiosity. "You never met anyone who smokes rainbows? "

"Oh, come *on*, " Nox snorted. I couldn't decide whether or not to be pleased that the appearance of this stranger had caused Nox to revert to his old, prickly self.

"They're rolled from the finest dried rainbow husks Rainbow Falls has to offer," Bright said. "Hard to get these days, now that there's not much trade with the mainland. But I hear Dorothy has a case or fifty stashed away for special occasions. They're all I smoke. Luckily I have a steady supply. Get 'em straight from the source."

A light bulb went off over my head.

"Wait," I asked, putting all of the pieces together. "Rainbow Falls? You don't know someone named Polychrome, do you? "

Bright's lips curled into a crooked, rakish smile.

"Know her? Yeah, I think we might have met once or twice," he said. "Cool girl. Crazy as anyone you'll ever meet, but there are worse things than crazy, right? "

"We're looking for her," I said. "Do you know where we can find her?"

"Ahh." Bright tapped his chin. "I might be able to help you out. Is there a reward?"

Nox was already seething. "Yeah, the reward is that we save the kingdom from an evil tyrant and *you* get to keep on smoking your rainbow cigarettes without a care in the world."

"Well, *that's* tempting," Bright said. "What else have you got?"

I figured maybe it was time to step in and lighten the mood.

"How 'bout a French One textbook? It's worth forty bucks." I was half joking, but if this dude thought he was getting my necklace or even my Argyle sock, he was dreaming. Which might not have been so far-fetched for a guy who smokes rainbows.

"Sorry," Bright said. "I already speak French. *Peut-être vous pouvez m'apprendre à embrasser en français à la place?*"

My old French teacher Madame Pusalino would have been extremely disappointed in how quickly I'd forgotten my conversational skills. It took me a good minute to translate what he'd said, and when I figured it out, all I could do was snap my head back and shoot him my most withering look.

"What'd he say?" Nox asked, narrowing his eyes.

"*Möchtet ihr deutscher Schokoladenkuchen?*" Ozma offered.

All three of us turned and stared at her. She smiled and shrugged.

"Look," I finally said. "Forget all this. Tell us how to find Polychrome."

Without mentioning it, I called forth a small spell. Something subtle. My fist began to burn with orange, smoldering flame.

"Jeez!" Bright said, taking the hint. "Don't get all hot under the collar. I'm just messing around. Although I have to admit, it's not every day that I meet a girl as beautiful as you who can do *magic*."

Nox made a move to step between us. "How about you back off?" he snapped, looking ready to actually punch the guy.

"Whoa there, *mon frère*," Bright said, now raising his palms in a show of completely insincere apology. "I'm a lover, not a fighter. Anyway, I didn't know the lady had a protector on call. As a gentleman, I stand down."

"And as a *gentlewoman*, I can protect myself," I said, glaring at Nox. Then to Bright: "If you think I'm pretty now, you should see me when I'm splattered with blood and entrails. I'm a ruthless killer, you know."

Out of nowhere, Ozma interjected. "Bring us to her," she said, slamming her scepter into the ground. All three of us turned to stare at her, momentarily united in amazement, and I realized that, with her scepter, she suddenly looked more regal than before. I wondered if finding it had somehow made her stronger.

"Well!" Bright said. "I didn't know it was a royal command! The way I heard it, you weren't doing much commanding at all these days, Your Highness. But I'm nothing if not a faithful subject. I'll try to be of service if I can."

"Yeah," Nox said, apparently still not ready to admit that Bright was harmless. "How about you do that."

"Whoa, chill, pal. The door to the falls will be around here somewhere—when I'm in the mood to go home, it's never too far away. Everyone else has a bitch of a time finding it. Meanwhile, half the time I feel like it's following *me*. When I'm not lost, that is. Go figure."

He began to shamble toward the trees, I guess expecting us to tag along.

"What an asshole," Nox said under his breath. I elbowed him in the ribs as a friendly reminder to let it go. I didn't disagree, but for now, we needed this guy.

After moving quickly through the palm trees, we found ourselves standing on a cobblestone street at the edge of the city. From the beach, we'd only been able to see a silhouetted skyline against the blue sky, but now that we were *in* it, it was stranger and larger than I had expected. It was like something out of a fairy tale—which I know is a weird thing to say when you're already in a fairy tale, but that was Oz for you.

Skyscrapers stood cheek by jowl with dilapidated shacks that in turn pushed up against huge, strange houses with cupolas built on top of porticos built on top of steeply gabled roofs. A strip of dusty, abandoned shops advertised strange things like baby teeth by the pound and a two-for-one deal on lost marbles. Everything was crowded so close together that it looked like the whole town was about to collapse in on itself. And the twisty, narrow cobblestone street snarled its way through it all.

The sun was setting again, and was just beginning to dip

behind the skyline, and, other than me, Nox, Ozma, and Bright, there wasn't a person in sight.

Nox looked at me, and saw me taking it all in. "I told you it was incredible," he said. "The whole time I was lost, I was hoping I'd get to show it to you."

It was the corniest thing I could ever imagine him saying. It was sweet, but it was unexpected.

He noticed my surprise, and looked a little embarrassed, but before he could say anything else, Bright interrupted our moment.

"Everyone loves the Beach of Misplaced Objects, obviously," Bright said. "But the beach is for tourists. The city here—this is the real deal. This is where the *really* lost shit ends up."

"Like us," I mumbled. After everything, the fact that we had made our way here felt fitting. Even though we were looking for the door out, there was something about the place that felt like a final destination.

"You said it, not me," Bright said. He leaned against a burned-out streetlamp, lit another cigarette, and regarded the streets, multicolored smoke wafting out into the dusk. "Let's try"—he let his index finger drift lazily through the air until it landed on a random point—"this way."

"Why that way?" Nox asked. "What's that way?"

"Dunno," Bright said. "Why not?"

He was already moving, headed toward the strip of storefronts facing the beach. He peered into a store that appeared, from the window display, to only stock old, broken doll parts, then shook his head.

"Nope," he said. "Not in there."

"How long does it usually take you?" I asked. "To find the door?"

"Depends. One thing about always being lost is you get a lot of practice when it comes to finding your way home. But you never know. Sometimes it takes five minutes. Sometimes a week. Look, my track record is way better than most people's. You guys could look for the door for the rest of your lives and never quite get there. You're lucky you found me."

I was still stuck on the numbers. "A *week?*" I asked. "I don't know if we really have that long."

"Well, let's hope it doesn't take a week, then. I'm telling you, it's unpredictable. One time it took me something like a year to get back to the citadel. Polly was righteously pissed. I was like, dude, maybe try not making your damn glass castle so hard to find."

"A *year?*" I asked incredulously.

Ozma, who had been silent since her earlier outburst, looked around and waved her newfound scepter. Suddenly I noticed an alleyway where there hadn't been one before, wedged between the doll shop and the place that sold the baby teeth. Maybe the suggestion spell Mombi had put in her ear was still at work.

Bright noticed the alley at the same time I did. "Well, what do you know?" he said. He cocked an eyebrow at Ozma. "I guess having a queen along for the ride has its uses."

He turned sideways and squeezed himself through the gap between the buildings, which was so narrow I wasn't even sure he would fit. But he did, and when I squeezed in after him, it turned out that it wasn't even as tight as it had appeared. When I looked over my shoulder, Nox was right behind me, with Ozma trailing behind us, her scepter slung over her shoulder.

"Do you really think we can trust this guy?" Nox whispered.

"What choice do we really have?" I responded.

We wove our way through the back alleys of the Lost City. Now and again, Bright would look inside a trash can or rap his fist a few times against a wall, checking for something I couldn't figure out.

I thought it was a little strange that Bright hadn't really asked us who we were, or why we were looking for Polychrome. Was it possible that he knew more about us than he was letting on? After all, he had recognized Ozma right off the bat.

Before I could worry about this any more, he stopped at the entrance to a nondescript office building. He looked up, examining the windows, and jiggled the knob.

"This one, I think," he said. The door swung open.

The inside of the building was the complete opposite of the city outside. It was the kind of place you'd find in any crappy office park in Kansas, complete with an unmanned reception desk and a sad little ficus in the corner. It was clean, lit by flickering fluorescent lights, and smelled like air freshener.

"How did a place like this wind up on the Island of Lost Things?" I asked, wondering.

"Hell if I know," Bright replied. "Someone must have lost it, I guess. Foreclosure?" He pressed the button for the elevator. It dinged, opened, and we all crowded inside.

Bright searched the buttons for the floors until his finger landed on one that, instead of bearing a number, was pulsing with color, cycling through the spectrum. "Here we go," he said. "Told you I was feeling lucky."

Bright punched the button, then turned to me and winked. "Next stop, Rainbow Falls."

I felt us going up, first slowly and then faster and faster. Finally, after both my ears had popped from the altitude, the doors slid open. But we weren't facing the empty hallway or a bank of cubicles you might have expected given the decor downstairs. Instead, we were looking out onto a blue, open sky, where a bright, vertiginous fall of rainbows, rushing just like water, crashed thousands of feet toward the ground.

It was breathtaking. It was one of those things that makes you remember, even from the elevator of a crappy office building, that you're really in fairyland. I tried to picture what my five-year-old self would have thought if she could see me now, about to enter a kingdom of rainbows.

That's assuming we were actually about to enter it. I sort of hadn't told anyone in Oz about my debilitating fear of heights. "Um," I said. "So . . ."

"What?" Bright asked. "I thought you wanted to see Polly? How else do you think you get to Rainbow Falls?"

"Are we supposed to *jump*?" I asked, my heart beginning to race. I'd already spent way more time than I cared to in a state of total emotional free fall, and here I was being asked to do it yet again, this time literally.

Instead of answering, Bright wiggled his eyebrows and leapt. "Cannonball!" he shouted, before launching himself out the elevator door.

Nox, never the type to be outdone, gave me a cocky, pitched smile and was right behind him with a joyful whoop, plunging into a raging sea of color.

Boys, I thought. *What show-offs.*

I knew that I had to jump too. And I knew that no matter how I felt, I had to push the fear away. There wasn't room for it.

I was working up the nerve to go for it when Ozma extended a hand.

"Come," she said. "Don't be scared."

Something in her tone made me want to show her that I wasn't.

So I took the closest thing to a running start the confines of the elevator would allow us, and sailed out into the colors of the sky below.

SEVENTEEN

The rainbows washed over me. It was like I was being spun in some Willy Wonka version of a washing machine. A neon palette swirled around me as I tumbled: hot pink, electric blue, candy-apple red, grape-soda purple, and every color imaginable in between, all of them zooming downward into infinity in a twisting, death-defying flume, carrying me faster than even seemed possible.

Once I got used to the nauseous somersaults my stomach was pulling—and figured out that I wasn't going to die—it was less scary than I expected it to be. It was actually sort of fun. Then the world flipped upside down, and instead of falling, I was flying, sailing upward into a radiant light, the colors becoming brighter and brighter until they all merged with each other.

When I saw blue, clear sky over my head, I felt myself swimming, and I realized the ride was over. I floated upward a few more feet and emerged into day in a warm, whirling pool of light that wasn't quite wet and not quite dry, and felt like all the sun-shine in the world had been poured into a jar too tiny to begin to contain all of it.

Of course: I'd spent enough hours studying with Glamora and Gert to know a magical portal when I saw one.

I rubbed my eyes, adjusting, and saw that Nox and Bright were already here. From the edge of the pool, Nox reached out a hand to help me, and I took it, climbing up to join him on a small, grassy patch of land, feeling like I'd just gotten off a waterslide at an amusement park.

"Fun ride, huh?" Bright asked, wiggling an eyebrow.

"I've definitely had worse. Most of them this week," I said, shaking myself off and spraying a shower of iridescent droplets from my body.

My jaw dropped at the scenery. We were on an island in the air, no more than thirty feet across, suspended high above the clouds. The portal I'd just crawled out of took up almost all of it, extending all the way to the edge except for the area we were standing on, its shimmering light spilling out into the sky like water in one of those infinity pools you see in ads for fancy hotels. Ozma was crawling out of it herself now, but all I could do was gape at the scenery.

The air was dotted with what could have been hundreds of the hovering islands, some huge, others as small as my trailer back home. They drifted lazily through the air as if being blown by a gentle wind. As they floated, a constantly shifting network of vibrant, shimmering rainbows appeared and disappeared randomly between them, momentarily connecting one to the next before fading away.

On the largest and highest of all the islands was a crystal palace with sharp, angular lines, reflecting and refracting the light at a million different angles like a diamond. A trio of glittering spires rose up so tall that they looked like they could have been scratching the edge of outer space.

"Come on," Bright said, pointing toward it. "Polly'll know we're here."

Like it knew our exact intentions, a rainbow appeared where we stood and shot up to the citadel, forming a long, steeply pitched bridge.

"Don't worry, they're totally solid," Bright said, stepping out onto it, "but watch your step anyway, they're slippery as hell."

I went next, bracing myself, and though I was expecting a long, nail-biting hike up to the castle, it turned out that the only thing I had to do was keep my balance: as soon as I had both feet on the rainbow, it began to carry me upward.

I laughed a little. This was like being on an escalator at the most surreal mall ever, heading from the food court to JCPenney. I breathed deep and tried to relax. The air smelled like honeysuckle and filled me with a deep, longing feeling.

It took me the whole ride to identify it as *hope*.

From up close, the palace was even more beautiful than before, with intricate floral patterns etched into all of its surfaces. The rainbow bridge took us over a moat of clouds and right to the castle's grand, arched entranceway, where the doors flung themselves open before we could even step up to them.

Standing behind them was a girl so beautiful that I was startled at the sight of her. She was tall and statuesque and willowy, wearing a loosely fitting caftan in a neon paisley print. Even though the dress was roughly the size and shape of a refrigerator box, it was translucent to the point of near abstraction, almost like the fabric itself had been woven from threads of light and color, and didn't do much to cover the shape of her slim, coltish body.

But it was her hair that was the most impressive thing about the girl. It flowed around her like she was being blown with one of those giant fans they use in music videos, and was so long that it was hard to tell where it ended. It was intertwined with beads and flowers and threads of color that shifted through the spectrum depending on the angle you looked at them.

I had a pretty good feeling that this was Polychrome.

"Welcome to my kingdom, visitors!" she exclaimed in an ethereal voice.

"What, no welcome for me?" Bright asked, stepping up and wrapping an arm around her waist.

"Oh, hello there," she said, batting her eyelashes coquettishly.

"Hey, babe," Bright said huskily.

"You've been gone too long. Lost again, I presume?"

"Yup. Saw a lot of crazy stuff this time. There's some serious business happening on the ground right now—we have a lot to talk about."

"I'm sure," she agreed, and she promptly swept him up into the kind of kiss that made me feel like I should probably look away.

Was he kidding me? I was pretty sure he'd been hitting on me back on the ground, and it was now clear that Polychrome was his girlfriend. Had he been trying to embarrass me before, or was he such a player that he just couldn't help himself?

Probably both, I thought. Nox must have known exactly what I was thinking, because he gave me a smug *I told you so* look and then a *gag me* gesture.

They didn't notice. Their makeout went on. And on. And on. And *on*.

About two minutes after it had gotten seriously uncomfortable, I cleared my throat, and Polychrome pulled away from Prince Charmless looking flushed.

"Forgive me," she said, remembering us. "What a bad hostess I'm being. I can't help it sometimes—we rainbow dwellers are a people who truly delight in the senses. But please! Come in and join me in my rumpus room. I've been so looking forward to your visit."

"She knew we were coming?" I whispered to Nox as we stepped into the castle, but I guess I'd been too loud, because it was Polychrome herself who responded.

"My sprites sent word of your arrival, of course," she explained as she led us up through a lavish foyer. "They got so excited when they saw you heading up the bridge. Tourism used to be one of our biggest industries here in the falls, but Dorothy's rule put an end to all that. Now we're reduced to selling those disgusting rainbow cigarettes on the black market to make ends meet. We never get visitors anymore. Especially none as *royal* as yourselves." She glanced over her shoulder at Ozma and gave a halfhearted little curtsy without breaking her stride.

"Come on, Polly. Everyone's a royal around here," Bright said. "Can't go ten feet without bumping into someone who claims total dominion over a patch of grass. Is it really such a big deal to have another princess in our midst?"

I was starting to agree with him, but Polychrome didn't look amused. "Please forgive my Royal Consort," she said, beginning to ascend a spiral staircase with translucent, floating steps and a thin silver, handrail. "He's a monstrous pain in the ass, and the absolute laziest person you'll ever have the misfortune to meet, but you have to admit: he's hot."

"Guilty as charged," Bright said.

The staircase went up and up, high into the castle, and opened up into a spacious, circular lounge that was entirely enclosed in glass, providing a stunning, three-hundred-sixty-degree view so expansive that I was pretty sure I would have been able to see from one end of Oz to the other, if my vision were sharp enough.

Ozma trotted over to the window and stared out at the kingdom, fully entranced. She turned to me. "The time draws near," she said.

I glanced at her in surprise. Her moments of lucidity were becoming more and more frequent—and more lucid.

"The time for what?" I asked. But she didn't reply.

On one edge of the room was a curved, chrome bar, its glass shelves fully stocked with hundreds of tiny jars and bottles of strange things I wasn't able to recognize. In place of any other furniture, the rest of the space was strewn with plush, oversize pillows in various shades of white. Bright immediately flopped down on one of them and leaned back, stretching languorously, his shirt rising to reveal an inch of stomach.

I caught myself staring and quickly looked away, hoping that no one had noticed, only to see that Polychrome was openly ogling him, too. When she saw me, she tossed her hair saucily, gave me a *just us girls* wink, and stepped behind the bar.

"Can I offer anyone a snack?" she asked.

"We're looking for the Order," I said. It was easy to get caught up in the strangeness of everything, but I couldn't forget I was here on a mission. "Mombi said we might find some of them here."

Polychrome raised a brow in recognition of Mombi's name, then shook her head as she continued pulling out jars and vials. "I'm sorry," she said. "It's true that this was once a meeting place for Mombi's cohort, but none of them has passed through here in as long as I can remember. Now would you care for some rose petals? A relaxing snort of poppy pollen? Perhaps a thimbleful of dew?" She drew out the last word into at least three syllables so it was almost hard to tell what she had said.

"No thanks," I said. "We can't stay long. Anyway, I'm not hungry."

"No one ever is," she said with a sigh. "I guess I just have a larger appetite than most. For now I believe I'll just munch on some freshly caught wasps."

My stomach lurched as she pulled out a large glass jar containing what looked like most of a fairly healthy hive of crawling, brown insects. She unscrewed the lid and reached inside to pluck one out with her fingers, then popped the still-squirming creature into her mouth—chomping down on it with an audible crunch.

Bright lit another rainbow cigarette. "She's just showing off," he said. "She knows it's disgusting, but she does it every time someone new comes around."

She gave him an unamused look. "*Must* you smoke in here?" she asked icily.

"Where else am I going to smoke?" he asked, deliberately blowing a smoke ring into her face. Instead of getting angry, she giggled and batted her eyelashes again. For a second, I was worried they were going to start making out again.

Instead, Polychrome sat down on the pillow next to him, tucking her legs underneath her body and gesturing for me and Nox to sit, too.

She tossed another wasp into the air, watched in amusement as it buzzed around trying to evade her, and then snapped her head forward to catch the bug in her mouth, looking quite pleased with herself. "So," she said. "Tell me about *you.*"

"Please," I said. "We need your help."

"All in good time. First, introduce yourselves."

"I'm Amy," I said. "This is Nox. That's Ozma over there."

"Oh, I know the princess, of course. Or the queen, I suppose. Everyone was always so vague when it came to her title."

She cast a pitying look toward Ozma, who was still occupying herself by looking at the view. "So tragic what happened to her, isn't it?" Polychrome said. "Before her troubles, we were the best of friends. Sure, she was always a little too serious—constantly worrying about tariffs and labor regulations and the dullest things like that, never seemed to have *any* time to *rip* off our clothes and go for a fully nude romp in the clouds, just us girls—but nevertheless, I adored her."

Polychrome saw the skeptical look I was giving her. "You land dwellers never understand," she said. "It's very important for fairy princesses to commune with nature. In the nude, the way fairies were intended to be. Anyway, forget about Ozma: the poor thing is a lost cause. Amy, Nox, it's lovely to meet you." A sudden thought swept across her face. "Oh!" she said excitedly. "Would you like to meet my pet unicorn?"

I groaned inwardly, wondering if we'd really come all this way to make small talk over thimbles full of dew. But I could also see that I was going to get nowhere unless I at least tried to humor her. "You have a unicorn?" I asked politely.

"I'm the Daughter of the Rainbow," she said in a voice that indicated she was beginning to think I was a bit of an idiot. "Of course I have a unicorn. You simply *must* see him. I guarantee he'll enchant you." She snapped her fingers in summons. "Unicorn!" she singsonged. "Unicorn, unicorn!"

When there was no response whatsoever, she rolled her eyes,

shook her head, and screeched at the top of her lungs. "Heath-cliff!"

That did the job. In the distance, I heard the patter of feet, and a large, snow-white creature came bounding from the stairway and settled into a dignified crouch at Polychrome's side.

She smiled and patted it behind the ears. It was not a unicorn. In fact, it was a huge cat—a panther, maybe?—with a long, sharp horn fastened around its head with a pink ribbon tied in a bow under its chin.

"Interesting unicorn," Nox said. "Never seen that particular species before."

"Look, I always wanted a unicorn," Polychrome said. "A fairy princess should have a unicorn, don't you agree? The problem is, purebred unicorns don't take to being made into pets. It's one of their biggest failings. Of which they have many, I might add. Ugh, they're awful creatures in the end. So haughty and headstrong, impossible to train, always making a mess in the house. They're very judgmental, too—always setting perfectly *ridiculous* rules about who gets to ride them and who can't. But the Daughter of the Rainbow should have a unicorn. And I am, above all things, a fairy of can-do spirit. So, you see, I had to fashion myself a unicorn of my own. And anyway, Heathcliff is so much better than another unicorn would be. He's very dear, he lets me pet him, and he can devour an entire human in just three bites if I need him to. So why should I have any regrets?"

She turned to the beast, who pawed at the ground looking, frankly, a bit humiliated at the charade he was being forced to enact. "And you love being my little unicorn, don't you? You're such a pretty, noble little loveykins, aren't you?"

Heathcliff gave a placating rumble of a purr as Polychrome ran her fingers through his fur.

"Does he grant wishes?" Nox asked. "Like a real unicorn?"

The fairy stiffened, and she sat up very straight. "He's extremely sensitive about that. I would appreciate it if you didn't mention the subject in his presence again. Or mine. Now, please, let's move on."

"He doesn't grant wishes," Bright said, blowing a smoke ring and looking amused.

"Shut up, consort," Polychrome shot back at him. "I'll remind you that you are allowed to stay here at my pleasure. Now"—she turned back to us—"what in the world has brought you to my kingdom? You're not the conquering types, are you? I would hate to have to fling you off the side of the Sunset Balustrade. I'm *so* not in the mood for a conquering today."

"We're not here to conquer. At least, we're not here to conquer *you*. We're with the Revolutionary Order of the Wicked," Nox said. "Mombi sent us. She thought you might be able to help."

"So you said. I wish I could be of more help—I do *so* love that old hag. Such a wit she has about her! I hope she's doing well. But as I've told you, I have been utterly alone up here, save for my sprites, for quite some time now. If Mombi thought her revolutionary friends would seek refuge here, she was mistaken."

I looked from Nox to Ozma to Bright, who seemed extremely bored by the whole conversation, and then back to Polychrome.

"Maybe I could speak to you alone," I said.

Nox gave me a sharp look, and I shrugged apologetically. It wasn't that I didn't trust him. At this point, of course I trusted him. It was just that there were still a few things I wanted to keep to myself as much as possible.

"Fine," Polychrome said. "Bright, show the others to the parlor."

Bright stood, looking disgruntled. "The work of a Royal Consort is never over," he said.

When they were gone, Polychrome walked to the bar and sat down on a high, glossy stool. "Now I'm intrigued," she said, patting the stool next to her for me to sit. "Mombi wouldn't have sent you to all the trouble of coming here if she didn't have good reason. What news can you give me of the world below?"

"Oz is at war," I said simply.

Polychrome sighed and ate another wasp.

"I can't say I'm surprised," she admitted. "It's been a terrible time for us. These last few turns of the sun, I've often wondered if the Rainbow Falls would survive at all. The wild unicorns all took off for god knows where; the sprites seem antsy. Several of my handmaidens have developed very destructive habits; I've had to let a few of them go."

I nodded.

"When Dorothy came back, you could just feel the color draining from this whole place. We've been hanging on, but black and white isn't a good look for anyone here at Rainbow Falls, as I'm sure you can imagine."

"It's Dorothy," I said. "She and Glinda have been draining Oz's magic."

"Precisely," Polychrome said. "Or, at least, she *was*. But is she still? I'm Ozma's distant cousin, you know—fairy genealogy gets complicated considering that none of us have parents, but we *are* cousins of a sort. We share the royal blood of Oz, and as the mistress of the falls, I am *intimately* attuned with Oz's mystical rhythms. It's easy to see that there have been recent changes afoot. The magic is returning; the falls are suddenly looking healthier than they have in ages. Dare I hope that Dorothy has been defeated?"

I shook my head. "No. But she's been driven out of the Emerald City. And I think there's something going on between her and Glinda. I'm not sure if they're quite the bosom buddies they were before."

"Well, that's an interesting development," she mused. "There have long been complicated political forces at work here in Oz, and Glinda has usually been at the center of them. With the witches of the East and South killed, it became easier for a while, but other factions have developed. Both Glinda and the Wizard have always been wild cards. No one has ever been able to tell quite where their loyalties lie, or what their goals are. And Dorothy *is* a problem. She's quite mad, you know."

"I know," I said. "I'm going to kill her. Things will be a lot simpler when she's dead."

Polychrome scanned me carefully.

"You're from the Other Place, aren't you?" she asked.

"Yes," I said.

"I see. Who brought you here?"

A change had come over her. She was no longer the airy, slightly dippy fairy who had greeted us at the door. Now she seemed older, more thoughtful. Her caftan had taken on a darker tone, and there was a glare in her eyes that was honestly a little frightening. I wondered if that earlier version had been an act. Maybe there was a steeliness to Polychrome that I was only beginning to see.

Heathcliff was pacing the room, and I could see that he was different, too. His white fur was glowing with an electrical sheen, and his horn was glittering. It looked like it was an actual part of him rather than just a stupid hat.

"I was brought here on a cyclone," I said. Before she could comment on the obvious, I said it myself: "From Kansas. Like Dorothy."

The new shift in Polychrome made me nervous. Suddenly I wondered how much I wanted to tell her. "Mombi thought I might find other members of the Order here," I said, choosing to go with the easiest part first. "Have you heard any word of Glamora?"

Polychrome shook her head. "In the past months, my scrying pools have been clouded. I've been able to see very little of the goings-on in the rest of Oz. All I know is what I feel. And while I feel great changes are afoot, you know better than I as to what has brought those changes about."

"I know some," I said. "But not everything."

I made a decision. I picked up my bag and emptied it onto the bar, displaying the trophies of my battles.

The Tin Woodman's heart. The Lion's tail.

"Where did you get these?" Polychrome asked, her voice quiet and surprised.

"I took them," I said. "From their owners. I know they're important, but Mombi thought you might be able to tell me more about them, and what they do."

The Daughter of the Rainbow was already on her feet. "Come," she said. "I need to examine these further in my Luma-torium."

EIGHTEEN

Polychrome's so-called Lumatorium was a dim, windowless chamber hidden deep in the castle's interior behind a revolving bookshelf. It was crowded with mysterious, vaguely scientific-looking instruments, long laboratory tables and beakers and flasks full of colorful liquids and powders.

Looking around the room, I was struck by how many different types of magic there were in Oz, and how many different ways there were of practicing it. For some people, like Mombi—and me, come to think of it—magic was something you just kind of *did*. It was all instinct, a power that came directly from within. For other people, it was a practice closer to science.

The first style seemed a lot more convenient to me, but, on the other hand, Mombi had sent me here because she thought Polychrome would uncover things that *she* hadn't been able to. So I guess there was something to all this junk.

Polychrome moved around the room efficiently, gathering up

her materials, while Heathcliff curled up in the corner, observing her lazily. When she had everything she deemed necessary, she gestured for me to empty my bag again.

"Let's take a look at those," Polychrome said, and I set the objects I'd taken from the Lion and the Tin Woodman on a table. Polychrome in turn placed each of them on either end of an old-fashioned scale, which indicated, improbably, that they were perfectly balanced with each other.

The metal heart thumped robotically; the tail continued to twitch as if attached to an invisible owner. Polychrome sprinkled them with a dusting of acrid-smelling powder, causing them to halt in their motion. She fastened a thick, old-fashioned set of goggles to her face and knelt to examine them.

"Just as I suspected," she said after a bit. She lit a candle and then, after some consideration, picked up a long, hollow glass rod tipped with a tiny, red orb. She touched the orb gently to the Tin Woodman's heart and held it there. The rod began to change colors, filling with a sort of pink liquid, which she emptied into a beaker before repeating the same process with the tail.

She held the beaker over the candle and we both watched as it began to heat up and bubble.

"What are you doing to it?" I asked.

"Just running a few magical tests," she said. "My methods are somewhat different from those used by the witches. I'm isolating the mystic elements of the objects to determine their origin, as well as—hopefully—to divine their purpose. It seems strange, of course, that they have any enchantment on them at all; when the Wizard granted them to their owners, he had no facility with magic to speak of. So one wonders that they should now be imbued with such energies. But indeed they are. Is it something that Dorothy did? Or is there another explanation?"

The liquid in the beaker boiled quickly over the flame, until all that was left of it was a thick, red syrup resembling blood. Polychrome selected a wide, shallow silver bowl from a shelf, placed it next to the scale, and poured the strange substance into it. She crouched and peered at it carefully through her goggles, swirling it around a little with her finger.

Next, she waved her palm across the surface and mumbled a few quick words that I didn't understand.

The liquid began to change color until it was transparent. Polychrome nodded to herself. "Look," she said, and when I gazed into the bowl with her, I saw that there was now an image in it.

In the bowl, as clear as if I was looking out through a window, was a flat, dusty prairie under a gray sky, tall grass blowing in the wind.

I recognized it immediately—maybe not the exact, specific location, but the idea of it. Back home, the prairie was everywhere. Even when you were standing in a strip mall, or walking along a busy highway, it was always still there, just out of sight. The flat, flat everything, the gray, dusty nothing seeping into your pores. So I had no doubt of exactly what I was looking at.

"Kansas," I said.

"Indeed," Polychrome said quietly. "And yet. Is it?"

I looked closer. It was Kansas, but it wasn't. It was like one of those games in the back of a celebrity magazine, where you look at two pictures of Jennifer Aniston, and in the second one, everything is just a little off. Except in this version, the difference wasn't that Jennifer Aniston was wearing a pink bracelet instead of a blue one. It was something harder to put your finger on than that.

It was something about the way the wind was blowing, something about the thick clouds that were rolling in. It didn't just look lonely. It looked sick. It looked evil. It sent a chill down my spine.

"What does it mean?" I asked quietly.

Polychrome was silent. Heathcliff padded over to where she stood and she peeled her goggles off, then knelt and touched her forehead to the cat's horn, staring into his eyes. She seemed to be consulting with him in a silent conversation.

Eventually she turned back to me, still kneeling.

"It could mean several things," she said. "I still have many questions about these items. But, certainly, it means that they bear a deep connection with the Other Place. Your home. The Wizard's home. Dorothy's home. I also sense something not quite right about them. Something evil, I suppose. There was something about these things that was corrupting their owners."

It was time to stop holding back, I knew. "The Wizard told me that until I gathered them, I wouldn't be able to kill Dorothy."

Polychrome twisted a lock of hair around her finger. She chewed on her lip. "It makes a certain sense," she said. "If these items were somehow holding a piece of Dorothy's essence, it could explain this connection to the Other Place. It might also explain the evil about them. And yet"—she dipped a finger into the pool—"I don't know. I sense nothing of Dorothy in the tincture. You would think . . ."

She crossed her arms and looked up at the ceiling, confounded. "I just don't know," she sighed. "Here in Oz, we understand so very little of the Other Place, or of how Oz is connected to it. We never have. It's a shame that the one person who does have knowledge of it is the one person we can't ask."

"Dorothy?"

"No. Nor do I believe the Wizard has much expertise when it comes to matters of the Other Place, despite hailing from there. But Glinda has made a study of your world. Of Oz's magic practitioners, she is the only one who has demonstrated an ability to summon visitors from the outside—though many have tried."

"Do you think she's the one who brought *me* here?" I asked. I was still struggling to put all the pieces together. Things were beginning to add up, but in a way I couldn't quite see an order to. It was like being halfway through a calculus problem, knowing you're on the right track, and having no idea of the answer or how the hell you're supposed to get there. This time, I didn't think I would get points for showing my work.

"It's possible. But part of me doubts it. What reason would she have had? And why would she have made an enemy out of you so quickly, if she had been the one to bring you here?"

She was right. It didn't really make sense.

"I'm sorry I could not have been more help," Polychrome said. "Perhaps if we had the third item—the Scarecrow's brain—it would complete the puzzle."

"I'm already on it," I said.

"And Amy? Do me a favor?"

"What?" I asked.

"When you cut him open, make it hurt."

I smiled. "It's a promise," I said.

With that, some of the girlishness returned to Polychrome's face. She gave me a conspiratorial look. "Even *before* Dorothy came back and turned everyone evil," she said in a stage whisper, cupping her palm to her mouth, "the Scarecrow was *always* a bit of a dick."

She giggled and tossed her hair, and some of the tension left the room.

"Now," she said. "Before we retire for the evening, I wanted to look into one more thing." She turned to her giant unicorn-cat. "Heathcliff," she said. "Fetch me our friend the queen."

Heathcliff stood up on command, took a powerful leap across the room, and, like a ghost, passed right through the wall.

When Polychrome saw my look of surprise, she pursed her lips. "Everyone doubts my unicorn," she said tartly. "Just because he doesn't grant wishes doesn't mean he's useless."

"I can see that now," I said. "But why do you need Ozma again?"

Polychrome pressed a finger to her chin. "When we were in my rumpus room, I noticed a disturbance in the princess's aura," she said. "Something that made me suspect there might be more to her . . . *condition* than I previously suspected. I would like to examine her. Is there anything about her that you would like to tell me?"

I couldn't tell if I was being tested. Is it possible she knew about Pete? Or knew that I knew? So I decided to hedge for the time being. "Mombi was hoping you would be able to . . . fix her. Make her more like how she used to be," I said, feeling guilty both for telling only half the truth and also for saying even that much. I'd been hoping to totally avoid the subject of Ozma. After my conversation with Pete yesterday, I was worried about what would happen if anyone started messing around with whatever magic was binding him to the princess. What if they were fused forever? What if Pete just . . . disappeared?

He had made good on his promise to help me find Nox, and I didn't want to betray him now.

A few minutes later, Heathcliff came padding back into the room with Ozma at his side. The princess looked sleepy and listless, like she'd just been woken from a nap.

"Hello, cousin," Polychrome greeted her. Ozma looked up with an open and curious face, and Polychrome gently removed her scepter from her hand. For a second, Ozma looked reluctant to part with it, but she didn't put up a fight.

"Stand over here, just for a moment." The rainbow fairy led Ozma to a small footstool, and helped the princess climb onto it. As Ozma stood there dutifully, Polychrome began to bustle around the room, pulling ingredients from the shelves in a way

that looked random and combining them haphazardly into a
small cauldron that she suspended from a small stand over an
eldritch flame.

"What's that?" I asked, watching her suspiciously.

"Oh, nothing much," Polychrome said. "Just a little Tincture
of Revelation. Old family recipe. Not to worry; it's quite harmless. Tastes quite a bit like Earl Grey, I'm told."

She sniffed at the cauldron, and when she was satisfied that
the tincture had been properly prepared, she poured it into a little teacup ringed with a delicate floral pattern and a gilded rim.

"Unicorn?"

She placed the teacup on the floor where Heathcliff could
reach it, and he bent his head and touched the liquid with his
horn. I didn't notice that it had any effect, but when Polychrome
examined the mixture again she seemed happy with the result.

She handed the cup to Ozma. "Drink up, Your Highness,"
she said. "And let all that is hidden be revealed. When all this is
over, I hope that we can be lovely friends again."

Ozma sipped tentatively from the cup, and then, appearing
to like the taste of it, gulped thirstily. As she drank, her move-
ments began to slow. The empty cup dropped from her hands,
and shattered on the floor.

"Never liked that pattern anyway," Polychrome said to herself.

I wasn't very worried about Polychrome's china. I was too
busy watching what was happening to the princess.

Her arms dangled lazily at her sides, her mouth went slack,

and her eyes were heavy-lidded in an expression of sedate peace-fulness. Meanwhile, something was emerging from her, a green smoke that curled out from her chest and hovered in the center of the room.

At first, it was just an indistinct cloud. Then its colors shifted, and the smoke condensed as it gathered itself into recognizable form. No: *two* forms, each of them hanging in the air next to each other, translucent but clearly visible as separate, familiar bodies.

One of them was Pete. The other was Ozma—a second Ozma, a ghostly simulacrum of the version who was still stand-ing in a semi-drugged state on the stool.

Pete looked utterly himself: slim and lanky and a little bit mischievous, his features sharp and strong, with an odd, mis-matched beauty.

This version of Ozma though, was different. Not in any way that I could really put a finger on, but in a way that was subtle and at the same time impossible to miss. Her eyes were bright and full of intelligence; her posture, even as she hung suspended above the ground, perfectly still, was regal and dignified. She had a power about her; an awe-inspiring grace that, even know-ing she wasn't real, made me want to kneel and bow my head to the ground.

She looked, in short, like a queen.

Behind them, the real Ozma—or, what I guess was the real Ozma—observed the two spirit forms that had been summoned forth from somewhere deep within her. She didn't try to move from the stool she was standing on, and instead was simply looking on with the confused, sheepish guilt of a little kid who's just been caught next to a broken cookie jar, the cookies scattered across the floor.

Polychrome looked back and forth between them and raised a knowing eyebrow.

"Interesting," she said. "There have been two life forces occupying the princess's body. But you knew that already, didn't you?"

She smirked in my direction, like she'd had a feeling all along that this is exactly what she would find.

I nodded. What else could I do? But Polychrome didn't seem to care that I had lied to her. "No matter," she said. "We all have our secrets. One of mine is that I'm not as dim as people often think. But, actually, I have a whole cabinet of secrets. So much more convenient not to have them rattling around in my head, you know? It's much safer to keep them all locked up where I can't leave them lying around by accident. Anyway. I could run some more tests, but I have a nagging little suspicion that you already have most of the answers we could desire. Who is this second soul?"

She stepped over to the spot where Pete's form hovered and circled him, looking him up and down wolfishly. "Is he as *charming* as he appears?"

I tried my best to explain the whole Pete situation—what I knew of it, at least—to Polychrome, who nodded along with the story as I related it to her.

"I see," she said. "When Mombi attempted to disguise the

princess, she inadvertently created the seed of a new soul. It happens! The trick is catching it and nipping it in the bud before it comes into itself. Mombi has always been so sloppy when it comes to the details. It seems simple, now that you explain it. When Ozma was restored all those years ago, she suppressed this other soul. Then, when Dorothy did her little number on the princess, the thing was allowed to flourish again. At any rate, it shouldn't interfere much with things."

"What are you going to do?" I asked. I wasn't sure I wanted to hear the answer.

"I can see now that the spell Dorothy cast on the princess was all anger and impulse. No sense of precision at all, but it was powerful, too. That makes it a bit more complicated, especially now that it's had so much time to put roots down. But I think with a little elbow grease, I can restore Ozma to her proper state—the state you see before you instead of the simpering, foolish nincompoop who has been occupying her place all these years. And *that* will certainly change the game, won't it?"

"What will happen to him? To Pete?" I tried to hide the panic I was feeling, but I don't think I did a very good job of it.

"Oh, dear." Polychrome gave me a sympathetic frown. "Did you develop a little crush on the rogue soul? Well, he *is* handsome, I'll give you that. But you can't let yourself get all mushy over it. I imagine it'll just disappear."

"Please," I said. "You can't. It's not a crush. He's a good person. I don't want him to die."

"Amy, sweetie. Listen to me. It can't *die* when it's not alive in the first place. And it's not a person at all—just a little bad witch-ery that got out of hand. No matter what happens, you'll always have your perfectly lovely memories of it, now won't you? And a memory is worth a lot, especially when Ozma's return will do so much for Oz. So you lose yourself a plaything. There are more fish in the sea!"

I didn't like the way she was talking to me. As if I was some dumb little girl and she was my big sister who had come back from college and thought she knew everything because she'd had sex a couple of times and had read some French novels.

But while people like me had been fighting for Oz, Polychrome had just been locked up here in her castle, doing practically no good to anyone while she played tonsil hockey with her vapid, rainbow-smoking boy toy. And now she was trying to lecture *me* about the good of Oz? Some people had a lot of nerve.

On the other hand, she had a point. Having Ozma back for real *would* change the game in a serious way. Was the risk of losing Pete worth it? And even if it wasn't, could I stop it from happening?

At this moment, the only thing I could be sure of was that Polychrome was annoying. "Would you like a hug?" she asked.

"No, thank you," I said.

She snapped her fingers, and the floating images of Pete and Ozma were instantly sucked back into the body of the *real* prin-cess, who doubled over at the shock of having all of her parts returned to her. She stumbled from the stool on which she'd been standing and landed on her hands and knees on the stone floor of the Lumatorium, and promptly began to retch.

Instead of vomit pouring from her mouth, a flurry of tiny rainbows came out, and pooled on the ground in a sick puddle of jumbled-up colors.

Polychrome ignored the fairy princess's distress, and instead directed her attention to me.

"Don't you fret over all this, at least not for now. The Ritual of Restoration will be difficult, and before I can perform it, I must ask my sprites to gather the necessary ingredients. Also, I need my rest—I can practically feel the dark circles forming under my eyes as we speak. And, not to be a bitch, but you look like you could use a little beauty sleep, too. I'll let Heathcliff take you to your room, and tomorrow, we'll get everything all settled, okay?"

"I'll take my stuff, first, thanks," I said. The things I'd taken from the Lion and the Tin Woodman seemed even more important than ever now, even if I didn't know why, and I didn't want to let them out of my sight.

"Of course," Polychrome said, and I gathered them quickly into my bag, wondering what to do next.

NINETEEN

"We need to get out of here," I told Nox. After leaving Ozma in the room Polychrome had given us—this whole huge castle, and that dumb fairy couldn't even give me my own room!—I hadn't been able to sleep, and so I had gone to find Nox. Now he was leaning against the wall in thought, staring out the window at the rainbows that swirled outside in the dark, and I was sitting on the edge of his bed as I related everything that had just happened.

"Get out of here and go where?" he asked.

"Back to the jungle to find Mombi," I said. "Or to find Glamora. I don't know. Anywhere."

"Well *that* sounds like a plan." Nox shifted his weight and crossed his arms at his chest. There was something else bugging him.

"What?" I asked. "Why are you looking at me like that?"

Nox took his time answering. "Why didn't you want me in there with you?" he finally asked. "What were you telling her that you couldn't tell me?"

"I . . ." I started. "I don't know. Nothing. It's just . . ."

"That you still don't trust me? Even now?"

At first I was hurt, and then I was angry. "Of course I trust you," I said. "I *want* to trust you. And I do. But there's only so much trust in a place like this, and I didn't come here to find a boyfriend. So get over it. I just wasn't sure. And I'm telling you everything now, aren't I?"

He looked surprised at my outburst, but then he just nodded. "Sorry," he said. "I get it. And you're right. I think I went soft when I was lost. I sort of—I don't know. Maybe I started to lose perspective. It's just . . ."

I waved him off. "Never mind," I said. "Just help me figure out how to get out of here. Whatever she's about to do to Ozma, I don't like the sound of it."

"Really?" he asked. "Or is it that you don't like the sound of what she's going to do to *Pete*?"

"What difference does it make?"

"It makes all the difference," he said.

"I don't want her to hurt either of them," I said. "We have no idea what kind of voodoo she's cooking up, or what could go wrong. For all we know, she wants to stick Ozma in a box and saw her in half."

"I kind of doubt that," Nox said. "But I'll tell you what *I* know. I know that Ozma's important. And I know that she's already acting different. More powerful. If there's something we can do to help her, we have to."

"Pete's my friend," I said quietly.

Now it was Nox's turn to look angry. "Do you know how

many friends I've buried?" he asked. "Have you forgotten Gert? She wasn't the first, and she won't be the last, unless we do something. Look, I hope Pete's okay after all this. But it's worth the risk."

It was pretty much exactly what Polychrome had told me back in her lab, but in nicer words.

"Not *it*," I shot back. "*He*. And if *he's* worth the risk, then who else is? Are you? Am I? Isn't there a point where we stop deciding to sacrifice anything and start saving people?"

Nox sighed and looked at the ceiling. "I don't know," he said after a bit. "I really don't."

"I'm sorry," I said, remembering back to the Fog of Doubt, and what Dorothy had said about becoming like her. Even if I hadn't admitted it before, it really was the thing I was most afraid of. "You might not know, but I do."

Nox looked me up and down with something I recognized as respect.

"Okay," he said slowly. "I'll help you. You've come this far without me. You've earned the right to make the decisions. Whatever you want me to do, I'll do. Your call. But do me a favor, and think about it first. Just sleep on it."

I stood up. "Fine," I said. Even if we were going to leave, I still had to figure out how. "But tomorrow, we go."

Back in my chambers, Ozma was already asleep in the darkness. I got under the covers and was still trying to put together all the events of a long, confusing day, when, from the other bed, a voice cried out. I sat up.

It was Ozma. She was screaming, writhing under the silk sheets, struggling with an invisible enemy. "No!" she was shouting angrily. "Go away!"

Half of me just wanted to ignore her and try to fall asleep anyway. Ozma talking to herself was nothing new, after all.

But I jumped up, and felt a now familiar darkness coming over me as I prepared to fight whatever was attacking her.

"Help me!" Ozma pleaded, but it wasn't her own voice now. It was a man's.

Then she was screaming again, still writhing in pain and fury. "I won't!" she said. That was when I realized there was only one person in the room. Whatever was attacking Ozma was coming from within her.

"Pete?" I asked tentatively.

For a moment, the princess calmed herself, and turned her face to mine. "Please," she said, and now I was sure it was him talking. "Amy. Please. You promised. Help me."

"Pete . . . ," I said. "I . . ."

"I helped you," he said. "And you promised. I'm begging you."

I had to make a split-second decision. I don't know if I would have done anything differently if I had that moment to do over again. It was true. He had helped me. More than once. He was my friend.

Despite what I'd said to Dorothy's Fantasm in the Fog of Doubt, and as wicked as I knew I could be when I had to, I had one weakness: kindness.

And kindness *is* a weakness. I can see that now. But it's a weakness I'm still not sure I'd want to give up entirely.

I didn't have a choice. He would have done the same for me.

I shifted myself, only for a moment, into the shimmering world of light and energy that I'd discovered, the world where all I had to do was pull a few strings to get what I wanted.

I pulled them, and Ozma's body began to contort.

She was Pete, then she was herself. Like she was melting, her figure began to deform itself into a grotesque mishmash: Pete's legs and chest, Ozma's arms and face. She was fighting it. But Pete was fighting, too, desperate to get out.

So I helped him a little more. I had promised him. I pushed a little harder, then pulled, giving the invisible magical skeins a sharp yank, and Ozma screamed one last time, at the top of her lungs, and was gone, leaving Pete in her place, sweaty and panting in the bed where she had just been lying.

He sat up. He was crying.

"I'm sorry," he said, rubbing his brow. "Thank you."

"No," I said, my mind made up. "I won't let them do anything to you. I promised, and I still promise."

"I'm sorry," he said again. "I don't want any of this. I never did. But I don't believe you. And I need to live."

He took the lamp from the table next to the bed, and before I knew what he was doing, he clocked me with it. Right in the face.

TWENTY

"Amy," Nox was saying. I felt a hand patting the side of my face desperately. "Amy, get up. You have to wake up."

My whole body shuddered as a sulfuric, noxious smell filled my lungs. It smelled like burning hair, but worse. I coughed, hacking, as my eyes fluttered open, and I saw Nox's stricken face looking down at me. Something had obviously roused him from sleep: he was wearing only a pair of loosely fitting pajama pants, and his hair looked even crazier than usual.

"Nox? What's going on? Why am I lying on the floor?"

"I don't know," he said. "You tell me. Whatever. It doesn't matter. You have to get up. Something bad is happening. Something *really* bad."

Then I remembered. Pete. Why I wasn't in my bed. I twisted out from underneath Nox and spun around, searching the room for my attacker. He was gone. Of course he was.

I racked my brain trying to remember every little detail,

trying to figure out why he had done what he had done, and where he could have gone. But my head was still spinning, and I could barely put the simplest thoughts together.

"Pete," I said. "He hit me. There's something . . ."

I stopped as my gaze landed on the giant, panoramic window on the other side of the room. The stars were still out but the sky was bright. In every direction I looked, all I saw were flames.

All across the horizon, the islands that made up Rainbow Falls were awash in a sea of fire—and not just any fire. The flames that licked the sky were every possible color of the spectrum, from pastel pinks to deep, royal indigo and sick, toxic green.

The sky was burning. It wasn't just the islands. The rainbows themselves were on fire. If you've never seen a rainbow burn, consider yourself lucky. It might sound pretty, but it's not. It's horrifying.

This was where the smell was coming from.

"Did Pete do this?" I demanded.

"I don't know," Nox said. "But we have to get out of here. Now."

But before we could figure out *where* exactly we were supposed to be going, Polychrome burst through my door, with Heathcliff at her side and Bright, clad only in a pair of hot-pink underpants, right behind her.

"We've been betrayed," Polychrome said.

"I'm sorry," I said. "I didn't mean . . ."

"They never mean to, do they?" she asked a shell-shocked-looking Bright.

He shook his head sadly. "This is it, huh, babe?" he asked, without emotion.

"This is it," she said. "We couldn't stay above the fray forever. We knew this day would come. I just wish you didn't have to be here to see it. If you've ever been good for anything, try to make yourself useful for once in your useless life. If you kill someone, I promise I'll give you a surprise later."

She flung the window open. "There," she said, pointing to the largest and most distant of the floating islands in the burning sky. "They're waiting for us. They want us to come to them."

"Who?" I asked. "Who's they? How did they find us?"

Polychrome looked at me in disgust. "Oh, don't be stupid," she said. "Your little friend got scared and went running to the only people he could think of. Don't tell me it didn't occur to you that this might happen."

The fact that it hadn't occurred to me made me feel even more foolish than I had before. But when I searched my pockets for the handkerchief that Queen Lulu had given me back in the forest and couldn't find it, I knew exactly what had happened.

Pete. He'd taken it. He'd used it to contact Glinda. He'd fallen for her trap—he'd gone to her for help, just like she'd tempted him to, and had brought her right to us.

Polychrome was right. How stupid could I have been? For that matter, how stupid could *Pete* have been? Did he think Glinda had even the slightest selfless intention in her entire body? Why hadn't he been able to see this would happen?

I guess sometimes things get bad enough and you just don't care anymore.

"Shit," I said under my breath.

"Yes," Polychrome spat. "Shit. We're all buried in it now. For years, the Rainbow Falls have stood protected by Old Magic, free of Dorothy's influence and incursion. It was charmed, protected from the outside, from those who wanted to find us. We were hidden. Now you've brought her to my doorstep, and all of Oz will suffer because of your idiocy."

"I'm sorry," I said. "I . . ."

Polychrome waved me off. "Forget it. There's nothing left to do but fight."

She began to glow. In the distance, out the window, a lone rainbow crept toward us, winding in and out of the flames.

"I can get there faster," I said.

"No!" Nox shouted. Too late. I was already slipping into shadow, moving through the nothingness toward an enemy that I could feel at the edge of it.

I felt my way through the dark. All I had to do was let myself become one with the shadows. I didn't know exactly where I was heading or what I would find, but there was a power out there, and it was calling to me.

Then I felt heat on my face, and sweat forming on my brow as it got hotter. I opened my eyes and saw that the shadows had brought me right to the center of an inferno: I was standing on one of the floating islands, and it was engulfed in flames of every color imaginable.

Anything else that distinguished it was impossible to say now. All that was left of it was smoke and fire.

Then, from out of the flames, stepped Glinda. She had

undergone a costume change since I'd last spotted her: now she was dressed for battle in a skintight, magenta bodysuit, complete with a gleaming armored bodice. Her strawberry-blond hair was pulled back into a neat, severe bun.

"Well, lookie loo," she said in greeting. "Amy Gumm is here! I think we just about have a quorum for a tea party!"

With a wave of her hand, the flames immediately surrounding her subsided enough to leave a ring of burned-out rock—revealing that it wasn't just the two of us.

To Glinda's right was Pete. He was wrapped in chains—and from the scarlet aura around them, I could tell they weren't ordinary chains binding him, but magical ones. In addition to being tied up, he was gagged. I tried to meet his gaze, but he looked away, and I instantly knew my suspicion about what he had done was the right one.

I didn't even bother being disgusted. Pete, and the way he had betrayed me, were the least of my concerns. Because standing to Glinda's left was none other than Dorothy Gale herself. She wore a menacing, self-satisfied grin, like the cat who had just eaten the canary.

Crouched at her feet, looking more like a cat who had just eaten one too *many* canaries, was the Lion. Like Pete, his body was wrapped in a thick, heavy chain, one end of which Dorothy was clutching like a leash. He was whimpering pathetically, hiding his face with his huge paws, quivering in fear. A coward.

"Amy Gumm," Dorothy said. "Just who we were hoping to run into. Somehow I had a feeling we might find you here—and

when I say a *feeling*, what I mean is that this guy told us." She
nodded smugly in Pete's direction. "Careful who you trust,
hmm? That's a lesson you could both stand to learn. Can you
imagine? He thought Glinda would actually help him."

"I'm glad you found me," I said, mustering more confidence
than I actually felt. "It's actually pretty convenient. Everyone I
want to kill, and you're all lined up in a neat little row so I can
pick you off one by one. Now who wants to go first?"

I couldn't help shooting daggers at Pete. "How about you?"
I asked. "Nah. Not worth my time."

At that moment, my reinforcements came bursting through
the wall of flames, the charred rainbow that had carried them
expending itself in a final sputter of exhaust as they landed: first
Polychrome, followed by Nox, Heathcliff, and, finally, a dazed-
looking Bright.

Polychrome didn't waste any time. In one quick move, she
jumped astride her cat, and they seemed to merge into one:
together, they were undulating with color, a panther and unicorn
and girl and rainbow all at once, a single form burning with even
more intensity than the flames that were everywhere around us.

"*Witch,*" the creature bellowed, rearing on sinewy haunches
and launching itself straight for Glinda, claws extended and long
as kitchen knives. As it flew through the air, its churning colors
shifted up the spectrum until it was a radiant beast of pure light.

Glinda simply flung her arms out, throwing up protection,
and the whole sky lit up in a blinding flash as the creature col-
lided with her in a shower of multihued sparks. It looked like

someone had just set off a whole entire barge of fireworks in one go. But the sorceress just let out an uncharacteristically harsh cackle as she stood there, unharmed.

The monster that had been Polychrome just a minute ago drew back, undeterred, and struck again, quick as lightning. The battle was on, and I had to trust that Polychrome could handle her part of it. I had another enemy to fight.

Suddenly Nox was at my side. "Ready to raise the body count?" he asked.

"I'm ready," I said. As if it would ever be a question. It had taken me sixteen years to figure it out, but this was what I had been born for: to fight. When I looked down on the knife that was already in my hand, I saw that it wasn't a knife at all anymore, but now a sword with a shining ebony blade.

Dorothy hadn't moved an inch. She was observing the scene in unconcerned amusement. She looked down at the Lion crouched at her feet.

"Cowardly one," Dorothy commanded. "Prove your worth."

"But . . . ," the Lion whimpered. Dorothy yanked at the chain that bound him, pulling it tight around his neck, choking him with it.

"Kill them," she said.

He roared, not with menace but with rageful anguish, and attacked, bounding for us. Nox hadn't come bearing a weapon, but he didn't need one: his magic was made for battle. His hands began to crackle with mystical energy. He dropped to the ground, letting the Lion sail over him, and then reached up and plunged his burning fingers into the beast's belly. The Lion yelped and rolled away as Nox bounced right back up.

"I've got him," Nox said. "You take Dorothy."

I teleported myself ten feet over Dorothy's head and dove for her, swinging my sword with both hands like a batter ready to hit the game-winning home run.

She just laughed and ducked.

I kept on going, feeling like a windup toy. I was hitting her from every possible angle, slicing and dicing and shooting off one fireball after the next, moving with the grace and precision of a ballerina. But every shot I took missed, and she barely seemed to have broken a sweat.

She was still holding tightly to the end of the chain that she seemed to be controlling the Lion with, and she kept glancing over at him, muttering things under her breath like she was giving instructions. Was she controlling him with magic? It was like she was fighting in two places at once, her mind—and maybe her power—divided between me and Nox.

It should have given me an advantage to have her distracted like this. It didn't. Nothing I did seemed to even come close to hurting her.

But I couldn't give up. I wouldn't give up. I had been brought here to do this. It was my only purpose, and I wasn't going to fail again.

Then a voice pulled me out of my fugue. It was Pete. "Amy!" he shouted. I snapped my head toward him, only to see Bright lying unconscious on the ground and Nox in the clutches of the

Lion, who had him by the collar of his shirt and was dangling him aloft. Nox writhed and fought, helpless in his grip.

Dorothy shot Pete a look of disgusted consternation. "Oh, shut *up*," she snapped, sending a bolt of energy flying for him. "You can't keep changing sides like that." As the magic connected with a ruby-red flash, Pete disappeared, replaced, once again, by Ozma.

That was the least of my worries. If I didn't do something fast, Nox was a goner.

"Kill the warlock," Dorothy cooed at the Lion, who was baring his fangs in threat. I realized he was trembling. Once a coward, always a coward. "I want to see him suffer," Dorothy said.

"I . . . I . . . ," the Lion stuttered. "I don't . . ."

Nox gave me a wide-eyed look of panic. "Forget me!" he shouted. "I'm not important."

I looked from him, to the Lion, to Dorothy, making a calculation. Nox was right—this wasn't about him anymore—but at the same time, what good would it do for me to keep on fighting hopelessly against Dorothy just to let him die?

For her part, Dorothy just looked annoyed at the Lion's inaction. "Do it, coward," she said. She gave a sharp yank on the chain she held the Lion with, and I saw a wave of energy ripple through it. So *that's* what she was controlling him with.

It gave me an idea: a cord can always be cut. So instead of striking directly at Dorothy again, or at the Lion himself, I stepped forward and brought my sword down on the leash.

A freezing jolt zinged through my body as the metal links shattered. The Lion collapsed to the ground, dropping Nox from his grasp, and Dorothy screamed, recoiling. Whatever I had done, it had wounded her.

I probably should have gone straight for her while I could— hit her while she was down. But I only had a moment to make my choice.

I was now certain that my decision to let the Lion go the last time I'd seen him had been stupid, and I could have weakened Dorothy before now, before she'd had a chance to bring us all together like this. And I should have put him out of his misery when I'd had the chance.

As he heaved on the ground, covering his face with his paws, I blinked myself to his side and in a single, determined stroke, sliced his head off.

I did it with no pleasure. I hardly thought about what I was doing at all, but I was surprised at how little resistance I felt as my dark blade tore through his thick, muscular flesh; at how effortlessly I drew blood.

At how little remorse I felt.

He didn't even have time to scream: a geyser of blood shot up from the stump at his neck as his head separated from his body and dropped to the smoking rock. It bounced once and rolled over to where Nox was crawling to his knees and staring in disbelief at everything that had just happened.

"Help Polychrome," I told him tersely. Nox nodded, springing instantly back into action. He teleported across the field to where the rainbow's daughter was still locked in combat with Glinda.

Based on what I could see of how she was faring, she needed all the assistance she could get. Glinda had surrounded herself behind a barricade of magical protections, and was crouched with a shimmering longbow from which she was letting loose one zinging arrow of pink energy after another. Each one flew through the air faster than the last toward the creature Polychrome had transformed herself into, which was flailing on the field, dodging in vain and stumbling to keep going as light poured from the many wounds that had already pierced its body.

And the moment that Nox materialized at her side was the moment it was all over. One final arrow sailed through the air from Glinda's expert hand and ripped through the creature's chest. The creature fell from the air and separated, once again, into two figures: Polychrome and Heathcliff, both of them now limp and inert, landing with two thuds on the ground.

"No!" screamed Bright, who had come to and was now on his knees, watching in horror.

Nox didn't let it give him pause. He spun toward Glinda, drawing his fist back and bringing it toward her, letting loose a torrent of purple bolts that rained down on the makeshift walls she'd built around herself and shattered them like glass.

I wanted to watch him take down Glinda, to relish her demise, but I had to deal with Dorothy. She had recovered herself, and was now smoothing out her dress. She glanced over at where the Lion's head lay and tossed her hair.

"Good help is so hard to find these days," she said. "Just as well, I guess. What use is a Lion who doesn't even want to eat people?"

She gave the head a kick with a cruelty that made me shudder. "Now, Amy," she said. "You and I have a score to settle."

I couldn't disagree. It was time to finish this. I just wasn't sure how I was going to do it.

Dorothy and I stared each other down, slowly circling each other. There was something crackling between us now, a repellent attraction that I couldn't ignore, and I tried to let the battle still raging around us slip away. She was the only thing that mattered right now. I had to fight smarter, not harder.

As for her, she wasn't concerned at all.

"You know one thing I miss from home?" she asked pleasantly as she reached up and pulled a red ribbon from her hair, letting her ponytail come loose and fall in shiny waves around her shoulders. "Malt shops," she said. "You have no idea how many servants I've been through trying to find the one who could brew me up a decent strawberry phosphate. They never quite get it right. Have you ever had a strawberry phosphate? Do you love them?"

I pictured all the different ways I wanted her to die.

I wanted to drive a stake through her heart like she was a vampire. I wanted to bring my fists together and smash her skull open. I wanted to drop a house on her. It was too bad that I didn't have one handy. I took a step back, unsure of myself, as she bit her lip and began to twirl the ribbon absentmindedly around her finger.

But it wasn't as empty a gesture as it appeared: as she twisted it, the ribbon began to take on weight and heft. It began to grow until it was twice and then three times the length of her body, and then she began to whirl it over her head, where it thickened, its satiny texture transforming into something metallic, until it was no longer a ribbon in any way, but instead a thick metal chain just like the one she'd used to bind the Lion, spinning above her.

Game on. I flung off a fireball as a warning shot, and was surprised that when it emerged from my hands, it burned not red but black as night. Dorothy watched it shoot toward her like it was moving in slow motion and, with her free hand, flicked it away as easily as a normal person would swat a mosquito. As it hit the ground, it exploded into a ring that surrounded us in a wall of black flames.

In the distance, I heard Nox howling in pain. I felt a wrench in my heart. I wanted desperately to help him, but I knew that he was now as much beyond my reach as I was beyond his. Dorothy wanted me alone, and so that was how we would fight.

And even as I felt my body pumping more power than I was sure I could handle, I also felt a spiraling sense of helplessness. All the training and fighting techniques and all the magic that I'd come to rely on felt suddenly like they were useless against her. I pushed my doubt out of my mind, but I knew that if I didn't come up with a plan, fast, I was a goner.

Dorothy didn't miss a beat as I teleported myself through the shadows to a place behind her. She just pivoted on her red heels to face me, her chain still whistling in the air as she twirled it faster and faster.

"Someone's getting awfully familiar with the darkness, isn't she?" Dorothy singsonged. She cracked the chain like a bull-whip, then swung it toward me.

I dodged, my magic pulsing in my veins like a drug, pushing me to move faster than she—or anyone—could ever possibly anticipate, so fast that it was hard to know if I was actually tele-porting or not. I sliced my sword through the air in a graceful arc. I'd used it to hurt her once before; maybe it would work again.

In order for that plan to work though, I would have to actu-ally make contact, and that was easier said than done.

As fast as I spun and dodged and blinked in and out of real-ity, she swung her chain faster. Whenever I thought I was close enough to slice the thing in two, it slithered out of my reach just in time.

Then it struck, shooting forth and grabbing me by the neck, where it coiled itself tightly around me.

Just like that, my sword disappeared from my hand, and I felt my windpipe closing up. I clawed at my neck, trying to break free, but the more I struggled, the tighter the chain pulled.

"What about tuna noodle hot dish?" Dorothy mused, caught up in some game she was playing with herself. "My aunt Em always made the most delicious hot dish. Tuna noodle hot dish and strawberry phosphate. Now there's a meal I'd waste a few calories on! It's not that I miss Kansas. It will be burned to the ground soon enough anyway. Just like this place. But, oh, there are a few things it will be a shame to lose for good."

If I'd been just slightly stupider, I would have thought she'd forgotten I was even there. And if I'd had any breath to speak, I would have asked what she meant about Kansas being burned to the ground. But at that second, it was all I could do just to keep breathing.

Dorothy's voice was filled with smug satisfaction and just a touch of wistfulness. "I'll need a new slave now that I've lost my dear, cowardly companion the Lion," she said. "And you, Amy Gumm, have more power in you that he had in one of his his teeny weeny pinkie-claws. You'll make a perfect hench-girl."

She curled a spindly finger toward me, beckoning, and, almost as an afterthought, gave a tug on my leash. As much as I wanted to stay where I stood, I couldn't. There was some kind of power the chain gave her over me. I felt myself walking obedi-ently toward her.

"That's a good girl. I can already tell that you'll make quite the little trained monster."

I was so tempted to just give in. Nothing could have felt nicer, in that moment, than to stop fighting for good. To let it all go, and be under her power once and for all. To not have to worry about this crap anymore. I kept moving forward, halfway relieved to have it all be over.

And yet, another voice in the back of my head was urging me not to give in. The voice was no one's but my own. *I couldn't give in*. As much as I wanted to, as good as it would have felt, I knew that I couldn't. Not after all this.

If anything separated me from Dorothy, it was that. We *had* been the same, once, except that she had given up. Had given in. To the magic, to her shoes, to Glinda, whispering in her ear.

I wouldn't.

Now we were eye to eye, so close that the stench of her breath was overpowering as she spoke. It smelled like rancid strawberries.

"I'll give you this," she was saying. "You've developed a certain *flair* in the short time since I last saw you. A sense of magical style, I suppose. You're really coming into your own. But, like I say, you're leaning too much on the same old, same old. The shadow teleporting thing is getting to be old hat, don't you suppose? A little predictable, hmm? Well, we'll just need to teach you a few new tricks."

New tricks. After I had made it to the Fog of Doubt, I'd thought for sure I had been sent there to fail. To lose myself; to give up. Now I realized that I had been wrong. I had been brought there by the Road of Yellow Bricks, and the Magril had been waiting for me for a reason. It was only because I had made it through the fog that I knew now what I had to do. It was simple. It was what the Magril had taught me. I just had to become myself.

I could. And I would. I didn't need my blade to do it, either. The blade was a part of me.

"How's this for tricks?" I croaked at Dorothy, tearing with my bare hands at the leash. From out of my fists, a swirling blackness enveloped the shackles that bound me, and the links in the chain began to crumble. There was a snapping sound as I freed myself, and the leash she held me by crumbled to pieces and fell to the ground, melting into shadow.

Dorothy recoiled in shock, and as my knife returned to me in a flash, a look of even deeper surprise crested her face.

In her moment of confusion, I drew the knife back and plunged it through her heart. I pushed it straight through her body until I saw the bloody tip come out the other side.

Dorothy screamed, doubling over in pain. Her mouth dropped open and her eyes bugged out; her smooth, china-white skin began to sag and wrinkle as she aged what looked like twenty years in the fraction of a second. She began to turn green.

I had done it. I had killed her.

I towered over her, raised my fist to the sky, and called down more of the darkness, letting it rip through me. I had done it. I had killed her. This was who I was. This was who I was meant to be.

Then she stood up.

TWENTY-ONE

Dorothy looked as surprised at her condition as I felt when I saw her get back up to her feet.

She wasn't dead. I had given her everything I had, and it hadn't been enough. She seemed as shocked I was.

She stared at me, then looked down at herself, where my knife was still lodged in her body. She began to laugh at the absurdity of it.

Then, with more strength than she should have had left in her, she kicked me in the stomach with a spiky heel and sent me flying onto my back. As I struggled to my feet, she flicked her wrist and shot a bolt of energy at me, hitting me square in the rib cage. My whole body seized in convulsions, pain shooting through my every nerve as I fell back down again.

Dorothy yanked my knife from her chest. Blood was squirting everywhere, but she didn't seem to be feeling any pain. She held the blade aloft, looking at it curiously.

She shouldn't have been able to do that. The knife was a part of me. No one else was supposed to be able to touch it unless I was using it to slice them open.

Then again, Dorothy shouldn't have been alive either, after what I'd just done to her.

"Well," she said. "I don't know *what* just happened, but I guess it didn't work. Cool knife, though." She rested the hilt against her palm. "Looks like magic. The black kind."

Now she was advancing toward me, brandishing my weapon. All I could do was lay there waiting for her, twitching. Her red shoes were sparkling with magic, and with every step she took she seemed to grow more powerful. Without even looking like she was trying to do it, she was drawing down a storm of lightning bolts from the sky, all of it flowing through her body and into her shoes like she was a living conduit for all the magic Oz had to offer.

Was it possible that I had somehow just made her *more* powerful?

"So. It seems that you have a bit of a problem. It *looks* like you can't kill me, now doesn't it? I think this is the part where you cry uncle."

"Not on your life. Assuming you even have one anymore," I said.

But I knew she was right. Maybe I still needed the Scarecrow's brains, just like the Wizard had said, or maybe something else was the problem, but I wasn't going to be able to beat her. Not like this.

All I could do was retreat to the one place I knew I would be safe. So, old hat or not, I pulled the darkness over me, feeling it envelope me like a familiar blanket. I burrowed into it as far as I could, closing out the flames, the smell, the screams—closing out the whole world until everything, everything, everything was pitch-black.

Everything except the one thing I was really trying to hide from. Against the utter nothingness of the shadow world, Dorothy looked Technicolor. Her eyes were so blue they vibrated, and her face—which had formerly been tinged with a sickly olive pallor—was now a vibrant, clownish green slashed with lips red as cartoon blood. Her shoes were the reddest of all. They were so bright I had to look away.

Even here, I couldn't escape from her.

"You think you're the only one who knows about the Dark-lands?" she asked, seething. "Oh, honey, this dimension might as well be my living room. Have to admit, I've never met anyone else who could get in here—even Glinda doesn't get it. I guess it's a Kansas thing!"

It's hard to describe the powerlessness I felt just then. This was a different kind of powerlessness than I'd felt when Dorothy had me wrapped in her chains. Instead of feeling hypnotized—held in her thrall—I just felt hopeless, like nothing I could do would make a difference, so why bother trying?

She looked down at my knife curiously. Watching her touch it gave me a strange, awful feeling, like when you're a little kid and you wiggle your tongue around in the hole where you just lost a tooth.

I could see that Dorothy understood my discomfort. "I doubt

I can hurt you with it," she said, "But I'm guessing as long as I'm holding it, you won't be able to put up much of a fight. Shall we test the theory?"

She extended an arm and touched the tip of my knife to my collarbone. I didn't resist. She drew the blade across my neck, pressing hard enough for me to feel pressure. But there was no blood, and no pain.

"I figured," she said. "You get a feel for these things after a while, you know? Anyway, it doesn't matter. I'll just have to get creative." She paused.

"Oh, never mind," she said. "You can't kill me, I can't kill you; how predictable can it get? There's probably some dull prophecy about it—there always is, isn't there? Chosen ones and blah blah blah. Who can keep track? Good thing I don't need to kill you anyway. Oh, I'd *like* to, but as Glinda's constantly reminding me, a girl can't have everything she wants. Not even me. But you've got your wants, and you've got your *needs*. And all I *need*"—she grabbed the strap of my bag and yanked it hard, snapping it—"is this."

"No," I said.

"*Yes*," she said, digging around inside. "Let's see. One mechanical heart. Check. One artificial tail. Check. And . . . a French textbook? I mean . . . I guess that could come in handy, too. You never know when a girl might want to aim for higher education." She brushed a lock of hair from her face and the blackness began to fade.

As the world returned, I saw that the battle was over. Really over. The floating island on which it had been waged was now just a scorched, charred husk of dirt and rock, with only a few small flames lingering in the wreckage.

Polychrome lay still in the middle of it, her delicate hand wrapped around Heathcliff's lifeless tail. Nox was kneeling beside them in defeat, his face bloody and covered in dirt and ash, his formerly wild hair singed to almost nothing.

The battle was over, and we had lost. *I* had lost. Glinda stood above us, arms crossed at her chest in a pose of both victory and impatience.

"*There* you are," she said as Dorothy stumbled out of the shadows to join her at her side. "I was just about to wonder if I was going to have to leave without you."

"I got what we came for," Dorothy said, holding up my bag triumphantly.

"And yet the girl lives. Curious."

Dorothy shrugged. "You know how magic can be. *Annoying*," she said, finishing her own thought.

"So it can," Glinda agreed.

"Must be some dumb rule no one remembers. She couldn't kill me either, by the way."

"It makes no difference. The girl is no more than a nuisance now. So what do you think? Should we take them with us?" Glinda asked. "Put them to work? The Order's little warlock can wash windows, the witch from Kansas can serve, and the beautiful boy behind the boulder"—she waved a hand and a large rock disappeared from the periphery, revealing a sheepish

Bright's hiding spot—"could make a *very* interesting play-thing."

Even as she said it, I could see that it was, at least in part, bravado. She and Dorothy might have won, but they hadn't come out of this unscathed. Dorothy looked aged and decrepit, her skin still a sickly green, and even Glinda looked exhausted. Her bun had come undone, her armor had been pierced in several places, and she had a giant gash running from her shoulder to her elbow. If she'd had the juice left in her, she could have done whatever she wanted to us. But she didn't. Which meant that this was a stalemate of sorts, whether or not either of them wanted to admit it.

Dorothy shook her head with an exasperated groan, trying to act like she seriously didn't give a shit. "They're too much trouble," she said. "Ozma is back in our control. We have the things we came for. The rainbow fairy and her familiar are dead, and this horrible so-called paradise has been burned to a crisp. Soon, we'll have done the same to the place I used to call home. I say, let's get out of here."

"Your wish is my command," Glinda said. She turned gloatingly to me: "Toodle-oo! Polly's been the *mostess* of hostesses, but even the most delightful teatimes must come to an end. And Dorothy and I are late for a very important appointment, aren't we, dear heart?"

"We sure are." Dorothy lowered her eyes toward the bodies on the ground, then shot a glance at me. "I hate to leave it such a mess, but I guess a girl from the trailer park has slung some slop in her day." She gave me a barely perceptible wink. "Not that I know what that's like."

Suddenly, out of nowhere, Ozma let out a screech from where Dorothy still had her chained, where Pete had been earlier. It had taken her this long to come to her senses, but now, she finally seemed to understand that she was being held prisoner.

"I command you!" she shouted. "With the Old Magic that . . ."

"That's the royal spirit we like!" Glinda said, looking like she wanted to explode with laughter.

Dorothy waved a hand, the chains pulled tighter, and Ozma was silent.

Then Glinda snapped her fingers and, in a puff of pink smoke and a shower of glitter, all three of them were gone.

TWENTY-TWO

Glinda, Dorothy, and Ozma were gone. The falls, and the islands revolving around it, had been destroyed. The sun was rising, and the purple sky was filled with floating ash and ember and the sad, wilted remnants of barbecued rainbows.

Off in the distance, the place in the skyline that had been occupied by the Rainbow Citadel now held only a billowing plume of blue-black smoke.

It all looked like the morning after a surprise party gone really, really wrong.

Nox and I couldn't even bring ourselves to look each other in the eye.

Meanwhile, Bright stood stoically, gazing out at the wreckage as the sun rose slowly above it. He shook a single cigarette from his case. "My last one," he said. "Ever, I guess. No more rainbows left. I guess I should savor it, huh?" But instead of lighting it, he put it carefully back into the case and patted it like a precious object.

He walked over to Polychrome's sad, limp body and knelt to touch her face. "She was something," he said. "Y'know, I never figured out what she saw in me, not really." He bent over and kissed her tenderly.

As his lips touched hers, her body began to glow one last time, and when he pulled away, a small, weak tendril of yellow light curled from out of her mouth and began to eat away at the rest of her until she had melted into a shapeless puddle that danced with color like an oil slick. When there was nothing left of her, the puddle began to unwind, rising—first slowly, then quickly—into the sky in a luminous, vibrant thread.

A rainbow.

We watched her go. And when the last of the last rainbow had faded, Bright turned his attention to Heathcliff. He carefully untied the ribbon at the giant cat's chin, and removed the horn that Polychrome had given him. "Here," he said, handing it to Nox. "This will come in handy. It's real, you know. It came from a real unicorn. Polly got it off one when it crashed through the window by the breakfast nook and died. Stupid things are dumber than birds. God, that was ages ago. Anyway, it's rare you find one of these. And it's magic. Does some crazy shit. You'll see."

"You don't want to keep it?" Nox asked. "It should be yours."

"Nah. It'll just make me sad. And what am I going to do with it anyway? It'll probably just get lost, like everything else. It's time for me to get moving again."

He reached behind his ear and pulled out a golden button.

"My only trick," he said, holding it up to the morning light. "But it's a good one. My parents always said I was bright as a button, and Polly knew I'd get bored if she tried to keep me cooped up, so she magicked these for me so I could get out whenever I wanted. *Don't want my bird in a cage*, she said. Didn't even care if I sometimes left without telling her when I'd be back. Anyway. I only have a couple of these left, but I guess I don't really need 'em anymore. Won't be coming back here, will I?"

He pulled out another button and handed it to me. "Do good, babe," he said. "Maybe I'll see you around."

"Where are you going to go?" I asked him.

"Where else?" he asked. "I'm going to get lost." He flipped the button up, and it spun a few times, then exploded in a shower of glitter, leaving in its place an ordinary wooden door, standing free amidst the rock, connected to nothing.

Bright turned the dull, glass knob, pulled the door open, and stepped through the frame. It disappeared as he closed it behind him, but I kept staring at the empty place where it had just been.

Instead of saying anything, I stepped to the precipice of our flying hunk of burned-out rock and sat down, letting my feet dangle off into the vast, empty sky. Nox slid down next to me and we just sat there in silence, watching the last of the sunrise.

"Well," I said to Nox when it was over. "I guess it's just us. What do we do now?"

"I don't know," he said. "I really don't."

"You know what I wish?"

"Yeah," he said. "I think I kinda do."

I knew he knew. I said it anyway. "I wish we could just stay here. Just the two of us. See if we could rebuild this place. Maybe not the same as it was, but, maybe like we would want it to be."

"Like it was ours."

"Exactly. Make it a home." I didn't need to say what we were both obviously thinking. The first real home either of us had.

"I wish that, too," Nox said. His voice cracked. "Maybe next time."

"Yeah. Next time." I turned away, and Nox stood and walked to where Heathcliff's body still lay.

"You were right," I said. "About Pete, I mean. I should have listened."

"It wouldn't have mattered," Nox said. "It was already done."

"I shouldn't have trusted him in the first place."

"Yes," Nox said. "Yes, you should have. Because that's who you are."

I hadn't thought of it that way, but maybe he was right.

"Maybe we should find Mombi," Nox offered. "Maybe she's better now. Maybe she'll know what to do."

No. I was sick of maybe. I was sick of witches, sick of searching, sick of chasing mysterious objects. Sick of being ordered around and used like a pawn. Now, if I had to trust anyone, it was myself.

"Forget Mombi," I said. "We're going to find Dorothy and kill her. And then we'll finally get a happy ending."

Nox seemed too tired to argue with me. I was tired, too, but I was also jittery and restless and suddenly not in the mood to waste time. I took the button that Bright had given me and tossed it up just like I'd seen him do. Like before, a door appeared.

Screw it. I didn't know where it would take us, but I stepped through it anyway. Maybe, I thought, the magic will be on my side for once.

Instead, it sent me walking right into a brick wall. Literally.

A *yellow* brick wall, to be precise.

TWENTY-THREE

Bright's portable doorway had deposited me back on solid, non-floating land, where the clouds were now once again hundreds of feet above my head rather than miles below my feet. Nox was just a second behind me, and as soon as he stepped through the portal, it slammed shut and disappeared. We both stared up in amazement at what was standing in our way.

Rising up out of the field in which we stood, the Road of Yellow Brick had turned itself into a gleaming wall. A wall so high that there was no hoping to see over it, and so wide in either direction that it appeared to go on forever, with no sign of any way through it.

I pressed my hands against it. "Does this count as lost?" I asked, wondering if maybe we should have found another way back down to earth than the one we had chosen.

"It seemed like a good idea at the time," Nox said, echoing my thoughts. "What do you think's on the other side of this thing?"

"I guess I'll find out."

Before I even tried teleporting to the other side of the wall, I had a feeling it wasn't going to be so simple. My gut was right. When I tried to melt into the shadows—what Dorothy had called the Darklands—and slither through the wall, some kind of force stopped me. Instead of finding myself on the other side of the barrier, I rematerialized ten feet back from where I'd started, with a woozy sensation and a sudden headache, like I'd just tried to butt my head against the bricks. I tasted something metallic in my mouth.

"Weird," I said.

"Not really," Nox replied. "The road is serious business. Mombi once told me it's as pure an expression of Oz's magic as there is—and now that the magic's coming back, I bet it's getting *more* powerful than it was before. You've seen how it can be. It has a mind of its own. I guess it decided that it doesn't want anyone going past this spot. And it looks to me like it's not going to give up without a fight."

I felt the wall, running my fingers along the smooth bricks, which were glittering golden in the sun. It was so beautiful that, under other circumstances, I would have been awestruck.

I don't know what I was looking for. A secret button that would open a door, like in a Nancy Drew book?

I laughed at the irony of that. Come to think of it, though, how nice would it have been to find myself in any other storybook world than this one, with nothing to worry about except missing heiresses and stolen jewels?

Next time, I promised myself.

For now, I was out of luck. Even if there was a hidden switch somewhere in these bricks, I had no way of finding it—it would take me weeks, if I was lucky, to cover every inch of the wall looking for it.

"So what do we do?" I wondered aloud, giving the wall a kick. "Know any flying spells?" Flying had never been my thing. Hovering, maybe, a little levitation here and there, fine, but actual flying was something I'd only seen Mombi do, and it took a lot out of even her.

"Nope," Nox said. "But there's no law saying we have to go through it. Who knows what's on the other side, you know? Maybe we should head the other way and try to regroup. Go find the Order and get a real plan together."

"News flash," I said. "There is no Order anymore. Mombi's sick, Glamora's probably dead. Who knows where the rest of them are? That leaves you and me. Look, I say Bright's doorway took us here for a reason. If something's trying to keep us from getting through here, there must be something important on the other side."

"Maybe we can climb it," Nox said thoughtfully. "I never was so great with horticulture spells but . . ."

He moved his fingers over the earth and a pair of thick, green vines sprouted up from out of it, quickly crawling up the sides of the wall.

I shuddered, remembering rope climbing in gym class, and how I'd never been able to even make it halfway. I wasn't sure I wanted to test my improvement on a day like today.

I didn't need to worry about it. When Nox tugged at the newly created vines to test their strength, they wilted instantly under his touch.

"Damn," he said. "No surprise, though."

I just stood there, trying to think of what to do. Maybe we *should* just turn around and head off somewhere else.

I was so exhausted. *Rest.* That was what I wanted. Somewhere to rest.

Not rest like sleep though. I could have used that, too, of course, but what I really wanted was rest as in, like, a break from always having to be on alert, never knowing what was coming next, a break from watching people die and not being able to do anything to stop it.

A break from being the one who had to kill them.

More than anything, I wanted this to be someone else's responsibility.

I let out a scream of pure frustration and slammed my fist against the wall. When that felt good, I did it again.

That was when I felt something inside of me snap. I kept on screaming and punching, and screaming and punching. It felt good, in a weird way. This was everything I wanted to do to Dorothy, and Glinda. To Mombi and Glamora, for getting me into this. To Pete, for selling us out. To the Wizard, for just being the Wizard. Screw it—to *everyone*.

This is what I'd always wanted to do to all the people who had ever underestimated me, to everyone who had ever picked on me, or cast me aside. Just hit them. I hadn't even gotten to hit Madison, but I'd been suspended for it anyway.

So I kept on whaling on it, not caring that my knuckles were bleeding, or that I knew it was all completely pointless. Actually, there was something about the pain, and the pointlessness, that was exhilarating.

"Amy!" Nox said, sounding shocked at what I was doing. I ignored him. I didn't care.

I was so caught up in my fury that I didn't notice that, as I kept on punching, the pain became less and less apparent. I didn't notice that, with every blow I took at the wall, I was getting bigger. Stronger. Or that, as I punched, the blood pouring out of my fists was seeping into the bricks, and that, one by one, they were turning black.

But then I realized my punches weren't just bouncing off it anymore. As I hammered blindly away, small pieces of rock began to fly. I don't know how long I kept going, but whether it was five minutes or an hour, or a day, the whole wall had turned black, infected with the dark magic I could no longer control.

When I gave another scream—a scream so loud that the wall actually shook just from the sound of it, a thin, golden fissure appeared, spidering across the wall's surface, and when I punched it again, there was a sound loud as thunder as that crack split wide open, and bricks came tumbling down around me like dominoes, first just a few and then hundreds and thousands. The wall crumbled around me.

I had torn it down. The whole damn thing was obsidian dust

in my hands, and I was kneeling on top of it.

Still, I didn't stop. Even when it was all gone, I kept slamming my fists into the dirt. I felt more powerful than ever, like I had taken its magic for my own, and I liked it.

"Amy," I heard Nox saying. I ignored him until I felt his touch on my shoulder, and then I turned around to face him, and I growled.

Growled. Like an animal.

"Amy," Nox said. "It's okay."

He knelt down next to me, wrapped his arm around my shoulder, and pulled me into his chest. I was still shaking, and I nestled into his body, which suddenly felt very small.

"It's just too much," I said. I felt like I would cry at any second. I *wanted* to cry, and at the same time, I couldn't. I was in a place past crying.

"I know," Nox said. "I know. But it will be over soon. It has to be."

I began to melt into him. There in his arms, I felt so secure—for the first time in maybe my whole life—that if I could have, I would have let myself become part of him. Just so I could feel that safe forever.

But then I looked into his eyes, and I saw how haunted they were, and suddenly I realized that he was afraid of me. At first, I thought it was only because of what he had just seen me do, but then, I caught a glimpse of myself—just a glinting image reflected in his pale gray irises—and I realized that it wasn't what I had done that had frightened him.

It was what I had become.

Startled, I wrenched myself from his grip and stared down at my own body.

Was this really me? My hands, my arms, and even my legs—all of me—were rippling with muscle and bulging veins, and were covered with a fine dusting of something like fur, a deep emerald green and the texture of velvet. Each of my fingers was tipped with a blood-red, razor-sharp claw.

Beginning to panic, I pressed an open palm to my forehead, hoping that what I had just seen had only been my imagination. It wasn't. At my temples, just below my hairline, two hard, curling nubs protruded. They weren't big, but they were there.

I had grown horns.

"Amy," Nox repeated. I jumped to my feet, but he grabbed me by the wrist and pulled me back toward him. I was so ashamed of myself that I just wanted to run away. And I could have. I was so much stronger than him now, and bigger, too—his body had seemed small because he *was* small now, at least compared to me. Because as I had been tearing down the road of yellow bricks, I had grown into something new. Something huge and terrifying. The very thing I had been afraid of turning into.

I had become a monster.

I didn't want Nox to see me like this, and still, I stopped myself from pulling away from him and hiding. I didn't want to hurt him by accident either. I didn't know my own strength. So I let him hold me.

"I didn't mean to . . ."

"I know," he said. "I know."

We stayed like that for a long time, me shaking in his arms while he held me and told me everything was going to be okay. As he said it over and over again, I felt myself calming down, and the thing that was inhabiting me began to slip away, leaving my body.

The most messed-up part is that I wanted to hold on to it. I didn't want it to go. But I forced myself to relinquish it, and soon I felt my horns shrinking away, my claws pull back into my fingers, and my skin return to normal. I was myself again.

"What happened?" I asked when I finally felt able to really speak.

"You got carried away," he said. "It was the magic. You let it take over. That wasn't you."

I wanted to believe him, but I wasn't sure that I did. What if it *was* me?

Then I let my gaze move past him, and all my thoughts of myself stopped as I realized where we were. In my temporary insanity, I had lost track of what I had been doing; I had forgotten why I had wanted to get through the wall in the first place. Now I turned and saw what it had been protecting.

We were sitting on the edge of the Emerald City. Or, I guess, what used to be the Emerald City. It was hard to say if you could still call it that—because it was different now.

It looked like it had been hit by a nuclear bomb. The once glittering, bustling thoroughfare was now empty, piled with trash and debris. The buildings that hadn't been destroyed were empty shells, with charred facades and shattered windows. The lavish, stately gardens that Dorothy had spent her time lounging in had been mostly destroyed, the fountains shattered, the flowers dead and covered over with vines.

But all over the place, when you looked a little more closely, traces of the city's former grandeur remained. Amidst all the wreckage, the streets had a sheen that I realized was coming from millions of scattered jewels—emeralds, obviously, but diamonds and rubies and amethysts, too. Here and there, pools of gold melted and then hardened again, like puddles lingering after a thunderstorm.

At the center of it all, the Emerald Palace rose up, its majestic towers replaced by a dense tangle of twisting, almost tentacle-like spires that stretched so high into the sky that the tops of them were obscured by a cover of dark clouds. The whole structure was covered in grime and dust and a thick forest of ivy, but at the same time, there was something about it that took my breath away. In the still silence of everything, it looked less like a palace now and more like a cathedral; like a monument to some ancient, long-forgotten god.

As I stared up at it, something jogged my memory, and I remembered something I was pretty sure I'd heard someone say. One of the monkeys on Queen Lulu's council.

For one thing, it seems to be growing.

At the time, I'd had no idea what that had meant. It had seemed so strange that I'd pretty much ignored it when I'd heard it. Now I understood.

It was true. Somehow, the palace was bigger than when I'd left it. *Much* bigger. Maybe it was still growing: when I stared at it long enough, I realized it seemed to be moving, like it was a living thing. It seemed to be breathing.

But before I could ask Nox what he thought had happened, I saw a movement out of the corner of my eye, and then from out of every crevice and alleyway and window, from the sewer grates and the gutters and out from behind every building, an army of monkeys emerged, coming toward us. Leading the way was Queen Lulu, who was dressed in army fatigues and carrying a small, silver pistol.

"Amy," Lulu said. "We've been waiting for you. And I'll tell you one thing. You sure know how to make an entrance."

TWENTY-FOUR

"You were right," Lulu told me as she approached. The rest of her monkey guard was hanging back, watching silently. "You told me we couldn't just sit up there in the trees, waiting for bad things to come to us. We'd been ignoring the rest of Oz for too long—and now look what happened. When I heard there was trouble afoot in the city, this seemed like the best place to come. I had a feeling you'd turn up sooner or later. I guess you chose later."

"What happened to Mombi?" Nox cut in. "Is she here, too?"

"Nope," Lulu said. "She disappeared from her quarters last night. Don't know where she got herself to, but there's no time to worry about that."

"What happened to the city?" I asked. "Where is everyone?"

Lulu let out a cackle. "Everyone? Everyone left, I figure. Or at least, everyone who hadn't left when you and yours attacked the place. With Dorothy gone, and the city ruined, wasn't much reason to stick around. And it's not safe here. Doesn't feel right. There's something going on in the palace—something rottener than week-old herring."

"I can see that," I said.

"I don't know what it's all about, but I've sent in three separate patrols to check it out. Last I've seen any of them. But we have seen a *few* signs of life."

My ears perked up. "Who?" I asked. "Who's been through here?"

"Dorothy and Glinda passed through a few hours ago—zipped right over the top of the yellow brick wall in a pink soap bubble. Not quite as impressive as blowing the whole thing to smithereens of course."

My stomach dropped as I looked around for signs of them. "Where did they go?" I asked. "We have to find them. Now."

Lulu bared her teeth and narrowed her eyes. "Honey, don't I know it," she said. "But we monkeys haven't just been sitting around on our heinies. The sorceress has been . . . dealt with. For now." She gave an oblique glance toward her pistol. "Dorothy got away. Took Ozma with her and headed straight for her old haunt. The palace."

"Did she say what she wanted?" I asked.

"What, you think we were making small talk? If you want to know what she's up to, you'd better find out for yourself. You have a job to do, sweetheart. My people and I will protect the city. You'd better hop to."

I clenched my jaw, with no idea where all this was heading.

"It's that way," Lulu said, stating the obvious as she pointed toward it. "Wish I had more time to catch up, but if you want my opinion, time's already wasting. Good luck."

I looked at Nox, who nodded back at me. The crowd of monkeys parted to let us pass, and we began to move on our way.

"If I were you, I'd head for the maze!" Lulu shouted after us. We were already gone.

"Now, I ask you," Nox said. "What the hell is going on?"

I was pretty sure the question was rhetorical. Even if it wasn't, I didn't know the answer. All I knew was that something had brought us here, and that whatever was going on, the palace was at the center of it.

As we rushed through the abandoned city streets, the feeling of dread that was emanating from the center became more and more palpable. When I looked over at Nox, he looked almost sick.

"There's something evil in there," he said. "I can feel it." He didn't say it aloud, but he was staggering a little, slowing down, and I could tell that he was fighting with everything he had just to keep going. "It's like it wants me to turn back," he said.

I could feel it, too. And I could tell that it was evil. But instead of repelling me, that same feeling was pulling me closer, like there was a party going on somewhere nearby, and I was following the music. Like someone was cooking a delicious roast and I was a starving woman following the scent.

I didn't mention that.

Nox put his head down and kept on moving.

Soon, we were there, and I saw exactly how grotesque the palace had become. It was covered in a slimy, filthy moss, and in place of the ornate, golden doors that had once served as the entrance, there was a kind of horrible sculpture: a gigantic, monstrous creature in bas-relief. Itlooked kind of like an octopus, but with more arms, and with a nasty, crowded mouthful of sharp, gritted teeth.

"What the hell is *that?*" Nox asked in disbelief.

I didn't answer, because I had just noticed something even more disturbing.

Lying on the steps like a broken, discarded rag doll, his arms and legs splayed out in every direction, was the Scarecrow. His head was hanging limply, lolling off to the side. He didn't look like himself.

"Shit," I said. "It's showtime."

I summoned my knife, hoping to make this a fast fight, and screamed in horror at what appeared in its place: somehow, from out of nowhere, a black, hissing snake was writhing in my grip. Before I could drop it, it had wrapped itself around my arm, where it pulled its head back and unhinged its jaw, ready to strike me.

Without thinking, I sent it away, the same reflexive way I had learned how to do when I didn't need my weapon anymore.

Nox was staring at me, his mouth wide open.

But I found that I wasn't exactly surprised by what had just happened. "It's this place," I said. "The evil in here. It's screwing with everything."

We didn't have the luxury to puzzle through it any more than that, because the Scarecrow was now moving. He sat up and looked at me with his painted-on little eyes and gave a weak grimace.

"Hello there," he said, without any of the sinister menace I was used to from him. Instead, he sounded like someone's weird, only slightly creepy uncle. "Do I know you?"

I saw immediately that there was something wrong with him, but it took a moment longer to actually see what it was. Then it dawned on me: his head looked misshapen and oddly deflated. Like there was something missing from it.

I was pretty sure I knew what that something was.

Without my knife to rely on, I felt a little bit unprepared, but I had other weapons to work with. At least, I *thought* I did. But when I tried to fire off a flame dart at him, all that came out of my fingers was a puff of noxious, green smoke that smelled like rotten eggs, and I realized with a sinking feeling that I wasn't going to be able to rely on my magic at all.

Luckily, for now at least, it didn't seem that the Scarecrow would be much of a threat. As I ran up the stairs toward him, he made no move to attack me or even get out of the way. Instead, he was just muttering something to himself. A spell, I wondered, reminding myself to keep my wits about me.

No, I realized as I got close enough to hear. It wasn't a spell at all.

"And so the imp says to the toadstool . . . ," he was saying. "No, wait. Let me start that again. Two young harlots and a fish walk into a . . ."

When he saw me racing for him, he looked up at me again,

as if he was seeing me for the first time. "Did I already tell you this one?" he asked. His eyes rolled back, and his canvas head dropped to the side, where it flopped at his shoulder.

"I used to be very clever, you know! Everyone said so. I was even king, after a fashion. Now look at me." With that, his painted-on face collapsed in a mask of grief and he began to weep silently to himself.

"Who?" I asked, already knowing the answer.

"*Dorothy,*" he said. "My dear old friend Dorothy. How could she?"

It was pathetic to see him—the cruelest and most terrifying of Dorothy's companions—in such a state. But I didn't feel sorry for him. How could I?

I grabbed him around the throat and picked him up, squeezing tight. His cross-stitched mouth let out a gurgling sound as he gulped for air. I squeezed harder, and then harder as he let out a gurgling noise. He flailed his stuffed arms, but didn't really resist. If anything, he looked relieved.

Then, finally, his eyes popped open and he gave a final, high-pitched whimper as his stuffed body went completely limp.

However much he had been alive in the first place was a mystery and probably always would be. But whatever it was, that life was gone. I had killed him.

Before I tossed him aside, I grabbed at the loose fabric of his scalp, and yanked his head clean off.

Second beheading in one day. I guess you could call that a record, huh?

When I examined what had been his head, turning it inside out and dumping the stuffing onto the ground, my suspicions were confirmed. All that came tumbling out was some straw, a few cotton balls, and some loose change.

Just as I suspected, the Scarecrow's brains were gone. Dorothy had already gotten them. Now she had a full set: heart, brains, and courage. But why? What did she want with them?

I tossed the Scarecrow's head onto the ground like the trash that it was, and stomped on it for good measure.

"Whoa," Nox said. At first I thought he was reacting to yet another act of brazen cruelty from me, but then he put a finger to his lips and said, "Listen."

I didn't hear it at first, but then, in the distance, from deep in the palace, I detected a rumbling sound. The ground beneath my feet began to shake, and as it did, the octopus statue before us came to life; its arms began to wriggle and its eyes began to glow with a nasty green light. Slowly, its mouth slid open, revealing an entryway just big enough to step through.

I glanced sidelong at Nox. I'd never seen him look so terrified.

"I guess we can take that as an invitation," I said.

TWENTY-FIVE

Inside, the palace was nothing like the place I'd gotten to know by heart when I'd been posing as one of Dorothy's most loyal servants.

In fact, it was no place I'd ever been before, outside of a nightmare. At first, it was hard to even understand what I was looking at. The vast entry chamber we were in had been turned upside down and inside out. No. Scratch that—inside out and upside down implies a certain order to things, and here, it was like none of the normal rules of physics applied at all. Like something out of an M. C. Escher drawing, there were entire staircases that floated in midair, leading to nowhere, furniture suspended from the slanted walls, and, overhead, an entire jungle looked like it was growing out of the ceiling.

I had no idea what this was all about, but I knew, on instinct, that Lulu had been right about where we had to go. "The maze," I said. It was the center of everything. It was where Oz had started. And now it was fighting back. "We have to get there."

Nox wasn't really listening. He appeared totally disoriented, like he didn't remember who he was anymore, and was looking around desperately, with wild eyes, as if searching for any way out. There wasn't one, at least as far as I could see. The door that we had just walked through had disappeared as soon as we'd stepped through it.

"Nox," I said frantically, grabbing his hand. "Get yourself together. I know it's hard, but we have to find Dorothy and Ozma. We don't have a choice."

"I . . . ," he started to say. Then he just shook his head. He couldn't make the words come out.

"I need you," I said. "I can't do this alone."

Somehow, that seemed to have an effect. Nox bit his lip, nodded, and steeled himself. "Okay," he said, taking a deep breath. "I can do it. It's something about this place. It just seems . . . wrong. It's messing with me."

"I know," I said, but I didn't quite get why it was affecting him so much more than me. It was true that it was disorienting—I could barely see straight, and, when I took a step forward, found myself moving backward instead, like I was on rewind. The main problem was that I didn't know how in the world we were going to find what we were looking for in all of this.

That is, I didn't know until a flash of red in the corner of my eye attracted my attention, and I spun around to find the source: Dorothy.

Across the room, Dorothy had Ozma on one of her

mind-control leashes and Dorothy was leading her up a moving staircase. They spiraled upward, toward a green door that hovered in midair what seemed like a mile above us. I wasn't even sure how it went so far up—the ceilings didn't seem all *that* high, but the way space seemed to be working in here, it obviously wasn't worth it to try to puzzle it out.

"There," I said, pulling Nox with me as I began to run. Or tried to run: the faster I tried to go, the more the strange physics of this place slowed me down, until it felt like I was moving through Jell-O. At this rate, Dorothy would get away long before I was able to catch up.

"Do you think you can teleport?" I asked Nox. It was a risk—who knew whether teleporting would even work in here, especially the way my magic had been working ever since we'd entered the city—but it was one I had to take.

"I can try," he said, looking uncertain.

"Are you sure?"

He gulped. "I think so," he said.

I didn't believe him. But what else could I do? Dorothy hadn't noticed me yet, but she was already halfway up the stairs. "We'll do it together," I said. Holding Nox's hand tight enough to cut off circulation, I held my breath and took him with me into the Darklands.

As soon as I entered the shadows, I knew I had made a mistake. His hand began to slip out of my grip. It was like trying to hold water. But through the hazy screen that separated me from the world above, I could see that Dorothy was almost to the door that would take her out of here.

So I rose back up into reality. It had worked. I was only a few paces behind Dorothy now, and she still hadn't noticed me.

But Nox was gone.

Ozma was already through the door, and Dorothy was stepping through it. Panicking, I looked over my shoulder, and saw Nox, still back on the ground where we'd started, gaping up at me with a look of abject terror on his face.

"Go!" he screamed. "I'll catch up."

I could have gone back for him. Instead, I dove through the green door after Dorothy a split second before it closed. I was standing on the edge of the palace's grand, formal garden, near the hedge maze where Pete had once told me was the place Oz had been born.

Dorothy and Ozma were walking toward the maze.

Long ago, Pete had told me that Dorothy was terrified to enter it: there was something about it that scared her, something that told her she would never survive if she tried to make it through to the center. But now, with brainwashed Ozma leading the way for her, she seemed dead set on getting in.

The maze didn't scare me. I had made it through before. I knew how to deal with it. But I also knew that if I tried to get through it again on my own, there was every chance that I'd get lost, or lose track of my targets for good.

I decided that right now, stealth was the best option. And so I shrouded myself in a misdirection charm so that Dorothy wouldn't notice me creeping behind her. I wasn't sure if it would work, but it couldn't hurt. Ozma waved her scepter and opened up a gap in the hedges, and when she and Dorothy walked through it, I walked close behind them.

Ozma knew where she was going. She navigated the dark twists and turns of the maze without ever hesitating at which way to go. Every now and then, she paused at a place that didn't even look like a path at all, waved her scepter again, and opened up yet another hidden passage. As Dorothy followed her, I followed them both, and soon we had reached the center.

It was different from the last time I'd seen it. Instead of the tiny cobblestone sitting area, with a tiny bench and a modest, sort of dirty fountain, we stepped through the bushes onto a giant, deserted plaza. The fountain at the center was now ornate and stately, with gorgeous, twisting designs carved into a huge marble basin, from which jets of water poured forth.

Standing next to it was the Wizard.

"Right on time," the Wizard said, seeing Dorothy make her entrance. He flipped his pocket watch closed and tucked it into his lapel. "I knew I could count on you, Your Highness. You've always had a way of getting what you want. The only trick is making you *think* you want it."

"Shut up, you stupid old man," Dorothy snapped. "I'm not here to play your games. Step aside, so I can finally do what I should have done years ago—destroy that horrible place once and for all."

The Wizard just smirked. "But *can* you?" he asked.

"Enough with your insolence," Dorothy said, slapping him

across the face so hard that the sound echoed across the plaza. "Do what I say and prepare the ritual you promised me, before I decide to stop being so kind."

The Wizard rubbed his cheek, but didn't seem injured. "The thing is," he said as Dorothy's scowl transformed into an unexpectedly complacent smile, "you're not the one in charge anymore. Not in here. Since you've been away from the city, I've been hard at work communing with the Powers That Be. Powers far greater than you, or Glinda, or any of the witches." He gestured toward the palace, which, even deep in the center of the vast maze, was towering over the hedges. "You see what's become of the palace, don't you? It's not just for show, you know. It's a symbol of all that I've become, and of all that I'll be."

Instead of arguing with him, or fighting, Dorothy regarded him curiously. "Tell me," she said. "What do you have planned?"

She sounded so obsequious and smarmy that I thought it had to be sarcasm, but when she dropped the leash by which she held Ozma and took a step back, I got it. The Wizard was working some serious magic, and Dorothy, who had always enjoyed enslaving people so much, was now at the other end of her own torture: from the glazed, vacant look on her face, it was clear that he had her under some kind of hypnotic spell.

As Ozma stepped to his side, the Wizard looked around. "Just a moment," he said. "There's something else, isn't there? Do I spy a witch lurking in the shadows?" he asked.

He fluttered a hand in the air, and, feeling strangely compelled,

I dropped my misdirection charm and moved forward, joining them.

"Ah," the Wizard said. "How lovely to see you, Miss Gumm! Tell me, what have I done here to deserve not one but *two* of my favorite people on a day like today?"

"I . . . ," I began to say. But I stopped. A certain kind of contentedness had come over me—not like my mind was being controlled, exactly, but more like I had been drugged, and nothing in the world could bother me now. "I don't know," I finally said. "You tell me, I guess?"

"Yes," the Wizard said. "I believe I shall."

He gestured to a place at his feet, and two small stools materialized, each one upholstered in green silk with a golden filigree. I took a seat, and Dorothy sat down next to me. It was unnerving seeing her behave so pliably. But, then, I was behaving the exact same way.

The Wizard gazed at us with fatherly kindness. "Let's discuss some things," he said.

TWENTY-SIX

"Have you ever—either of you—looked at the American state of Kansas on a map?" the Wizard asked.

Before either Dorothy or I could answer, or even nod a yes, he went on. "If you have, I'm sure you've noticed the shape that it is. Dorothy? Amy?" he prompted us like a doubting school-teacher. "What shape is Kansas?"

Dorothy answered with confidence. "Oh, something like a round blob with a funny little hole shaped like a jolly fat woman cut right out the side of it," she said.

I looked at her like she was nuts. If it was anyone except her, I would have felt almost sorry for her to be humiliated like this.

Not that I was in much better shape. I had no idea why the Wizard cared what shape Kansas was, or why I felt so strange, but it wasn't exactly a hard question, if you were from there. And I knew the answer.

"It's a rectangle," I said. "With a little missing chunk out of the top right-hand corner. I don't know why." That missing bit had always bothered me; it seemed to set everything a little off balance.

The Wizard smiled dotingly. "Correct," he said. "Amy gets a gold star. Dorothy wears the dunce cap for spinning foolish taradiddles."

"But . . . ," Dorothy said, sounding like a kid in school who just can't believe she's spelled an easy word wrong in the last round of the spelling bee. "They must have changed it," she muttered.

The Wizard shook his head impatiently. I could see that he was getting to a point here—I just didn't know what it was.

"Now, girls, can you think of another place that's shaped like a rectangle—wider than it is tall—with a little chunk cut out of the corner?"

It struck me immediately. This time, Dorothy knew what he meant, too. We both answered at the same time.

"Oz," we both said.

The Wizard gave a golf clap.

"Ding ding ding. Oz is exactly the same shape—and, it just so happens—exactly the same *size* as the great state of Kansas. There's only one small difference, which is that in Oz, that little chunk missing from the corner is in the *west*—right where the legendary valley of Oogaboo would be if it existed, which it doesn't and never did."

I glanced at Dorothy, feeling a strange camaraderie with her. She looked as confused as I was.

"Look, just forget Oogaboo for now—that's a long and extremely boring story that I barely remember myself. It's something to do with tariffs and Winkie bylaws, if memory serves. In any case, it's not important. Here's the important question: why do you suppose that Oz and Kansas are so similar, geographically speaking?"

The answer came to me out of the blue. "Because they're the same place," I said.

I hadn't even really thought about it; it was just sort of *there*, something that seemed obvious and familiar, even if it was absurd. Sort of like the concept of pi, I guess.

"Or something like that," I hedged quickly, embarrassed at how stupid it sounded.

But the Wizard was looking at me with something like respect.

"Indeed, Miss Gumm. They are, in a way, the same place. Oz and Kansas occupy the exact same physical space, but on two separate vibrational planes.

"You see, when the fairies created this fountain, and called forth the Old Magic that would be Oz's lifeblood, they weren't just pulling it from out of nowhere. They were pulling it from Kansas."

He gave me a meaningful look. "Explains why Kansas is so *very* dull, doesn't it? The fact is, it used to be a place of power. Dark power. All this time, it's been feeding Oz. Giving up all its magic so that this place could live. And yet, the balance has never been perfect. It's always been a bit inefficient. I'm going to change that. I'm going to finally open up the door between here and there—merge them into one glorious place. And, of course, I'm going to put myself in charge."

I was trying to piece together everything he was saying, but I still felt too muddle-headed.

The Wizard continued. "Now," he said, "let's have ourselves a little ritual. Well, not so little actually. You have no idea how complicated it was to arrange all this. Dorothy, may I have the items?"

Dorothy didn't resist—she unstrapped her satchel and handed it over to the Wizard, who opened it and glanced inside, nodding with approval when he saw what he was looking for.

"Wonderful," he said, first pulling out the heart. "I thought Amy here would be able to gather these for me, but when she became too much of a loose cannon, I decided that I needed some insurance. I'm glad I did. You did such a good job bringing me what I needed."

The heart was pulsing with a strange golden energy, and the Wizard held it out and placed it in front of him, at the level of his chest. Instead of falling to the ground when he took his hand away, it stayed planted in the air, vibrating.

Next, he did the same with the Lion's tail and the Scarecrow's plush brains, which were glowing purple and blue, respectively.

"I had no idea when I gave these silly things to your friends that I was unwittingly working in the service of the fairies," he said. "Creating the key that would unlock Oz's true potential. Now, Dorothy, I believe it's time for you to do your part."

"Yes," she said, zombie-like. She stood and took her place, standing next to the glowing objects. She suddenly looked uncomfortable, and the Wizard snapped his fingers in front of her face, freezing her like a statue where she stood. "Just in case she gets squirmy," he said. "Are you ready, Amy?"

I stood up from my seat, ready to obey him. But I *wasn't* sure what he wanted.

"Yellow, blue, and purple. What's missing?" the Wizard asked.

"Red," I replied. "The color of the Quadlings."

"That's right. And what's red?"

Then I understood.

"Blood," I said. It came out in a whisper.

"Good girl. It's your big moment. Isn't this what you've been waiting for?"

"I . . . ," I started to say. But even in my blissful, hypnotized state, I knew this wasn't how it was supposed to go. It didn't feel right.

The Wizard noted my hesitation. "You've always been so strong-willed," he said. "It's what makes you so special, and I respect that. But it's your choice, Amy. This is what I promised could happen, if you brought me everything I needed. And you've succeeded—after a fashion, I suppose. So go ahead, take your prize. Everything's in place, so fetch yourself a weapon."

My blade appeared in my hand of its own accord, and I held it out in front of me.

"Just a moment," the Wizard said. "Before you get carried

away. Just *one* more piece of business. In order for me to draw upon the Old Magic that comes from Kansas and rule over Oz as its rightful king, I'll need a queen. A *real* queen." He turned his attention to Ozma, took her hand, and kissed it in a way I guess was supposed to be gentlemanly. It made my skin crawl.

"How would you like to reclaim your throne?" he asked her. "Would you like to be yourself again? Would you like to be my bride, and sit at my side as Oz's fairy queen?"

Ozma looked confused. But she was already beginning to change. A pair of huge, shimmering, golden butterfly wings— *fairy* wings—had unfolded from her back. Her green eyes were glowing, and her black hair was whipping wildly in every direction. She began to hover a few inches from the ground.

"Ah, yes," the Wizard mused, looking admiringly at her. "I've always wanted to see the true aspect of a fairy. Even in my past dealings with them, I knew that they were only revealing themselves in a form that masked their true selves. I can't wait to see what you blossom into once the Old Magic is truly unleashed."

Ozma didn't say anything. But she looked into the sky, where slowly and then quickly, a whirling, black vortex appeared. As it grew in size, I saw what it was: a tornado. A *cyclone*. Except that it was upside down and inside out, and we were on the other side of the funnel, as if looking down on it from above.

The Wizard was staring at it almost lovingly. "Right on time," he said. "It's always so nice when things go as planned. Now, Amy, as someone who hails from the Other Place, from the very spot where the fountain draws from, and who has learned to channel its Old Magics with such ease, I'll let you do the honors. It's time for Dorothy to die."

I held my knife over my head, and felt power pouring into it from out of the funnel in the sky.

I felt the Wizard's spell in the back of my mind urging me on. I felt the darkness calling to me, too. *Rise*, the voices seemed to be saying.

Dorothy stood there in front of me, her face frozen into a silly, shy smile, and I almost thought I could see the person she had been: the girl who had come to Oz, stopped the witches, and saved the kingdom. Not because she wanted power, but because of her innocence. Because she was good.

I knew what would happen if I killed her. I would be accepting the mantle I'd been promised. Finally, I would be Wicked. Really Wicked. And there would be no going back.

Rise, the voice hissed again.

It was time. I drew my knife back to do it. To kill her.

But just as I was about to bring it down, I heard Nox's voice. "Don't do it!" he screamed. "It's a trick! He's fooling you!"

I spun around to see him pushing out from the hedges.

"Do it!" the Wizard hissed. "Do it now."

Then Ozma began to scream, her gossamer wings flapping wildly, and Pete burst out of her chest.

It wasn't like the other times he had transformed. Ozma was still there, still wailing and clutching herself in agony. But Pete was here now, too. He tumbled across the cobblestones, jumped up, and grabbed the Wizard's throat.

The maelstrom above us swirled. The Wizard cried out—like that, his spell was broken. I blinked and dropped my knife. It clattered to the cobblestone ground. I wasn't feeling so calm and contented anymore. I was feeling pretty terrified.

Dorothy emerged from her trance.

"Traitor," she said. She flung a hand out, and, like she was pulling a marionnette string, Pete flew away from the Wizard. She wanted the Wizard to herself, and now, as she approached him, his face went white. "I should have done this long ago," she said. "Now, let's hear you scream."

She clapped her hands together, and the Wizard *did* scream. His body began to ripple and twitch as Dorothy's spell moved through it, and then it was like something was eating him from the inside. "No!" he yelled. "Help me! Amy, help!"

But there was nothing I could do. The spell was quick. In an explosion of blood, guts, and glitter, the Wizard was no more.

The sky opened up. And Kansas rained down on us.

TWENTY-SEVEN

Have you ever looked at the American state of Kansas on a map?

The answer, at least for me, was, of course, yes. Obviously. In fourth grade, we'd spent at least a month of social studies on what Mrs. Hooper called our "Kansas Unit." During which, we'd had to memorize the Kansas state flower (the wild sunflower), the state bird (the western meadowlark), the state song ("Home on the Range"—that one was easy), and stupid trivia like where the name *Kansas* was derived from. (Either Native Americans or French people, or both; I forget).

In addition to memorizing all that trivia, each one of us had to give an oral report on a famous Kansan in history.

Until now, I had completely forgotten it, but in this moment the memory came back to me fully formed.

I had wanted to do my famous Kansan report on Dorothy from *The Wonderful Wizard of Oz*. I'd had my heart set on it, in fact. But Madison Pendleton had gotten to school early and had called dibs on it before anyone else could even get a chance.

Then, when I'd asked Mrs. Hooper if I could do Mary Ann from *Gilligan's Island* instead, Mrs. Hooper had told me it wasn't allowed, because Mary Ann Summers isn't a real person.

Dorothy Gale from *The Wonderful Wizard of Oz* isn't a real person either, I'd said.

But Mrs. Hooper loved Madison Pendleton. She loved her so much that she would sometimes let her sit next to her at lunch so that they could brush each other's hair.

Mrs. Hooper hated me. "Dorothy isn't real, but she's *important*. She's one of our most famous Kansans," she said. "Mary Ann from *Gilligan's Island* is not important. In fact, Amy, I always thought Mary Ann was from Oklahoma. Are you sure you're not thinking of the Howells?"

I knew it wasn't worth arguing, so I asked if I could do Amelia Earhart. If you thought about it, she seemed, at the time at least, to be a little bit like Dorothy, except real. But Mrs. Hooper gave that one to Candy Sinclair, her second favorite fourth grader after Madison Pendleton, and finally assigned me Bob Dole just to be mean.

Kansas had never been particularly kind to me.

And now I was back there. I was back home— if you could still call it that—and I had been brought there the way I'd left it: through a tornado.

The only thing is, it didn't feel much like Kansas anymore.

And I wasn't alone.

The two of us stood there, together: me and Dorothy, right

where we had both started. In Kansas. In the Dusty Acres trailer park, to be exact. Not that there was much left of it: I guess when the tornado had taken me to Oz, it had made quick work of this place. Now it was just an empty expanse of gray dust, with a sign: *Dusty Acres*, it read. *If You Lived Here, You'd Be Home Now.*

The only other thing that remained of the place I'd once lived was the concrete barbecue that no one ever used except for on the Fourth of July. Only now, it was blazing with fire, and a single dark figure was hunched over it. The figure was both clear and indistinct at the same time—solid, but blurry at the edges. Then the figure broke apart, and I saw that it wasn't one but three: from out of the darkness, a trio of women emerged, each of them wearing a heavy cloak in a different color: red, gold, and blue. Another cloak, a purple one, was lying in the dirt next to them, without an owner.

Witches. I recognized the one in red. It was Glamora.

In the distance, I thought I heard another voice calling my name—a voice that seemed familiar, but that I couldn't quite place. It was a boy. A man. It was someone important, someone who mattered to me, but I couldn't remember why.

"Rise, little witch," Glamora said. "Take your place among us."

I stepped forward.